Choker
قن ت خ مل

Books by Frederick Ramsay

The Ike Schwartz Series
Artscape
Secrets
Buffalo Mountain
Stranger Room
Choker

Other Novels
Impulse
Judas: The Gospel of Betrayal

Choker

لمختنق

Frederick Ramsay

Poisoned Pen Press

Library of Congress Catalog Card Number: 2008937737

ISBN: 978-1-59058-851-2 Trade Paperback

Poisoned Pen Press
6962 E. First Ave., Ste. 103
Scottsdale, AZ 85251
www.poisonedpenpress.com
info@poisonedpenpress.com

Printed in the United States of America

To Pastor Gary Hess:
You asked for it, you got it.

Acknowledgments

Once again, my thanks to all the folks at Poisoned Pen Press, Robert, Jessica, Marilyn, Nan, Geetha, and, of course, Barbara, our demon editor, who makes us all look better than we really are. Thanks, also, to Glenda Sibley for her diligence in text editing, and to my wife Susan for her endless patience and support in this giddy business. Finally, a nod to the gang at Toshi's Roast for their encouragement and friendship.

A caveat: I am not a pilot. I do not fly except in the economy section of large, anonymous, commercial aircraft. The few allusions in the book relating to flying and the death spiral were gleaned from articles and vetted by real pilots who affirm the descriptions are accurate—or close enough. My acquaintance with the occult, satanic practices and their dark ancillary preoccupations was gleaned from some limited experience in my previous life as a clergyman and from generally available information. I did consult secondary sources, had conversations with retired police officers on the subject, and am persuaded that the problems they present are real. I believe it is always a mistake to trivialize dangerous behavior simply because the odds may be against a bad consequence or, worse, because it is considered gauche to do so.

The terrorist program described is the figment of my overactive imagination, a necessary part of any novelist's equipment. I have been assured, however, by Col. Max Newman and people who regularly deal in these matters that the plot hatched here is frighteningly plausible.

Finally, slavishly following the latest fad in mystery story writing, I append a recipe: Agnes' Asparagus Roll-ups. Enjoy!

Chapter One

The ancient freighter inched closer to the shore. Its depth finder beeped softly as the bottom rose rapidly toward its keel, with a nearly empty hold, twenty feet below. Any false move on the helmsman's part would put them on the mud. That could spell disaster for all of them. An inquiry by the Coast Guard would not go well. People would have to die.

A gentle breeze blew in from the east, from the shore. He imagined he could smell honeysuckle over the stench of diesel oil, rusted steel decking, and sweat. He mopped his brow with a dirty sleeve and peered into the gloom. He could just make out the red flashing laser. When it stopped flashing and showed as a steady glow, he would have to stop the ship's forward progress immediately—no mean feat for a rusted out World War II-era freighter with an iffy boiler, slack steering, and a displacement of nearly sixteen thousand tons.

He rang all stop, then reverse, and the ship churned to a halt. The anchor, heavily greased and muffled with sacking, bumped through the hawse and dropped with a splash. The steam ship *Saifullah*, its name painted in white on its stern and prow in both Arabic, and English, heaved to, bow into the current, and thumped against a barge moored some fifty yards from shore. Except for the binnacle's glow, no lights showed—no running lights, all of its portholes painted over—nothing.

When the ship settled, a second anchor was let go aft. He peered off to the starboard. A series of intermittent flashes, this time green and difficult to see, were directed toward him. He murmured into the microphone attached to his headset. The forward anchor chain was allowed to play out. The one aft hauled in. The ship shifted toward the stern.

He signaled for the crew to complete unfastening the hold's hatches and to swing the ship's crane amidships. They would need lights now. The fog that allowed them to move in earlier had started to lift. They would have to work quickly.

Nick Reynolds had too few hours to fly at night with any degree of competence. That's what his instructor had said. Nick conceded he might be right at some level, but he, like many thirty-somethings, had become a risk discounter. Six years in the Navy, four in nuclear submarines, made him confident, perhaps too confident. Flying an airplane provided fewer degrees of freedom for mistakes than say, sailing a boat, a skill he also possessed. He'd brushed off attempts to dissuade him from night flying.

"I can do it, no worries. I have my IFR rating, I'll be fine." He smiled at his instructor and finished his preflight walk-around. He handed in his flight plan and took off, serene in the knowledge that if he followed the channel buoys to a point two miles south of the Chesapeake Bay Bridge, then swung southeastward, he'd raise Cambridge. From there he would have an easy final leg to Salisbury.

Nick's bravado faded when, minutes into his flight, he ran into thick fog. Had the weather report mentioned it? If so, he'd missed it. A moonless but clear night did not intimidate him, but flying blind in fog under those same conditions brought him to near panic.

He called the tower at BWI, Baltimore-Washington International, and felt better when they described the fog bank as only a few miles across. They also reported he'd drifted a few miles from his course. He'd need to correct it. He tried to remember what he should do in fog; rely on his instruments, climb, or descend? Climb seemed the most logical but he had an assigned altitude and climbing might put him in the path of a commercial jet on its approach to Baltimore-Washington International Airport. He decided to drop down to five hundred feet, skim the water at that relatively safe altitude, and see if he couldn't spot some lights from shore or ships out in the channel.

Moments later, he broke out of the fog bank. There wasn't much to see. To the east and west he saw the flashes of bright lights and the spreading star shells from a half dozen firework displays. The headset and engine noise kept him from hearing them, but he could imagine the thumps from the explosions. *Happy Fourth of July.* In front of him and a little to the southwest he could just make out the dim outlines of a ship. He should be over Eastern Bay, he thought, south of the Chesapeake Bay Bridge, and not near the channel at all. As he drew closer he saw the ship had a loading crane positioned on its starboard side and in the process of offloading or retrieving something from a barge. What looked like a buoy dangled from the crane's cable.

Funny, that. The Coast Guard usually handled buoys. And as far as he knew no ships' channel came this far into Eastern Bay. The ship below him did not have the classic white hull and bright red-orange marker stripe of a Coast Guard vessel. It looked more like a tramp steamer from an old movie, barely showing either running or marker lights. And what would anyone be doing on the Fourth of July, in the middle of the night, and so close to shore? Not positioning a buoy, certainly.

He put his right wing over and started a lazy turn around the ship. The fog bank still lingered over most of the bay behind him. Nearby, a fireworks display had started, pop...hiss...flash...boom, pop...hiss...flash...boom—the last very close. Where would that have come from? When he had completed a little more than half of his turn he recognized the object suspended in the air beside the ship's hull. He scrabbled for his cell phone, aimed the phone's camera lens toward the ship and pressed the "capture" button repeatedly. He opened the phone and speed-dialed. One ring, two.

"Come on, come on."

"Hi, this is Lizzy. I can't come to the phone right now…"

"Lizzy, pick up…pick up."

"…but if you leave a message…"

"Lizzy, pick up."

"Beep."

"Lizzy, call your uncle Charlie. Tell him that there is something really bad going on…" From the corner of his eye, Nick saw the orange trail of yet another rocket arc up and toward him. A very big rocket. Too big for the Fourth of July. The plane lurched. He dropped the phone. It slid under the pedals at his feet.

◇◇◇

"What was that?"

"What was what?"

"I heard an explosion."

A brief flash of light flickered through the port hole, just enough to light the tiny V-berth. A thump followed a second or two later. He rolled toward the girl, and the thirty-two foot Jeanneau sail boat rocked to port.

"Like that one?" he said.

"Yes, only louder, and then there was all this splashing outside."

"Splashing?" More flashes and thumps followed the first one. "It's the Fourth of July, Deedee. There'll be explosions all night somewhere. The splashes were probably caused by a school of fish breaking the surface."

"Hell of a big school, then. It sounded more like people doing cannon balls off a high board—louder even."

"If a school of big fish, rock fish say, were after a bunch of smaller ones and they all broke at the same time—"

"You think?"

"I don't know. Maybe."

"I'm going on deck to see the fireworks. That's why we sailed over here in the first place, isn't it? If it hadn't been for the fog… If we can see the flashes it must have lifted or something."

"Stay here, I'll show you some fireworks."

She laughed and stood up on the berth. The forward hatch was open so her head and shoulders cleared the deck line.

"Wow, you should see this, Ralphie."

She climbed on deck and he felt the boat rock as she made her way to the cockpit. He grabbed a torch, wrapped a towel around his waist, and climbed up after her. The fog had lifted. The flotilla he'd planned to join in the bay had disappeared hours ago when the fog bank rolled in. Watching fireworks from boats rafted up in Eastern Bay had become a local tradition, but fog had ended this year's gathering. They were alone.

"Look at that," she said and pointed westward in the general direction of Gibson Island. Flash...pop...thump. "Hey, let's skinny dip."

"No, not in the dark." He noticed for the first time that his marker lights were out. He'd forgotten to run the generator and the battery must have died. He hoped there'd be wind tomorrow. There was no way he'd get the little diesel started if both the cabin and engine batteries were dead. "The tide is running out. If you go over the side you could be caught in it and with no light—"

"Don't be such a wuss. Turn on the torch thing and we can home in on it." With that she dove into the inky black water and disappeared. He swung the light around looking for her. No sign. The light arced back and forth as he looked for her head to break above water.

"Deedee," he called, "where are you?" His heart began to race. Then he heard her laugh. She'd swum under the boat and surfaced on the other side. Idiot! With a four and a half foot draft under the keel and in the dark...

"Come on in, you big sissy," she shouted and stroked away into the night.

He dropped his towel and positioned the light so he could see it from the water. He'd lowered the swim ladder and started down when she screamed.

"What?"

"Ugh, I think something touched me," she said and swam back to the boat. "I'm done here. Yuck."

He pulled her aboard. He could feel the goose bumps on her body. She took a towel from the boom and dried off.

"Rockets red glare in the forward bunk," he said and she giggled. He doused the flash. In the dark he scanned the horizon. A hundred yards out he thought he saw the outlines of a small freighter. He frowned and then shrugged.

Their lovemaking caused the boat to rock gently, bow to stern. They were too absorbed in it to hear the gentle thump as a Zodiac came along side, or to hear the muffled footsteps aft. Only the flash of light in their eyes told them they were not alone, but by then it was too late.

Chapter Two

A brisk wind blew out of the east and across the deserted beach. Late September in Dewey Beach meant few people, except for the weekenders down from Washington or Baltimore to winterize their properties before the big nor'easters blew down the coast, tossing beach equipment and sand against the sea walls and jetties. The chilly early morning air smelled clean and salty. Months before it carried the cloyingly sweet smell of coconut-scented sun block and the voices of hundreds of people trying to squeeze one more day, one more hour, of vacation from the time allotted them. Ike Schwartz placed his coffee cup on the deck railing, propped his feet up next to it, and watched, fascinated, as the sun struggled to clear the horizon.

Sunsets he knew. Sunrises were a relative rarity for him. In the Shenandoah Valley, sunrises were screened by the mountains to the east. The sun didn't make a sudden appearance as it did at the beach. It seemed to just materialize and then the day began. But this…this was spectacular. The sky reddened, turned orange, and golden light bathed everything. Looking at it one could believe that every day arrived clean and innocent in that brilliant bath. Clouds trailing southward glowed pink and orange against a lavender sky, and then, pop, "Here comes the sun, here comes the sun…" I should do this more often, he thought. His only regret? No Ruth.

"A month's vacation is what you need," Ruth had said. "When was the last time you just kicked back?"

"I had that long weekend with you in Toronto."

"That doesn't count."

It didn't. They had spent the days talking about where they were headed. How could they blend two widely divergent careers and still make a go of it? She had a college to run, she'd said. President of Callend College, now Callend University, or not, she had to pitch in with the rest of the faculty. Next year would be a "make or break."

"You will not always be the president of Callend," he'd said.

"And what about you? Will you always be the sheriff of Picketsville? We have a way to go, Ike. We should take time out," she'd said. "We are not in a place or at a time when either of us can commit to anything permanent." Her voice had nearly cracked then. He'd let it pass.

He watched as the sun continued its ascent. The gold light faded to pale ginger ale and then flat daylight. He wished he'd persuaded his father to come to the beach with him. But Abe Schwartz's ebullient and garrulous nature seemed to have died with his wife in December. Theirs had been a storybook love affair, and with her no longer a part of his daily equation, Abe looked old and worn. Nothing Ike could say would convince his father to accept his help.

"You go on down there, Ike," he'd said. "I'll be all right. I just need to say goodbye to your Momma my own way."

He'd been saying goodbye for nearly ten months.

So, Ike, who had not had a vacation in years, rented a cottage off-season at Dewey Beach, Delaware, and now sat contemplating the stretch of deserted sand and the Atlantic Ocean beyond. Somewhere across the horizon he imagined an Irish fisherman might be staring back at him.

He missed his routine, missed his friends, and missed Ruth. She had said, barely glancing up from piles of paper on her desk, "Maybe a weekend, Ike. I'll try for a weekend. No, I can't say which. Send me your address after you settle in, and if I can, I'll surprise you. I've got your cell number."

Grains of sand danced across the porch decking, urged along by the steady breeze and collected in miniature dunes beside his empty boots. He shivered and folded his arms across his chest. His coffee started to cool, and he still needed to make a decision about breakfast. Breakfast was his favorite meal, but he had never acquired the skills to make a decent one. He could fry eggs and bacon; who couldn't? And making coffee only meant measuring the correct amount of grounds and water in the basket and pot, respectively. After that things became more complex. He tried to make those crispy diner hash browns and ended with greasy mashed potatoes. And you can forget fried tomatoes. His grits were invariably lumpy and had the consistency of Portland cement so, back home in Picketsville, he ate breakfast at the Crossroads Diner, where regulars gathered to be fed and abused by its proprietor.

The telephone rang. He'd been told the land line service had been discontinued. That bit of information had pleased him very much. He had his cell phone for emergencies and had instructed his staff not to call. He intended to leave it off but would check his voice mail a few times a day. A real emergency would require catching him when he had it on, or a call to the Delaware State Police. The phone rang again. Nobody he knew could possibly have the number, even if it was in service. He'd picked it up to listen for a dial tone when he first arrived. There had been none. But now…it rang again. Finally, to stop the noise and satisfy his curiosity, he looped a finger through the handle of his coffee cup and shuffled indoors.

"Yeah," he said into a phone so permanently lubricated with a season's worth of sun screen it nearly slipped from his hand. He half expected someone asking for the previous tenant or the owner.

"You had breakfast yet?" Charlie Garland asked.

"I won't even guess how you did this, Charlie, but I have to tell you, it's scary what you spooks can do."

"I tried your cell phone but all I got was voice mail. You should stay in touch."

"I had the reverse in mind, actually. What do you want?"

"There's a nice breakfast place in Rehoboth Beach. I could meet you there."

"Meet me? Where are you, Charlie?"

"I am sitting in an official-looking black SUV on Ocean Highway about ten miles out. Can you join me?"

"Sure, why not. Are you going to tell me why you're in Delaware at this hour, or will that be the price of breakfast?"

"The Avenue Restaurant, on Rehoboth Avenue, a block or so from the beach, I'll be there in five minutes."

◇◇◇

"Trasker, fetch!" Barney threw the stick—farther this time. It sailed over the edge of an embankment and out of sight. The big German shepherd galloped away and disappeared over the rim of a streambed. He waited. The seconds ticked by. By now the dog should have come crashing back to him, stick in mouth. That worried him. He knew the dog was probably okay, but ever since the Dumonts' two shepherds, Fritz and Otto, disappeared the previous month, he'd become slightly paranoid about Trasker. He knew he could take care of himself and, unlike Fritz and Otto, rarely strayed far from home.

"Trasker!" he called. The dog's head appeared briefly. It stared pleadingly at him and dropped out of sight again. He heard low whimpering.

"Trasker, here boy." The dog barked loudly. He walked toward the sound.

"What is it?"

Whimper.

The embankment dropped away sharply to the streambed. The dog seemed to be worrying something—the stick? Wet leaves piled up at the brook's edge. It had risen with a late September thunderstorm the previous afternoon, and now splashed over and around a series of flat rocks which seemed to have been placed in it like stepping stones. They appeared oddly out of place.

He sidestepped down into the swale and walked toward the dog. It looked up at him, uncertainty in its eyes. He stepped forward to see what it had in its mouth. It didn't look like the stick he'd thrown. The dog growled as he drew closer—a low rumble. Trasker never growled at him. Something was amiss. The dog turned sideways, dodged away a few feet, and wheeled to face him again, its jaws still clenched around the object. The man looked at the ground just vacated by the dog.

Bones. He couldn't be sure. Human, animal? He couldn't tell. He leaned forward and looked more closely. A skull of some sort, sloping head, certainly not human. A dog? No sharp canine teeth, not a dog. His limited knowledge of biology in general and skulls in particular, led him to believe that a predator, a dog or meat eater, would have sharp teeth. A dentist would know. An arrangement of long and short bones. It wasn't so much the bones that worried him, but their seeming placement on the ground—as if they had been set out with some sort of plan in mind. Something was not right. The dog seemed to study him.

"Trasker, drop it." He said. The dog hesitated. He repeated his command. The dog retreated a few steps, snorted and dropped the bone—a large bone—too large to be a rabbit or any local wildlife. He slipped the leash back on the dog and climbed back to the meadow floor. He hurried to his car, put the dog in the back seat, and called the Sheriff's office. He was no expert, but some those bones could be human, or not. Either way, the whole scene had a spookiness about it. He did not consider himself to be either superstitious or intuitive, but he sensed something bad, perhaps even evil, had happened there.

Chapter Three

Ike found the restaurant and slipped into a booth across from Charlie Garland. He and Charlie had a history. After Ike left the CIA, Charlie had soldiered on in his job as a public relations man—a position Ike knew provided a cover for what Charlie really did. Ike never asked what that was, but he knew.

"So, to what do I owe the honor of this visit?" Ike said, and studied the menu. He didn't know why he did so. He always asked for the same thing.

"You don't need that. I've already ordered for you," Charlie said, and sipped his coffee. The place was filled with breakfast aromas and sounds, bacon frying, coffee gurgling in large stainless steel urns, and toast. Ike inhaled. Surely it beat any scent manufactured by a Paris *parfumerie*. If women were serious about snagging a man with scent, he thought, they might try something called Diner #1.

"Of course you have," Ike said. He knew from experience that in many ways he was distressingly predictable. That Charlie knew his breakfast preferences and probable bar order did not dismay him anymore, but he sometimes worried that if he were so predictable he ran the risk of being compromised? The waitress brought him his coffee. "I ask again, Charlie, what—"

"In a minute, Ike. I am studying the people with the mirror over the counter."

"Studying? As in looking for someone or somebody?"

Charlie turned to face Ike and grinned. "Just practicing. Are you enjoying your vacation?"

"I was, until you called. I watched the sun come up this morning. Lovely. But you didn't drive down here from Langley to ask me that."

Charlie studied Ike like he would a steak at a butcher's shop. Finally, apparently satisfied with his choice, he nodded and pulled a folder from a soft leather case lying on the bench beside him.

"No, you're right. I need a favor," Charlie said, voice lowered and serious.

"And that would be?"

"My niece's fiancé disappeared three months ago. I want you to find out what happened to him."

"He disappeared? Disappeared, as in missing person, disappeared, as in snatched, or just disappeared, as in mysterious?"

"The latter. He had his pilot's license and filed a flight plan from Martin State Airport—that's north-east of Baltimore—to Salisbury and took off. He never made it. That was the Fourth of July."

"An accident, surely. No, you wouldn't be here asking me to track him down if that's what you believed. It's something else, isn't it?"

"I think so, but the FAA, the Coast Guard, the National Transportation Safety Board, Maryland officialdom, have all washed their hands. As far as they are concerned, it was an accident. He flew on a moonless night into a fog bank. He was an inexperienced pilot and they think he probably drove himself into the bay. Death spiral. No wreckage has been found, and no body. I need you to find out what happened."

"What do you think happened?"

"No idea, but there's this." Charlie pulled out a small tape recorder and punched play. Ike listened as a tinny voice pleaded on the phone, "Lizzy, call your uncle Charlie. Tell him that there is something really bad going on—"

"You notice anything in that message?"

"You mean besides the static and thump at the end?"

"The message, Ike, the message."

"Did he know what you do for a living?"

"Sort of, yes. Enough obviously."

"He said call you. Not the police, not the Coast Guard, just you. He thought he saw something that belonged in your bailiwick, and judging by his tone of voice, something that frightened him."

"So it would seem. Will you help me?"

"Charlie, helping you begs the question. What do you want me to do."

"I don't want to screw up your vacation but—"

"Not to worry. The truth is, I have been on my vacation for exactly three days. Never mind what I said before, I am bored to the proverbial tears. I can give you three and a half weeks, that's all. But I have to tell you, I don't know what I can do that others haven't already done."

"You used to fly, didn't you?"

"Not exactly. The ops planners, in the wisdom born of chronic isolation, got it into their collective pointy heads one year that it would be a good thing if their field agents could fly—watched too many movies, I think. We all qualified, twin engine, IFR rated. But I never really did much with it after that."

"But you can or could if you had to?"

"Yes, probably."

"Back track, Ike. Start with Martin State Airport. Talk to the flying instructor up there. His name is Trent Fonts. Maybe he knows something. Fly the same course and see where it takes you. You know how to do this stuff better than I."

"I'm a little rusty."

"I'll buy you some oil."

"You can't do this yourself?"

"You know I can't. If Homeland Security, the FBI, or any other involved agencies found out a CIA employee was working a case on their turf—"

"Right." Ike sat back and contemplated his coffee cup. "I don't know. A guy flies out one night and disappears. No wreckage—"

"There may be wreckage, just not visible."

"What do you mean, just not visible?"

"He owned an old war bird, a Korean War spotter plane, a big heavy-duty Cessna high-wing. It was painted camo. If it splashed and sank in the mud in the Chesapeake Bay, there'd be no way—"

"I thought all those planes had orange Day-Glo nosebowls."

"He and his co-owners painted it over with more camo."

"That legal?"

"No idea. They did it, though. I think they had a notice from the FAA to correct that, but I can't be sure."

"Great, so the top side would be lost in the mud, The underside of the wings would have been light blue and—"

"Ike, there was no wreckage sighted, period."

"I'll do what I can, Charlie. Three and a half weeks, max."

Charlie pushed his eggs and hash browns aside, slipped Ike a thick envelope and the folder he'd removed from his case earlier, and stood.

"It's all in here. Money, credit cards, IDs, names, reports, some photos, everything I have. I'll check in with you in two days," he said, and vanished through steamed up glass doors.

Frank Sutherlin's new sister-in-law, Essie, waved at him on her way to the ladies' room. It was the third time in the last two hours. Frank was a bachelor. He'd asked his mother if there was something about women's plumbing he missed in biology class. He described Essie's frequent trips by his door. Dorothy Sutherlin had raised seven boys and counted her blessings that six of them were still alive and that Frank had moved back home when her son, Billy, married and moved in with his new bride. She beamed.

"I'm fixing to get me a grandbaby," she said.

So that was it. The phone rang and he picked up. Essie, who normally sat at the dispatch desk, had not returned and no one else was available.

"Sheriff's Office, Acting Sheriff Sutherlin speaking. No, it's... Frank...Billy's off today. Out buying booties if I hear right." He listened to the caller, said he'd be right out, and hung up. Essie rounded the corner.

"Do you have something to tell me, Essie? A little secret, perhaps?"

Essie stared at him wide-eyed. "I don't think so. You know maybe I should see a doctor. I am spending way too much time in the can lately."

"That'd be a good idea, Sis. Or you can save yourself a copay and call your mother-in-law."

Essie frowned. "Mother-in-law...Ma?"

"Yeah. Listen, I just took a call from a Barney Dunhill. He's a professor up at the college, I think. He found a stash of suspicious looking bones out in the park. I don't think it's anything, but I'm going to drive out there and see, just in case. Tell Charlie Picket to watch the store while I'm gone."

"Yes sir, Mr. Acting Sheriff, sir. How're you making out with Ike being away?"

"Well, to tell the truth, I would have been happier if he'd given me a couple more weeks to get used to this place before he took off for vacation. What's that place he's at?"

"Delaware someplace, is all I know. Billy said to call him if you need anything."

"He's okay with Ike making me the acting and not him?"

"Billy? Shoot, yes."

"Okay, I'm off."

Chapter Four

The Reverend Blake Fisher made a point of never interfering with the ladies who prepared the altar for Sunday. They reciprocated by never telling him what they were doing. It wouldn't have made a difference in any case. The great divide that separates altar guilds and clergy is traditional, historic, and inviolable. A few guild members across the world are convinced it is even Biblical. So, it came as a modest surprise when one of their number rapped on his door and asked if he had a minute to talk.

"Come in, Mavis," he said. He assumed she had a personal problem to discuss. He was wrong.

"Father Blake," she said, worry creasing her forehead, "it's the silver cruets."

"What about the cruets?"

"They're missing."

"Missing. When did they go missing?"

"Well, that's the thing, you see." He didn't. "The first one disappeared two weeks ago."

"Two weeks ago?"

"Yes, but it didn't seem important at the time. We, that is, I…just substituted the crystal ones instead. But you probably noticed that already. Actually, they are much easier to work with and…You don't have to worry about which gets the wine and which gets the water when you use them."

Blake shook his head. Which cruet received the communion wine and which the water introduced a wholly new concept to him. He didn't know that it mattered. He reckoned if he thought about it for a while he would uncover yet one more example of a tradition whose origin is lost in time and has now become canon in the minds of altar guilds. "No one said anything about a cruet gone missing."

"No. I figured one of the other girls, women, had taken it home to polish."

"Just one?"

"Yes. Now that you mention it, that is odd, isn't it…to polish just one, I mean."

"So, one cruet went missing two weeks ago. You said 'they're missing.' The other one is gone, too?"

"Yes, just now. Well, I noticed it just now, and since no one seems to know about the first one, I guess it's safe to assume they may have been taken."

Blake stood and accompanied Mavis Bowers into the sacristy. Sure enough, the safe stood open, and only protective cloths lay in the place usually occupied by the cruets.

"You've called around, I assume. No one remembers missing the silver?"

"No."

"Is anything else missing?"

"I don't think so. Let me see." Mavis peered myopically into the safe.

"Check in the back."

Mavis rooted around in the back. "Oh dear! The little cup is missing, too."

"Little cup? What little cup?"

"We were given a silver cup—goblet, I guess you'd call it. Someone thought it could be used as a chalice. We've never used it, but…"

"It's missing, too? We should call the sheriff's office."

"Oh dear. I don't know."

"Problem?"

"Well, suppose a guild member has them and…I don't know. It would be so embarrassing."

"But you said you called around and no one knew anything about the disappearance. You did, didn't you?"

"Yes, but…Oh dear."

"Mavis, something is bothering you. What is it?"

"It's just that…well Esther Peepers has been on the guild for, mercy, sixty years and she's a little pixilated. It would be such a shame if the sheriff came and then…you understand."

Blake understood. Esther Peepers qualified as a matriarch. Senior pastors, rectors, and clergy in general, even bishops, learned, usually in the first months of their first call, that matriarchs are never to be crossed. Absent-minded or not, he'd be treading on thin ice if he were to ruffle the petticoats of Esther Peepers. He frowned at the mixed metaphor. He guessed the first symptoms of trivia-stress had arrived. Not that Esther would do anything herself; she sailed through life as a delightful octogenarian ditherer. But her guild colleagues would be upset for her; and he'd have several months of fence-mending ahead of him.

"Suppose you and I drop in on Esther and ask," he said.

Mavis looked doubtful. "What would we say?"

"Indeed, I don't know, Mavis, but we have to do something. If the silver has been stolen, we need to notify the police. If, God forbid, it's lost, we need to call the insurance company. The longer we wait, the worse it gets. Two weeks, you said."

"Dorothy Sutherlin would be a better choice to make the call," she said with something akin to fear in her voice. "Two of her sons work for the sheriff. She'd know how to…you know…ask."

Blake realized there would be no convincing Mavis to do otherwise, and on reflection, thought she might be right. Whether Dorothy Sutherlin's sons, and daughter-in-law for that matter, worked in the sheriff's office weighed less on his decision than Dorothy's well known common sense. She, he believed, could penetrate the murky recesses of Esther Peepers' mind better than anyone in town.

"Fine. Good idea. I'll call her and see if she will do it."

Mavis Bowers looked as if she'd received a last-minute pardon from the governor. He retreated to his office and made the call.

Dorothy Sutherlin answered the phone on the third ring. Blake held the receiver away from his ear. Dorothy had raised seven boisterous boys and in the years of their upbringing had been forced to communicate with them in a voice which could only be described as stentorian.

"Hello. That you, Father Blake?"

"Yes, Dorothy. Listen, we have a problem here at the church. Mavis has discovered the silver cruets and a small chalice we evidently never use are missing. Before we call one of your boys in, she thought we might call on Esther Peepers first...on the outside chance she might have taken them home to polish and forgot to return them."

"And Mavis said maybe I'd be a better choice to brace Esther than her?"

"Yes."

"Figures. Mavis has the backbone of a slug." Blake spun around to see if Mavis was within earshot. He doubted Dorothy would care if she'd been overheard, but Blake tended to assume the embarrassment of others. Mavis was nowhere in sight.

"Oh, my, the old gal isn't there, is she?"

"No, she's not."

"Well, that's good, I guess. When do you want to call on Esther? I'm tied up 'til three. We could go after that."

"We'll plan on meeting here at three, then. I'll call Esther and set it up. If you don't hear from me in the next twenty minutes, it's a go."

A call to Mrs. Peepers resulted in her agreement to see Blake.

"Oh, gracious, do come by. Can you take tea? I'll make tea. I hope regular tea is acceptable. So many of you young people want decaf these days, or green, or something new, you know... herbal. But it isn't the same is it? You're not one of those people are you? It's not a church thing, I hope. No, of course it isn't, we have a coffee hour, don't we? Would you rather have coffee?"

Blake assured her that he did, indeed, drink regular tea and coffee and had no feelings for or against the use of caffeine, nor did the church. Mrs. Peepers seemed relieved by that.

"You haven't seen Ogden, have you?" she asked.

"Sorry. Who?"

"I'm missing my cat, Ogden. I named him after my first husband. He was so sweet. My husband, I mean. And the cat, too. That's why I—"

"Yes, I see. No, I haven't seen your cat, I don't think. What does he look like?" Cats for Blake were an amorphous category. Seen one, seen them all.

"Black. Black as the ace of spades, Father Blake, and sweet."

"I'll try to remember to look around. See you after three."

He hung up and stared out of his office window. The leaves were beginning to turn. He made a mental note to invite Mary Miller, for an afternoon drive along the Skyline Drive to look at the fall colors. Officially, Mary was the church's organist. Unofficially, to Blake, she was considerably more.

Except for drug money, why would anyone break into a church and steal silver that is only used in a church ritual. What other possible use could it have?

Chapter Five

It had been a while since Ike had run down a preflight check list. He circled the Cessna 170S pausing to inspect, adjust, and study the plane and its exterior. The agent from Delmarva Aviation stood off to one side with his hands in his pockets, watching. In addition to serving as a local fixed-base operation, the company rented planes and gave flying lessons. The latter transactions produced a certain level of anxiety for them. The planes represented an important asset, and even though they viewed renting one to a stranger as a business transaction, they fretted over them, like parents who worry about the family sedan when the resident teenager takes it out for the first time.

They'd taken Ike's credit card, and a few eyebrows shot up when he'd slid it across the counter. They hadn't dealt with that many government credit cards in the first place and certainly none like the one Charlie had supplied. He'd wondered if Charlie would catch any Agency flak for using government assets in his, so far, personal investigation, and then decided he wouldn't make it his problem. He'd waited patiently while a few long-distance phone calls were placed and a smiling acceptance granted. He'd signed an open-ended contract. He didn't know how long he'd need the aircraft; no more than three weeks, though.

Satisfied, he gave the agent a thumbs-up and climbed into the cockpit to continue his pre-flight. The plane had been fueled. He snapped on the radio, adjusted the squelch, and signaled to

the ramp attendant to pull the chocks. The big engine turned
over easily, and he taxied to the end of the runway.

Cleared for take-off, he turned onto the runway and sent the
Cessna rolling down its length. The plane lifted gracefully from
the ground and Ike was airborne. *Up in the air, junior bird men.
Up in the air...upside down.* Upside down—not good.

Ike made three wide turns over the airport with a touch and
go on each loop. His hours in the air had been scant, but he still
had the skills. *Like riding a bike.* He needed practice, and that
was his excuse to fly to Martin State and take some instruction.
Nick Reynolds had received his at Brett Aviation. That would be
where Ike would register for lessons. He set a course to Martin
State and settled back in the left seat. BWI traffic control called
him twice to request he change altitude. The corridor over the
bay carried a lot of commercial traffic, it seemed.

There wasn't much to see out by the streambed. The bones were
gathered in a tight grouping. He studied a skull in the center of
the pile. Barney's description of an "arrangement" eluded him.
It was just a pile of bones. A goat, he decided. He stepped back
to take in the area and noticed the stones in the stream bed.
They had been placed there, of that he was certain. He looked at
the bones and then at the stones again. Barney's "arrangement"
popped out at him. He couldn't be sure, but he sensed the bones,
or at least the skull, had been placed to point toward the stones
and by implication the field beyond. He crossed the stream,
careful to keep his balance as he stepped gingerly on the stones
in the stream. They were neither set firmly nor designed to bear
his bulk. A path led away from the stream uphill and at an angle
toward a wood farther away. He followed it, his eyes scanning
the ground as he moved toward the trees. The grass had been
trampled. He could not tell how recently or how often.

The area's karst topography had created a sinkhole many years
ago. Frank recognized it as a gathering place for teenagers in his
past. The Passion Pit, they'd called it. He supposed it must still

serve that purpose. He worked his way down into its depth. At the bottom he realized he would be invisible to anyone walking in the fields above. The sinkhole had to be twenty feet deep, at least, and sixty across at the top.

In its center, someone had erected a low table or perhaps a high bench from three rock slabs. Two unmatched shorter blocks formed the base or legs, and a larger flagstone its top. Because the two upright stones were uneven in length, the table-bench sloped left to right as he faced it. He glanced down at a trampled fire pit at his feet. To his right and left he could make out two more. He circled the area and discovered another two. All five seemed roughly equidistant from the table and each other. If he connected them in his mind's eye, they formed a five sided figure with the table/bench in its center. He kicked at the ashes in the first fire site and saw what appeared to be the burnt end of a stake in its center. The other four seemed to have the same. Someone had measured the positioning of the fires with more than casual accuracy.

He didn't need any help identifying rusty stains on the table's surface. Blood.

"Essie," he said into the microphone on his shoulder, "I need you to call the lab and have them send out a crew to the State Park."

"Where you at?"

"Tell them to come out the Covington Road. After the second little hill look for me on their right. There's a sinkhole out here I want them to look at. If they can't come pretty quick, call me back."

"Roger that, Frank. I know that place. Everybody does... or did. Didn't you used to go out there when you was in high school?"

"Not much, I mostly missed out on the sinkhole action back then. Why'd anybody go there anyway?"

"Oh, yeah, I guess you might not know, since you never was much of a lady's man. Say, what did you mean I should talk to Ma?"

"Not now, Essie. Just get the lab boys out here."

He strolled back to the stream, to the bones, and with some care, moved them to the side. After he'd moved a half dozen he realized someone had already tried to do that and the plastic trash bag which apparently held them had split. He carefully lifted a corner. Beneath laid the remains of what he took to be a cat. A black cat, as nearly as he could tell. He stood and scratched his head.

His radio crackled. "Frank, the lab is on the way. They said they knew the place."

"Good, Essie, you know of any body missing a cat? A black cat?"

"Nope, but Ma might. She knows near everybody. Speaking of which—"

"Later, Essie. Oh, and tell the ETs to be sure and bring a camera and a tape measure, if they weren't already planning to anyway."

He paced the distance between the fire sights, placing his heel on the stake. Six steps exactly to have his toe on the next stake. A pentagon, a table with blood on it, and a black cat. He scratched his head, unsure what any of that meant but whatever it was, he guessed, it was not good.

Chapter Six

Ike got a visual on Martin State Airport and began his approach. Cleared to land, he set the plane down on the runway and pulled into the taxiway. He found Brett Aviation and eased the plane to one side, where a ramp attendant wig-wagged him to a tie-down at the side of their building. He shut down the engine. He asked to see the manager. The ramp girl pointed to the office entrance. Inside he asked to speak to Trent Fonts and was referred to a tall, balding man in a back office.

"I'm Trent Fonts." He extended his hand.

"Ike Schwartz. I'm here to sign up for some refresher lessons."

"Fine. We can surely do that. How'd you hear about us, if I may ask?"

"I heard about you from a friend of a friend, you might say."

"Friend of a…who might that be?"

"Nick Reynolds. I guess you remember him?"

"Good kid, too bad what happened."

Ike nodded and glanced around the room. Pictures of airplanes, the vision of the late Glen L. Martin's jet sea plane, and a smattering of 'B' list celebrities covered the walls. "Any thoughts about what put him in the drink?"

"Who'd you say you were?"

"Ike Schwartz."

"And you want flying lessons?"

"Yes."

"You were close to Nick?"

"A friend of a—"

"Friend. Yes, I heard you. It's just that since his accident, all kinds of people have come around asking about him…and it."

"All kinds?"

"Family, 'friends,' police, FAA, you name it, and others."

"Like who?"

"Like you, for example. And some spooky people who could be ICE, FBI, or CIA for all I know. What's up with Nick? Was he an undercover somebody?"

"Okay, I'll need your help. Truth is, I really would like some lessons. It's been a while. Also Nick's fiancée's uncle, who is one of those spooky people you mentioned, thinks something is not quite right about the disappearance. So it's semiprofessional but also a personal call. I volunteered to poke around, that's all."

"Credentials?"

Ike dropped his ID, badge, and Air Force certification on the table.

"You're ex-Air Force?"

"No. I used to be one of those spooky people, too. Air Force taught us how to fly. Long time ago."

Trent studied Ike for a full minute, shook his head and signaled for Ike to take a seat.

"Nick. Good kid, good pilot too, for a newbie, but, like all young kids, he thought he was invincible. It was the Fourth of July, you know." He paused and sipped from the coffee cup on his desk, made a face and put it down.

"It was like this. I didn't want him to fly that night. He was a good pilot, like I said, but night flying can be tricky. Well, you know about that, I expect." Fonts' eyes focused on the wall behind Ike. He took another sip of coffee, put the cup down and shoved it away.

"Coffee's in that pot behind you."

"No, thanks, not now." The aroma of badly burnt coffee convinced him he could wait. "What do you remember about that night?"

"That night…well, okay. The sun had set and with no moon; it got dark in a hurry. We were standing right out there," Trent pointed to the T hangars, "and I argued with him. I warned him, but he was itching to see his girl, and he had this fancy box…had a present, one of those little necklaces, you know, a choker, he called it. 'You don't approve?' he says. Nick knew what my answer would be but must have figured he'd better get the argument over with as quick as possible. Like, he was late already or something. I was angry and worried. His flight plan is letter-perfect, but he wasn't asking me about that. He wanted my blessing for the flight. 'Well, you won't get it.' I says.

"'Look,' he says, 'I can do this. It's no big deal. I fly south past the Bay Bridge and turn southeastward to Cambridge, then south to Salisbury. I could do it flying by the seat of my pants.'

"Seat of his pants! I told him he wasn't ready for it. 'You've logged the minimum hours to fly at night. There is no moon so you will not have a visual on the horizon.' 'I've got instruments,' he says, like that would be enough, like some real experience flying in the pitch black didn't amount to anything. 'There will be lights on both sides of the Chesapeake and fireworks. No problems.'

"I practically shouted at him. 'Will you listen to me? You are a good pilot. But this is different. Too many new pilots like you think they can fly over water at night. I got instruments—there will be lights—yahda, yahda, yahda—but then no one ever sees them again. Junior Kennedy had more hours and experience than you, and he's gone. You think you're better?'"

Ike let Fonts rant on. He obviously had an emotional investment in the situation and needed to vent. Expiation.

"'I've done this one many times. No moon won't make a difference. Worst case, I follow the channel markers.' Worst case, my foot.

"'I'll be on BWI radar the whole way down. I fly straight and then east. If I slip off course, all I have to do is head southeast and turn on the transponder. When I am in range, the runway lights at Salisbury will go on and I just make my approach and land.' Like he knew all about it. I should have stopped him right then and there. I could have done it, you know."

Ike heard the guilt and grief in Trent's voice. He knew the feeling, remembered the times years ago in the field when he'd let someone go into a high-risk situation, when he knew no was certain it might go south.

"'This may be my last chance to fly this bird. Do you have any idea what I had to do to get the plane for the Fourth of July weekend?' He tells me that and, I don't know, I guess I just caved in.

"Sitting on the apron in the dark outside the hangar, that plane was damn near invisible. Only the white stars amidships and wing tips showed up in the light from inside the hangar. It practically disappeared in the moonless night. I never saw him again. I wish—"

"That he'd listened to you? He was young and cocky. There wasn't anything you could or should have said that would have made any difference."

"Yeah…still, I wish…"

Ike waited for Fonts to regroup.

"His plane was a beefed-up Cessna 172, high wing, an old war bird, painted olive drab, and had seen action as a spotter plane. Vietnam, Korea—I don't know which—never asked. He, and two of his pals had purchased it from a woman down on the Eastern Shore. They kept it hangared here and flew weekends mostly. Anyway once he's in the air, the tower at BWI picked him up and assigned him an altitude. I don't know anything else."

"Your best guess, Trent, did he slip into a death spiral or some other rookie screw-up?"

"Guess? Okay, I would say, no. He was raw, maybe a little rash, but not easily distracted in the air. You get to know things about people when you fly with them. He'd call in and ask for help, turn around before things got too dicey. He was Navy, you know, not a pilot, but smart and not reckless."

"Will you help me?"

"Do what?"

"Fly the course he took that night, like it's a lesson, only we scan the land and bay all the way down to where he dropped off the radar at BWI. There has to be something. Planes don't just disappear into thin air."

"Maybe. See, I already flew that patch and…" Trent's voice trailed off.

"And?"

"It's just a maybe, but I thought I saw something the next day."

"Did you report it?"

"It was in the wrong place. It didn't make any sense. I figured it must have been something else."

Ike let it pass. If Trent connected it to something later, he'd say so. In the meantime, he felt sure he was missing something important.

Chapter Seven

Trent Fonts cleared the clutter from his desk, unfolded a large aeronautical chart, and spread it out.

"I pulled his flight plan and made a tracing." He put his index finger on the chart. "This was his course and here, the check points." He tapped the map and traced a line he'd drawn with a red felt-tipped pen. Ike looked at the line, which ran from Martin State straight down the center of the Chesapeake Bay, then, south of the Bay Bridge, turned easterly toward Cambridge, then veered again south-southeast to Salisbury. "The X shows where he dropped off the radar at BWI."

Ike studied the map. The X covered an area a mile or two off the northwest tip of Kent Island, a heavily developed area. If the plane had gone into the water there, someone must have seen or heard something.

"Nobody said anything about hearing or seeing a plane in trouble north of Kent Island?"

"Nope."

"If his engine had stalled, how far could he have glided?"

"It was a heavy Cessna, and at that point he'd still have most of his fuel, so not too far—a mile or more. It would depend on his altitude, of course."

"But still, there are several small strips on the island. Here and here." Ike put his finger on the marks indicating landing fields.

"The only real choice would be at the Bay Bridge field here." Trent put his finger on a spot just south of the bridge. These others are private and not lighted. Add to that there was no moon. Nick knew the strips, but I don't know if he could have found them in the dark, and if he overshot them he'd end up in the bay opposite Annapolis. He'd have to triple-click to get the lights on at the Bay Bridge field. If he was trying to stay aloft he might not have thought of that in time. No way, on a moonless night he'd have found the field otherwise."

"Triple-click?"

"Yeah, they don't light the field twenty-four seven. If you need to land after dark you raise their frequency on your radio and click the talk button three times, quick. The lights come on for fifteen minutes. It takes some practice."

"Had he ever done that?"

"I made him do it once before I'd sign off on his ticket."

Ike studied the map some more. There had to be a glitch somewhere. "Is there a time stamp when he disappeared from the radar?" Trent pulled a sheaf of papers from a pile on his desk and withdrew a piece of foolscap.

"Twenty-one thirteen."

Ike drummed his fingers on the desk. Twenty-one thirteen, Zulu, nine thirteen at night. He opened his phone and dialed Charlie on the private line he'd been given.

"Charlie, is there a time stamp on the call your niece got from her fiancé?"

"Geeze Ike, I don't know. Hold on, I'm in the middle of something here. Is it important?"

"Until we figure this thing out, everything is important. But in this case—yeah, very important." Ike could hear drawers opening and closing and an exasperated Charlie searching for wherever he kept his information. Ike had visited Charlie's office years before, remembered the confusion of papers and empty Styrofoam cups on his desk, and reckoned it might take more time than Ike had. He was wrong.

"Nine twenty-five. Of course that's not one-hundred percent reliable. The answering machine's time stamp was set by my sister-in–law. Nice lady but..."

"I got it. Thanks."

"Anything else you need, Ike?"

"You can check that time stamp if you get a chance, but I'll assume it is close enough."

Ike snapped the phone shut.

"His plane was a Cessna 172, modified as a spotter plane, you said?"

"Right."

"Any idea at what speed it cruised?"

"Maybe 110 miles per hour. But he might have been going faster or slower. Like I said, he's a baby pilot in a hurry to see his girl."

"But he dropped off the radar at twenty-one thirteen, right? And he made a phone call to his fiancée that night at twenty-one twenty-five. Allowing for some inaccuracy in the time register on the answering machine, he must have been in the air an additional ten to twelve minutes after he dropped off the radar. Where would that put him on your map?"

"Ah! Now that's interesting."

"How so?"

"In a minute. First I need to tell you that his plane had a tendency to drift to the left. So he could have been off this line by a couple of miles by then. He'd be on the right heading, just running parallel to this one."

"He knew about that?"

"Yeah, but in the dark he might have compensated for it—or not—or even over compensated a little."

"So he could have been several miles to the right and some distance to the left?"

"Correct. Now, assuming he was cruising and not playing jet jockey, he'd be on the south side of Kent Island, somewhere over Eastern Bay." Trent drew a large circle on the map.

"So if they were looking for Nick north of Kent Island—"

"They wouldn't find anything." Ike waited. Something in Trent's voice indicated there would be more.

"See, after the kid disappeared, like I told you, I flew this course the next day. I fixed up this map and went down the line, so to speak. After I reached the area they thought he might have ditched, I kept on over Kent Island to make my turn. That's when I thought I saw something—the 'maybe' I mentioned before."

"You thought you saw…what?"

Trent pointed to a spit of land on the map. "This map isn't the greatest, you know. The Chesapeake Bay is fickle when it comes to where the land is. Anyway, right about here there's a little sandy beach that goes with a small house and pier. I thought I saw a piece of airplane there—like it washed up."

"A piece of—"

"If I had to guess, tail section. But, see, it was in the wrong place, so I let it slide, but it has bugged me ever since. Now, it makes sense."

Ike punched the redial button on his phone.

"Garland."

"Charlie, we have a satellite in synchronous orbit over the Washington, D.C., area and coast line, right? I need satellite photos of the Chesapeake Bay."

"We have the Littoral Scanning System, yes. What pictures exactly?"

"I need distance and blow ups of the area known as Eastern Bay on the day before and the day after Nick disappeared. I might need more, I'll start with those, as many as you can get."

"I'm on it. Have you turned up something?"

"It's just a maybe," Ike said, and grinned at Trent. "I need those photos ASAP, Charlie. Can you messenger them to me at the beach?"

"Can do. This is important, correct?"

"I wouldn't ask if they weren't. I'll call you tomorrow." Ike ended the call.

Trent frowned and studied the chart again. "If they were not even looking in the right sector…it's no wonder they couldn't find anything. What do you want to do?"

"I want to study the photos as soon as they arrive, and then I'd like you to fly this line with me tomorrow. No, tomorrow's Sunday. Maybe the next day and show me that beach." Trent hesitated. "We'll call it a lesson, and you can bill me at your hourly. That way you don't use up your vacation time, tick off your boss, or both."

Trent looked relieved. Ike asked for a fuel top-off. When the refueler pulled away, he started the engine, adjusted his gauges and radio and, cleared by the tower, taxied onto the runway and headed south following the course Nick Reynolds flew in July. He wanted to see Eastern Bay while the light was good. Once he had a look, he'd turn eastward at Cambridge and go back to Delmarva Aviation.

Chapter Eight

Blake passed along the row of kneeling communicants. Into each outstretched hand he placed a wafer and repeated: *The body of Christ, the bread of heaven.* The ritual had become rote and often his mind wandered as he looked into the eyes of one or another person, trying to read their thoughts. Indeed, parishioners sometimes assumed he must be able to read their minds. More than once he'd been confronted by one who complained he'd not visited them in the hospital. And more often than not they, or a family member, had neglected to tell Blake they were scheduled for surgery, or even had been admitted. So he studied each face seeking clues as to what they might tell him if he were to ask.

While caught up in one of those mental tangents, he nearly missed the young man's pendant. A heavy silver chain bore what appeared to be an over-large, upside-down cross. At the crux, instead of a crucified Christ or some other Christian symbol, he saw a ram's head, its eyes set with red stones that might have been rubies but were probably glass. Blake stopped in mid-sentence and stared at the pendant and then at the boy. He couldn't have been much over sixteen. His hair, cut shaggy and moussed, had been dyed an unnatural black, which only emphasized the pallor of his skin and the rather prominent acne on his face. His clothes were ill-fitting—not that that was so unusual. Most boys who were dragged to church by their parents wore clothes that looked, to Blake, like they'd been rummaged out of their older brother's closet or the reject pile at the Goodwill store. His eyes returned to the pendant. Lanny Markowitz, who had been trailing along behind Blake as chalicist, nearly bumped into him. The boy looked up and extended his hand forward to receive the Host.

"Son," Blake said as softly as he could, "I'm going to ask you to leave the church."

Lanny's eyebrows shot up. The boy looked quizzically at Blake.

"Excuse me?"

"You can come back, but only after you've ditched that thing around your neck."

"What's wrong with my cross?"

"It's not a cross. It's a satanic symbol, and I won't have it in here."

Confused, the boy stood and walked back toward his pew. He started to sit. Blake pointed to the door.

"Jesus," the boy said, "what's up with you?" Red-faced, he stomped to the narthex doors and exited. He was followed by his girl friend who, Blake assumed, had brought him to church in the first place. She, in turn, was followed by her parents.

"What was that all about?" Lanny whispered.

"Satan."

Lanny frowned.

"Later."

The stir caused by Blake's action carried over into the coffee hour. With reluctance, he slipped out of his robes and descended the back stairs to the basement which served as the church's fellowship hall. Lanny sidled up to him.

"Barbara Starkey is looking for you," he said. "She's the mother of Peachy Starkey, the girlfriend of the boy you bounced from church."

"I know who she is."

"Before she shreds you with her tongue, would you mind telling me what happened at the rail?"

"The kid was wearing a satanic cross. Didn't you see it?"

"I saw an upside-down cross. I thought it was a peace symbol, or something like a protest deal. You know? Like flying the flag upside down—that sort of thing. Help, save the church from the House of Bishops, or whatever.."

"Maybe that's what the kid thought, too. I hope so. But the figure in the center was a ram's head, not a peace symbol. I know about peace crosses. I wore one of those once, myself, back in the day. I'd know one if I saw one."

"Okay, so what's the problem with the thing on the kid?"

Blake spun and looked at his friend. Lanny hadn't a clue. Like so many good church-goers, his idea of evil was largely cerebral. Yes, evil is real but…and there would follow a dissertation on a felon's feelings of low self-esteem, an unhappy childhood, abusive parents, perhaps just the inevitable product of a dysfunctional family and a conflicted society. The list was endless and, in Blake's view, made excuses for behavior that crossed the line, irrespective of its cause. He recalled an old seminary professor of his, near retirement, who described a trip to Nazi Germany in the late 1930s. He'd said that evil, real evil, was palpable in the air then. He was about to expand on the theme when Barbara Starkey braced him with a look that would etch glass.

"Mr. Fisher," she began. Blake knew he was in trouble when a parishioner addressed him as Mister. "Just what were you thinking about making Chad leave? In front of everybody. He's very upset. So, I might add, am I. I have been a strong supporter of this church, both financially and personally. My ancestors were instrumental in building this—"

"Yes, I know, Barb. And I appreciate all you've done. I told… Chad?…I told Chad that he could return if he removed his pendant and left it outside."

"His cross? I'd have thought you'd be pleased to see a young person wearing a cross to church."

"It isn't a cross, Barb, it's a satanic symbol, and it has no place in the church. Sorry."

"Satanic sym…oh, come on. Surely you don't believe in all that mumbo-jumbo."

"I do, and so should you."

"Well, of course…I mean yes, there's evil in the world, but what harm can come from a silly little cross thing. He just wears it, he said, because he thinks it's cool. You know how kids are."

"I do know. And I know the consequences of well-meaning but dangerous behavior."

"Dangerous? Really! Chad isn't a Satan person."

"Do you remember being in school and someone pinning a 'kick me' sign on another person's back?"

"Yes, but…"

"Chad's pendant is a kind of 'kick me' sign. It's an invitation. He doesn't realize it, but he's advertising for the devil, and in a way, inviting him in." Barbara opened her mouth to speak, but Blake cut her off. "I am serious, Barb. It begins with ignorance and ends in tragedy."

"Oh, really, Mr. Fisher, I thought you were smarter than that. The Inquisition was in another century. This is not Salem. I think you owe Chad an apology."

"Send him around. We'll talk, certainly. In the meantime, think about this—how would you have reacted to Chad if he'd first been introduced to you wearing a swastika…perhaps had one tattooed on his neck?"

Barbara Starkey stared at Blake for a split second, her mouth agape, closed it.

"I hardly think that's the same thing, do you?"

"I think it is exactly the same thing, as a matter of fact."

Barbara Starkey marched off, her back stiff, head held high, a vision of moral rectitude. Lanny, who'd stayed to listen to Blake's explanation, squinted at him, a frown on his face.

"You meant all that, didn't you?"

"Every word."

"I don't know…" Lanny looked doubtful.

"Lanny, maybe this is a better example. Suppose you lived in a very tough section of town, gangs, crime, all that. Would you leave your front door unlocked and open at night? I guess you might never be bothered. Years could go by and nobody would attempt to hurt you. But would you risk it?"

"No, I guess not. No, definitely not. So the kid may not have any investment in the thing around his neck but why take the chance."

"Exactly. And in the example I just gave you, would you advertise the door was unlocked?"

Lanny squinted at the ceiling for a second as if trying to remember something. "It's funny, you know," he said.

"Funny? How funny?"

"Up at the school the kids talk, you know, brag about this and that and..."

"And?"

"I hear rumors that some of them are into that kind of stuff. The Goths, mostly but some other kids as well. You're serious about this aren't you?"

"Serious as a heart attack."

"I need to think about it. Could you meet with the principal, if I set something up?"

"Yes."

"Ram's head. Why do I think I've heard that before?"

Chapter Nine

Good to his word, Charlie had the photographs delivered to Ike in the morning—Sunday morning at that. Ike spread them out on the kitchen table and studied them. The resolution was remarkable. In addition, Charlie had sent three blowups of random shoreline. In them, he could even see bits of driftwood on sandy beaches. He made a mental note to ask for a blowup of the area where Trent Fonts thought he'd seen the piece of tail assembly. It might be helpful, particularly if he also could get a tide chart for that day. Trent said it wasn't there the next week so why, he wondered, hadn't someone reported finding it? Given the fact that the missing plane was on the news for days, you'd think a piece of tail section, if that is what it was, would at least generate a call to the police if not the FAA. Strange.

He shuffled through the images. He didn't really know what he was looking for, but he hoped something would jump out at him. Nothing did. Just boats and ships—big ships, little ships. Ships sitting or moving—ships at anchor, cargo ships and container ships waiting south of the Bay Bridge for a pilot to come aboard and take them into port. Boats sailing, boats motoring—nothing out of the ordinary. He lined up the pictures of successive days side by side and compared them. Except for one small freighter that seemed to have repositioned itself in the night, the pictures for the morning of the fifth of July were not remarkably different that those for the fourth.

He turned his attention to the shoreline of Eastern Bay. It was formed by the southern peninsula of Kent island on the east and the shoreline of Delmarva Peninsula to the west. As with most coastlines in this part of the country, it was characteristically erose. Inlets, rivers, creeks, and small harbors increased the total shoreline measurement by a thousand-fold or more. No wonder sailors and watermen loved this country. There must be thousands of fishing spots, hunting grounds in any one of those rivers, and they were not the only ones around. What he couldn't see was the water's depth. That would be important if he ever hoped to locate Nick Reynolds' plane. He locked up and went to breakfast.

As a breakfast venue, The Avenue Restaurant compared favorably with his usual haunt in Picketsville, the Crossroads Diner. He maintained, as a faith statement, that no one but a culinary incompetent or a drunk could possibly ruin breakfast. On reflection, however, he remembered one he'd been served in Grants, New Mexico, that qualified as a breakfast disaster. But those experiences were rare. Breakfast was one of America's great achievements and a major contribution to the world. Gourmet or Denny's, one was rarely a disappointment. For Ike, the advantage of the Rehoboth facility lay in the fact that it was not run by Flora Blevins, the proprietor of the Crossroads, and, therefore, Ike could order anything he wanted without her vetoing his choices or lecturing him on the benefits of deep-fat frying in bacon grease.

He slathered butter and syrup on a short stack with scrapple on the side. A fruit cup was his nod toward good nutrition. He might or might not eat it. A vision of Flora rose up in his subconscious and he felt guilty—for about two seconds. Three cups of coffee and a block of green melon, which he assumed was honeydew, and he was on his way.

A marine supplies store on the ocean highway supplied him with a boating chart of Eastern Bay and its surrounding area. The Exxon station next door sold him a road map of Maryland.

Spreading the maps and photographs side by side turned out to be a problem. He didn't have enough table space. He found a card table behind the front door, and by positioning it next to the dining room table and pushing them both to the kitchen counter, he managed to create sufficient surface to assemble a display of three maps and the photos in approximate order. He spent the next hour studying one and then another. Not enough information. He called Charlie.

"Ike, it's Sunday morning, for God's sake."

"Why aren't you in church, Charlie?"

"What? You're joking, right?"

"I never joke about the Almighty, Charlie."

"Okay. Why are you calling me at this hour on Sunday? I just might have been going out the door to church, for all you know."

"And I might have been having breakfast with Angelina Jolie and Brad Pitt. Have I got that pairing correct?"

"Who knows? I haven't had my supermarket check-out line update lately. So, what's up?"

"I'm looking at maps. Three different kinds of maps, all depicting the same area. It's fascinating."

"Really? You called me on Sunday, the only day I can catch up on my sleep, to tell me about maps?"

"I have an aeronautical map, a road map, and a local boating chart side by side. I have your satellite pictures arranged in the same order. I am studying the Eastern Bay—that's a part of the Chesapeake Bay south of Kent Island."

"What is so interesting about that?"

"I think that's where your almost nephew-in-law went in. I can't be sure, but that's what it's beginning to look like."

"I thought the search was north of Kent Island."

"It was. That's why they never found anything. Since he disappeared from the radar over that bit of water, they figured that's where he must be, but according to your sister's answering machine, he flew another ten to twelve minutes. That would put him south of Kent Island somewhere near, in, or about, Eastern Bay."

"Wow. What do you need? I assume you need something since you called me on the Sabbath—my Sabbath, not yours, of course."

"I'm touched by your piety, Charlie. Okay, I am studying these maps and pictures, and each tells me a different story. The topography is the same, but the information each gives up is different. As I said, it's fascinating. What I need—what I think I need—is more comparisons. Send me pictures of the area over time. Today, last month, August, last year, and a blow-up of a bit of shoreline."

"I'd need to know where on the shore."

"Right, hold on a minute." Ike opened his laptop, clicked on Google Earth, and found the scrap of beach where Trent had indicated he'd seen the tail piece. He rattled off the coordinates. "I need the pictures for the three days following Nick's disappearance."

"Anything else?"

"Yeah. If your sister has not reset the time stamp on her answering machine, I want to know how accurate it is compared to the atomic clock."

"My sister's answering machine is important?"

"Very. I want to know exactly how many minutes and seconds elapsed from the time Nick dropped off the radar to when he made that call. That could produce a smaller area for us to look at."

"You're onto something, Ike."

"I'm just digging, Charlie. It may be something and it may be nothing. Stay tuned. Oh, and light a candle for me, while you're at it."

"Candle?"

"In church. You said you were—"

Charlie hung up.

◇◇◇

Frank spread the photos the evidence techs had provided him of the sinkhole. He laid them out on his desk and opened a topographical map. The sinkhole appeared obvious on that map. He marked the spot where he'd seen the bones and the path up the hill, and then down to the bottom of the hole. Then he tried to place the fire pits. He didn't know why, but he figured since they were equidistant, it might be important. He squinted at the photos, searched for and found a magnifying glass. Next to one fire pit he saw what looked like a surveyor's marker. He drew a circle and then spaced the other four in a pentagon. He drew in the bench at the center.

His mother called him to dinner. She wanted to tell him about Esther Peepers' cat and the missing silver from the church.

Essie and his brothers, Billy and Henry, were already at the table. Essie's face seemed locked in a chronic blush, but she had her hundred-watt smile on high beam. Apparently, Ma had filled her in on the probable cause of her bathroom addiction.

There would be a celebration that he guessed would last for the whole year. Grandbaby, Ma had said.

Well, good.

Chapter Ten

Blake had interviewed the altar guild members after church. His confrontation with Barbara Starkey had taken time and he missed a few, but he felt certain that one of them knew where or how the silverware might have disappeared. The following morning, he called the Sheriff's office. By then, Frank Sutherlin had already heard about the possible theft from his mother. He said he'd look at the safe and check the building security that morning. Blake had to smile. The church, as everyone except Frank seemed to know, was a sieve when it came to security. He'd ordered the locks changed once the previous year, much to the consternation of over half the congregation, who believed that they had an intrinsic, if not canonical, right to possess a key to their church. Within six months, the number of keys in circulation had returned to, indeed, exceeded the original number, and any hope of security went away.

The unhappy truth was that within their memories, churches had never been locked. In the past, sacred places were considered safe from pilfering and petty theft. Not so anymore. Now churches routinely locked their doors and in many cases had installed elaborate security systems. Blake knew of one that had a pressure sensor placed under the church's expensive antique chalice, which had been on display in the side chapel. Lift it from its spot, and it triggered an earsplitting siren. One night a thief stole both the chalice and the alarm system that went with it.

Frank Sutherlin was as soft-spoken as his mother was loud. He looked at the safe, declared it pointless to take fingerprints, and said he'd ask around. He suggested a preliminary call to the insurance company might be in order.

"You know anybody missing a cat?" he added.

"A cat? What kind of cat?"

"Black one, I think."

"Esther Peepers is missing a black cat. Answers to the name of Odin. No, that's not right, but something like that, though."

"Old Mr. Peepers was named Ogden. You think she named it after him?"

"Ogden. That's it. It's been missing for maybe a week. The cat answers to Ogden."

"Not anymore, it don't."

"How's that?"

"Deader than a chunk."

"That's too bad. Someone will have to tell her."

"I reckon that falls into your purview, Rev."

"Maybe it wasn't her cat. There must be dozens of black cats in the area."

"And dogs too. Don't forget the dogs."

"True. Someone told me a couple up at the college are missing their dogs. I think I'll wait a week or so, in case the pussy shows up. No sense in alarming the old lady for no reason."

"Right. Say, Rev., what do you know about pentagons?"

"Well, it's been a while since I studied geometry. Five sides, very difficult to bisect the interior angle, and...why do you ask?"

"No reason right now. Just ran across one and I can't explain what it's doing in the bottom of a sinkhole is all."

Frank left, and Blake stood staring out the window. He still had to ask Mary about the trip up the Skyline Drive. He dialed her number at work.

"When can you pry yourself loose from the job to go for a drive?"

"Where?"

"Up on the parkway to look at the leaves."

"Just the leaves?"

"Well, we might take a picnic and a walk on one of the paths and…"

"A walk?"

"And whatever."

"I'll think about the 'whatever' and let you know. Not today, though. Wednesday I have a half-day. Is that good?"

"Perfect. Wednesday it is."

"I meant to say something to you Sunday, but you were pretty tied up. You need a haircut."

"I do?"

"You're shaggy."

"You think? I like shaggy."

"It makes you look like a superannuated hippie."

"I don't like the barber in town, and Roanoke is too far to drive just for a haircut."

"You go see Lee Henry. She'll fix you up." Mary gave him the address and directions and said she'd set up the appointment.

"Ask her for the story."

◇◇◇

Blake looked at the scrap of paper in his hand and then at the mailbox. The address on the paper matched that on the paper. Something didn't compute. Mary had sent him to get his hair cut by Ms. Henry. He expected a salon of some sort, but he found himself on a country road on the outskirts of Picketsville staring at an ordinary split-level house with an oversized garage attached. Between the garage and the house he thought he could just make out a doorway, and it had a sign hanging in it—one of those ready-made available at the hardware store—black with florescent orange letters that spelled OPEN.

He turned into the drive and pulled forward to the garage where a graveled parking area had been created. He glanced at the door and its sign, shrugged, and exited his car. Over the door he saw another, smaller sign, hand-painted, he guessed, in similar hues as the house paint, declaring *Lee Henry—Stylist*. He'd found the right place.

Once inside he recognized the chair and smells of a barber shop/beauty salon—wet hair, mousse, and an olio of scents, some left by previous customers, others lingering in the air from hair sprays, conditioners, and shampoo. A woman in her fifties, he guessed—he couldn't tell her age with any certainty—greeted him with a smile.

"You must be my friend Mary's man. She called for your appointment."

"Yes, that would be me. How'd you know?" She lifted an eyebrow and wagged her hand, palm down, across her throat. "Ah, the collar. I forget sometimes." She waved him into the chair.

"That thing will have to come off, honey," she said. "You let the clock run too long since your last cut and I gotta work on that neck of yours."

He eased the clerical collar from the gold-plated collar buttons at the back and front of his shirt.

"Well, land's sake, will you lookit them? I didn't know they still made them collar buttons. My old granddaddy used to have some of them in his dresser drawer. He said they was for when he had to wear a boiled shirt, whatever that is, to some fancy do at the Elks."

"She said I should ask for 'the story.'"

"The what?"

"She said I should expect to hear a story sometime during the session. She said I should try not to seem shocked—that you sometimes got a little bawdy. Is that true?"

"Bawdy? Well, now that you mention it, bawdy might be the word. But I don't go over the line, well, not with Mary and…well, you being a preacher and all. I'll have to be careful there, too."

Blake wondered sometimes at a societal attitude that sometimes criticized clergy for not being of the world and then systematically refused to include them in it for fear of offending them. Men, and women, too for that matter, would tell the most outrageous stories to their doctors, lawyers, coworkers, barbers even, but clammed up the instant a clergyman or woman hove into view. The Caesar's wife syndrome, he supposed.

"I promise you, I will not be offended. Before I started wearing my collar backward I spent time in locker rooms with football players, and you'd be surprised at the jokes seminarians tell."

"When was the last time anyone took a look at this mess?"

"Sometime in August, I think. Mary said I looked shaggy and I should have you trim me up a bit."

"Shaggy ain't the word I'd use here, Rev. And trim won't cover it by half. Okay, I'll just put on some good old Johnny Cash. You just relax and let Lee work her magic."

She punched buttons on a CD player in the corner, and The Man in Black began a gospel tune. Blake wondered if she'd saved that one for "the preacher" or if gospel happened to be the next in the selection. She clucked disapprovingly while she combed and snipped at his hair. Johnny segued into "Will the Circle Be Unbroken?"

"You hear about the blonde in the bar and the suicide?" she said.

At last—the story. "I don't think so."

"It's a blonde joke. I can tell it on account of this month, I'm a blonde. See this man comes into a bar one night and orders a drink. There's this good-looking blonde next to him, and he's thinking up a good pick-up line to use on her. The late news is on the TV over the bar, and they're showing a scene where this guy is on a building ledge fixing to jump. Cops is talking to him, folks are yelling 'jump, jump.' Never could understand that, yelling for someone to kill themselves. Well, anyway, there he is teetering over the edge. The guy turns to the blonde and says, 'I'll bet you twenty dollars he jumps.' And she says, 'You're on.' So they watch a while, and sure enough the guy jumps off the building.

"The woman slides a twenty down the bar to him. 'You win,' she says. 'Hey,' he says, 'I can't take your money. I already saw this on the five o'clock news.' 'Me, too,' she says, 'I just didn't think he'd do it again!'" Lee dissolved into laughter. As with many story-tellers, she was her own best audience. Blake smiled. He had a repeatable story.

"So what's up with your missing silver?"

"You heard about that?"

"I hear most things in my line of business. People like to talk and somehow don't think telling me counts as lettin' out a secret or such."

"Well, Frank Sutherlin says he'll ask around. That doesn't sound like much, though."

"In this town, askin' around will get you more information than that CSI routine."

"Mmm...he wanted to know what I knew about pentagons."

"Why'd he do that?"

"Says he found a bunch of fire pits in a sinkhole out in the park."

"Oh? Out in the sinkhole?"

"You know it?"

"Well, sure. Back in the day when we was kids, that's where we'd go to...you know. We called it The Passion Pit, ain't that something?"

"Kids still go there?"

"I expect so, but of course the whole game is changed. Kids don't have to sneak around like we done, so maybe not so much any more."

Kids in the sinkhole.

Chapter Eleven

Ike flew to Eastern Bay and circled the area he'd marked on the map as the most probable location for Nick's downed aircraft. He hoped to find an altitude that would enable him to penetrate the water's surface visually and perhaps catch a glimpse, a hint, of the plane. At one point, he thought he saw a shape that would serve but it was fleeting. Still, he jotted down the coordinates. Later he'd have Trent Fonts fly the plane, and he'd look again. He turned north and headed for Martin State.

As he made his turn, a flash of light caught his attention. It came from the land. Nothing remarkable in that, a windshield reflecting the sun, perhaps. It could also be a pair of binoculars aimed skyward. He shook off the thought. Too many days and nights in the Company had rendered him permanently paranoid. He settled into the routine of guiding the plane toward its destination and let his mind wander. Nick Reynolds had seen something in or on the water, and it seemed sufficiently important to try to warn Charlie. On the water meant a boat or ship of some sort. A submarine would be out of the question. The Navy's tracking system would have located, identified, and probably made it surface long before it made its way into the bay. But Nick had seen something and deemed it important enough to make the call. A boat doing what? Dropping someone or some people off? To row ashore and…or maybe picking someone up? But why would that result in his plane being downed, if in fact, that's what happened. Was he so absorbed in the object on the water he lost altitude and spiraled in?

Martin State loomed on his horizon. He cleared for landing and taxied to Brett Aviation. Trent waited for him in the hangar's shade.

"I may have something for you," he said, as Ike climbed down from the high-wing's cockpit.

Ike smoothed out his slacks and breathed in the smells of kerosene and engine exhaust. Without much in the way of skyline to provide some shade, the airstrip shimmered in the late September sun and caused him to squint, in spite of his sunglasses. He ought to get a set of real aviator sunglasses. After all, if you're going to be a pilot, you ought to look like a pilot.

"What would that be?"

"I located the beach on my map, you know, the one where I thought I saw the tail section washed up, and then went online to a website that plotted the bay's tides. They had an archive section, and I found the tides for the time we think Nick went down. Then—I'm guessing now, you understand—I plotted them, like, backward and got a fix on where that piece of tail section may have gone into the water."

Ike was impressed. "They have web sites that do that? Show me."

The two men went into Trent's office, and he spread out his chart. Ike took his out and did the same. Trent's smaller circle would fit neatly into Ike's larger one.

Progress. Maybe.

It also coincided with the general area where Ike thought he'd seen the shadow.

"We should get some divers and go look," Trent said.

"Too soon. Look, the radius of that circle, as small as it seems on the map, is at least three and a half miles. I make that out to be about eleven square miles. Maybe more if you allow for the possibility of a greater or slower air speed that night, or wind. No, we have to narrow it down a whole lot more before we call in divers."

"But if you spotted the wreckage, wouldn't that narrow it down?"

"I saw a shape, a shadow, a…something, in the water. I didn't see the bottom and it could have been anything—an old island that hasn't quite washed away—anything."

"If it were that, wouldn't your boater's charts show it?"

Ike realized they would. He hadn't brought that map along and he regretted it. He'd have to check on it when he returned to the cottage that afternoon.

"I'll check, but first, let's fly Nick's line and see if you can see what I saw."

◇◇◇

Trent's voice crackled over the head set, "I don't think you need any more flight instruction, Ike. Maybe more hours would help and, of course, since I don't know what the Air Force put you through, I don't know what your emergency plans might be."

"Bail out, mostly."

Trent grunted.

Eastern Bay appeared on their horizon and Ike dropped down to five hundred feet.

"How low can I go before I get into trouble with the FAA? What's the limit? We weren't taught that in the spy flying school."

"None—if you're crop dusting—otherwise, prudent and nonintrusive."

"Meaning?"

Trent rolled his eyes heavenward and recited: "Except when necessary for takeoff or landing, no person may operate an aircraft below the following altitudes: (a) an altitude allowing, if a power unit fails…oh, never mind, I'll keep you legal."

"How about you take us down as low as you can and fly us like a crop duster back and forth over this area?"

"Roger, that."

Trent was a skillful pilot and sure enough, he handled the plane like a crop-duster—no mean feat as those planes are designed with a huge lift-to-drag ratio that allowed them to climb quickly and fly slowly. On the fourth turn, Ike thought he saw the glint of light from the ground again. It seemed to come from the land near a wooded plot that bordered the water.

"Did you see that?" he asked.

"See what?" Trent flew the plane with absolute concentration. He wouldn't have noticed.

"Thought I saw a flash of light."

"Water sparkles, and up here it'd look like a flash."

"No, it came from land."

Trent shrugged. "I don't see the shadow or whatever either."

"Tide's running out. Silt from the rivers and creeks muddies things up."

"The photos taken the day before and after showed a barge over there." Ike pointed toward the shore.

"Not there now."

"No, there's something else in about the same position. What is that?"

Trent took a pass at the object in the water. "Duck blind."

"Like for hunting?"

"Right. You have to get a permit to use them, and they are limited as to how many and when you can shoot."

"Funny place for a duck blind. It faces the deep water. I thought duck hunters shot over shallow water."

"Not my hobby. Bow and arrow for deer, now that's hunting."

"Fly over the place where you saw the tail section."

"Where I thought I saw the tail section, you mean."

"If you think you saw a piece of airplane, I'm guessing you saw a piece of an airplane."

Trent turned the plane inland and pointed to a narrow strip of sand a mile in. "Over there just beyond the pier."

The narrow strip extended on either side of a pier. A work boat was moored to the end, but Ike didn't see anybody on or near it.

"Not there now."

"Nope, it was gone the next day."

"Nobody reported a piece of wreckage even when the missing plane was on the news for days?"

"Nope."

Ike shook his head. "Something's amiss here. Why wouldn't you report something like that?" Trent shrugged again.

"About your tide charts...there's a problem. Unless you know for certain when the piece of airplane touched land—"

"I know. I can't be sure enough to backtrack...it could have floated further in, then washed ashore on the way back out when the tide turned." Trent looked disappointed.

"We'll stay with your best guess for now. I think we'd better get back to Martin State. I'll come back here later by car. I need to talk to the people on the ground. Someone must have seen something."

Chapter Twelve

Lanny Markowitz's note said that he'd arranged an appointment with the school's principal after football practice. The previous fall Blake had volunteered to help with the football program as an informal quarterback's coach—if time allowed. He watched the boys jog around the track on their way to the locker room and walked with Lanny toward the school's main building.

"What's up, Lanny?"

"I talked to Principal DiComo about the business with the cross last Sunday, and he said he needed to talk to you. I guess it's about that. I don't know. He didn't sound too happy."

Roger DiComo had an office next to the main entrance. His predecessor had his at the rear of the building but DiComo, who prided himself on his ability to communicate with students, "the guys" he called them, said he needed to be "near the action." One week after the move his secretary promptly retired and the new one seemed perpetually frazzled. The outer office door's base was chipped and badly scuffed, evidence of multiple kicks and abuse. Blake and Lanny were ushered in to the inner office. DiComo waved them into chairs without taking his eyes off a sheaf of papers in his hand.

The room reeked with musk aftershave. Blake rarely used the stuff himself but had several bottles of cologne on his dresser, annual Christmas presents from his nieces. He didn't consider himself an expert, but he guessed DiComo wore the good stuff.

The walls had pictures of football teams and a slightly deflated football sat tiredly on his desk.

"So, Reverend, you think I've got ourselves a coven of witches or something in my school?"

DiComo peered at Blake over a pair of half-lens reading glasses. He had one of those voices that was grating and condescending at the same time. He still held the papers he'd been reading in his hand as if they were, on whole, more important than his visitors. Blake fought the temptation to return rudeness with rudeness.

"I don't know what you may or may not have, Mr. DiComo. What I do know is that one of your students turned up wearing a satanic cross in my church last Sunday, and I told him he had to leave. He could come back, but he had to ditch the cross first."

DiComo closed his eyes and shook his head. "And on that basis you believe the school may have a problem?"

"I have no idea. Do you? Have a problem, I mean?"

DiComo laid the papers on his desk. He took several seconds to align them carefully, their edges precisely even. He did the same with three pencils, so that his desk appeared neat and perfectly symmetrical—feng shui for the obsessive compulsive. He shook his head again and smiled like an adult indulging a small child.

Blake felt his blood pressure start to tick up. "You asked to see me, I believe. If a coven is not your problem, may I ask what is?"

DiComo's expression shifted from annoyed to supercilious.

"Your treatment of Chad Franklin Sunday implies he is into this satanic thing. Now let me set you straight on that." He paused and corrected a flaw in his paper pile. Blake bit the inside of his cheek. "We believe in, no...correction...we, that is the school board and I, are governed by Supreme Court rulings on the separation of church and state. That's in the Constitution, you know. And I can't have you harassing my students about their rights to the free practice of religion."

"First of all, Mr. DiComo, let me say that I, too, affirm the separation of church and state and, therefore, will not let the

Supreme Court, or the local school board, or you tell me what I can and cannot do in my church. Secondly, if you read your Constitution with care, as I am sure you will, you will discover that the phrase 'separation of church and state' is not in it. The phrase 'separation of church and state' is traceable to a letter written by Thomas Jefferson in 1802 to the Danbury Baptists, and refers to a 'wall of separation.' The constitution, on the other hand, reads, 'Congress shall make no law respecting an establishment of religion, or prohibiting the free exercise thereof…' Now, I understand that the two are often considered synonymous, and I am fully aware that the government has ruled that the 'free exercise of religion' may include satanism, Wicca, devil worship, and all kinds of other marginal religious practices. But having said that, I will also tell you, government poobahs, well-meaning school boards, and others, notwithstanding, evil is evil in any of its forms, and you run a risk when you trivialize it."

"Mr. Fisher," DiComo said, back to shaking his head, "I know your kind would like us to quiver in our boots at the thought of some old codger in a red union suit carrying a pitchfork and taking over our lives, but this is the twentieth century—"

"Twenty-first."

"Right. As I was trying to say, nowadays we celebrate diversity, encourage inclusiveness, and, frankly, concepts of overarching evil and bogymen are, well, from another era."

"So you will dismiss Columbine as the result of what…low self-esteem on the part of a few misguided young men? You have a responsibility to your students—"

"I am fully aware of my responsibilities, Mr. Fisher. You can hawk that line of gibberish from your pulpit, but in this school, we are of this century and this culture." It was DiComo's turn to get angry.

"Nazis," Blake pressed on, "Skinheads, do you see a problem with them?"

"If we have any, appropriate action would be taken."

"Because?"

"What do you mean? They are a negative influence—"

"Negative? How?"

"They represent…"

"What…evil? Mr. DiComo, you can't have it both ways. There is evil in the world or there isn't. You've read *The Brothers Karamazov*?"

"That's by…what's his name…Tolstoy."

"Dostoyevsky. Reread the conversations Ivan has with his 'visitor' and see if you share his conclusion. In the meantime, I and 'my kind' will persist in calling a spade a spade and give fair warning to those who insist there is a correct psychosocial answer even to questions that fall into an area, in which, by the way, they have no competence or understanding, that the world can be a dangerous place made more so by muddled thinking."

Blake rose to go. "Sorry, Lanny, I thought I might help here, but I guess not." Lanny studied his shoes. DiComo plastered a smug smile on his, by now, red face.

"Thank you for stopping by."

Blake let himself out, Lanny close on his heels.

"Blake, wait a minute." Blake slowed and took some deep breaths. 'Look. I know the guy can come off sounding like a jerk, but he's under a lot of pressure. I know the Starkeys have been on the phone about Sunday. She is the PTA's president, and he heads up the booster club which, as you know, raises a lot of money for the football team. He wants you removed as coach, even."

Blake stopped short. "Removed? Why on earth for?"

"He didn't…well, you know how some people are…"

"No Lanny, how are some people?"

"He thought…um…ah…"

"He didn't want some Holy Joe proselytizing the kids."

"Something along those lines. See, most people don't see what the problem is. You go on the Internet and half the sites that deal with Satanism, devil worship, are over the top on the terrible things they say and do. Baby-killing, cannibalism—stuff like that. And the other half is pretty reasonable articles about people's rights and, you know, disclaimers about…well, anyway, the consensus is the whole business is a tempest in a tea pot."

"The Internet? You look for truth and guidance on the Internet? Lanny, you might as well throw yourself under a bus. There is no screening on the Internet. You can post anything you want about any subject you want. You can start a website, a blog, and whatever you say will stand as gospel. Of course there are apologetics for all sorts of behavior. I can show you several advocating pederasty, bestiality and child abuse as a God-given right of parents.

"But rationalizing stupidity, bad behavior, and evil doesn't make it intelligent or good. Black is not white, I don't care how many times it says so on the Internet." Blake paused and took a breath. "I'm sorry, Lanny, I'm taking out my frustrations on you. It's your principal that needs to learn to weigh ideas without societal bias."

"But the devil…"

"Devil, Satan, misdirected choices, all the perversions of what you and I hold as a standard for righteousness, whatever—call it what you want. Evil is real and it threatens society everyday. Psychobabble and good intentions will not allay it, and may even promote it. But my concern, here, is for that kid. He has put himself in harm's way and your idiot principal needs to do something about it."

"What can he do?"

Good question. In a secular society that does not permit spiritual intrusion in its governance, DiComo could do nothing. "Look, I am not pushing religion here. Maybe I should be. It's what I'm paid to do, in fact. I am not one of those bible thumping, mousse-haired televangelists, and I am not proselytizing students or anybody else, for that matter, more's the pity. He doesn't have to believe me, but he should at least acknowledge the possibility I'm right. Then there might be some chance he'd be ready if, and when, something really bad happens to the boy or to his school."

Chapter Thirteen

Ike taxied the plane to its tie-down position on the flight line and shut down the engine. The prop shuddered to a stop, and he completed his postflight check. The lineman stepped up to the cockpit door as he climbed out.

"Boss wants to see you."

"Trouble?"

"FAA called is all I know."

The FAA had, indeed, called. They'd grounded Ike.

"Why?" he asked, when he entered the office.

"Don't know, they just said I was to pull your ticket. Problem is, you don't have, like, a real license so I'm not sure…" The facility's manager stood behind his cluttered desk and looked embarrassed. "They said they had a complaint from someone over in Maryland about you buzzing some sailboats."

"There wasn't a boat in sight. Well, not within a mile, anyway." Ike sighed. "Consider the ticket pulled."

"Okay. Sorry about that. I guess you won't be needing the plane any more."

"We have a contract. The plane is mine for at least two more weeks."

"But—"

"I expect you'll be receiving a call in a few hours or maybe by early tomorrow rescinding the grounding. I won't need the plane again for a few days, anyway, so I'll see you Thursday or Friday."

Ike walked to his car and called Charlie.

"I need your help."

"Again? I'm beginning to feel like a scout master. What now."

"You'd make a very fine scoutmaster, Charlie. You ought to volunteer."

"What do you need?"

"A call to the FAA. They grounded me today and it's bogus. Even if it weren't, I need to get back in the air in a few days. Either that or send me an unmarked plane that I can fly off the beach."

"You can do that?"

"No."

"I'll make some calls. Do you have anything to tell me, any progress? Your bills are piling up. The suits upstairs are beginning to wonder what the PR department is doing with all its money."

"PR my foot."

"It's what we call it. What were you doing that got you grounded?"

"Actually it was Trent Fonts that did the questionable flying, but I took the rap. We were flying at a low altitude looking for what I thought was wreckage. Then we flew over a piece of shoreline where Trent thought he saw a bit of airplane the day after Nick disappeared."

"You thought you saw wreckage?"

"Operative word, thought. I can't be sure. It's a maybe at best, but we're getting somewhere, I think."

"Talk to me."

"Okay. The original search turned up no evidence of a plane crash because they were looking in the wrong place. Nick went down near, or in, Eastern Bay. That's south of Kent Island. You know Kent Island? So, they were looking north of Kent Island."

"Why north...or why are you looking south...you know what I mean."

"I do. North, because the original search supposed Nick went down when he dropped off the radar. But your phone call says he flew on several more minutes so, south."

"That's why you wanted me to check the time stamp."

"Correct."

"So, that meant he went down south of where they were looking and you thought you saw something—south."

"I hope so."

"You'll need divers and salvage equipment."

"Not yet, but you might get that ball rolling. I'm going to spend tomorrow scouting the bay's circumference. I want to know why no one reported a missing piece of airplane, and I can't believe no one saw anything that night. Somebody has to know something. By the way, what happened to my pictures?"

"On your kitchen table even as we speak."

"On my table? You were able to activate my phone, and now you have a key to my place."

"Don't be silly, Ike. Using a key breaks the spook's code. The messenger picked the lock."

"Right—spycraft. You guys never give up. I'll be back with you after I look at those pictures and check my navigation chart."

◇◇◇

The photographs were, indeed, on the kitchen table when Ike returned to his cottage. The messenger had picked the lock but forgotten to lock up on his way out. He'd have to mention that to Charlie. He didn't want to rat out the guilty party, but sloppy spycraft could cost someone his life.

He shuffled through the images, sorting them into piles chronologically. He paused and frowned. Something was not right. Why did Charlie tell him about the picked lock in the first place? If he'd come into the room and found the pictures on the table, he wouldn't have been surprised. A diversion. Make me think that the messenger lacked finesse and I won't look elsewhere. He let his eyes scan the room. Ike wasn't the neatest person in the world, but he knew his own clutter. During his time with the Company, he'd learned to keep track of everything irrespective of its place in the apparent disorder. His messes had fooled more than one counterintelligence agent in the past.

A chair had been moved. Not much. It sat almost exactly where it had been in the morning. Almost. There were small impressions in the carpet where the legs had been and the chair now sat a few inches over. The bedroom seemed to be undisturbed, but the phone with its layers of sunscreen felt suspiciously clean, as if it had been wiped down. Someone would have to do that to remove the mouthpiece and plant a bug. He turned his attention to the TV. So far he'd only been strolling about the place. If he were being surveilled, his watchers would soon know he'd tumbled to them when he turned the TV around.

He swung the set on its stand, peered in the back, and saw the small box that converted the set into a sending unit. He did his best imitation of singing; tone deaf did not even begin to describe him, "*Ye watchers and ye holy ones…* Hey, I'm the good guy here, okay?"

He draped a beach towel over the set and stuck a half of a banana into its concealed microphone. Then he lifted the air duct cover behind the chair and yanked out a second microphone. The phone bug he sent down the toilet. The phone rang. He screwed the mouthpiece back on and waited.

"That's very expensive government issue property you're manhandling there." Charlie said.

"Tough darts. You want me to work your patch, you trust me."

"Sorry, Ike. As I told you, the brass upstairs got wind of your…um…unauthorized expense account and ordered the surveillance. I didn't find out in time. Then I thought, let's see if he still has the chops. I guess you do. I would have told you in an hour or so if you didn't."

"Yeah, yeah. Now you know why I quit."

"I do know why you quit, and I know that wasn't the reason."

"It helped. Now are there any more surprises for me?"

"In the ceiling fan—little camera. Be careful, it cost a fortune."

"You're lucky I don't sell all this stuff to the Chinese."

"No market. They made all of it in the first place."

Ike hung up.

He hung a pair of jockey shorts on the ceiling fan and turned his attention to the pictures. The blowup of the pier showed a scrap of flotsam that could have been part of a tail. The work boat moored to the pier showed a man on the deck. The comparison shots confirmed that the barge, if that is what it had been, had been replaced by the duck blind. Why a duck blind?

He spent the next three hours studying the pictures, hoping for a pattern to emerge. He fixed himself a sandwich and a pot of coffee and retired to the porch to think. The ocean turned gray and then black as the sun sank in the west behind him. An offshore breeze picked up sending salty air across the beach. Except for the phone call to Charlie's niece, death spiral still seemed to be the best answer for Nick's sudden disappearance. Something, an image of something out of place, tried to push its way up from his subconscious. He waited. His subconscious stayed silent. At ten he shuffled off to bed.

Chapter Fourteen

Frank Sutherlin read the ET's report, turning each page with care. A methodical man, he wanted to be sure he hadn't missed anything when he visited the site earlier. He had been correct. The stains on the stone table were blood—animal blood. The lab couldn't be sure what kind or how many different, if any, without further, more sophisticated, tests. He called and told the director not to bother. He didn't know what the kids were up to. He assumed they were kids, given the sinkhole's traditional use, but he sure didn't want to spend any more of his time and the taxpayer's money just to find out the kids were parceling out raw hamburger to cook on the fires. He shoved the report in a drawer.

Essie sailed by on her way to the restroom looking triumphant. His brother Billy sauntered in and flopped down in the corner chair.

"Aren't you supposed to be on patrol?"

"Made one loop, thought I'd check in on momma-to-be 'fore I took another. My coffee tank's a little low, too, and I don't want to pay some Seven-Eleven guy two bucks for a cup of burned coffee. I got to be saving up."

"So you come in here for your burned coffee instead."

"Essie made us a fresh pot. You should try some instead of that herbal tea you drink. What do you see in it anyway?"

"It's green tea and it's good for you. It's got antioxidants that have been shown to reduce the risk of cancer, arthritis, high cholesterol, heart disease, and to pump up your immune system."

"Yeah, but will it wake you up in the morning after an 'all-nighter'?"

"Get out of here. Essie, make your husband get back on the road before I dock his pay."

Essie rounded the corner and gave Billy a smack on the back of his head.

"You heard the man. We can't afford no lollygagging around. Baby needs shoes."

"You wasn't so flaming conscientious before."

"Yeah, well back then I wasn't married, pregnant, and looking at real estate neither."

"You're looking at what?"

"You can't expect us to be raising children in a trailer park, Billy. First off, there ain't room enough to swing a cat in that place of mine, as you most surely know. Second, even if there was, there's the other kids we're having, and schools and—"

"Other kids? Whoa up there, Missy. Let's us just take them one at a time."

Frank stood and pointed first toward the door and then to Essie's desk.

"You two, you can have this out at home. Billy, git. Essie, sit."

The phone rang. Frank picked up before Essie had reached the dispatch desk. Blake Fisher asked for Deputy Sutherlin.

"You got him."

"I guess this will sound like a strange request, but can you tell me more about that sinkhole place?"

"I can tell you a lot. I had the evidence techs photograph it and map the site. It's in a report in my desk. You're welcome to have a look. What's up?"

"I'm not sure, but there is something going on at the high school, and since that has been a place where the kids meet, I thought I might get a hint if I looked it over."

"I'll put a copy of the report in an envelope for you. You can pick it up any time."

Frank hung up and shook his head. First the college guy with his bones, now the Reverend. Funny he didn't ask about his silverware.

Blake read the report twice. The bloody stone disturbed him. What kind of activity called for blood? And then what about the bones and the dead cat—Esther Peeper's cat more than likely. The map showed the location of the fires and the stone construction in the center. The lab techs referred to it as a bench. A bloody bench? The distance between the fires had been measured at eighteen feet. Why eighteen? Why not twenty? There seemed to be plenty of room. Why eighteen? A number like twenty seemed more usual unless there was some significance in the number eighteen. Eighteen feet was two hundred and sixteen inches, six and two-thirds yards, about five and a half meters. So what did any of that mean? Frank had paper clipped a sheet of paper to the report with directions to the sinkhole. Blake scanned the report again. Maybe he should go look at the place. It was nearly three, time to pick up Mary and look at the leaves on the Drive.

Mary stepped out of her door just as he pulled up to her house.

"Do you mind if I make a little side trip before we head for the hills? There's something I want to check out."

"No, of course not. Where're we going?"

"There's a sinkhole out in the park I want to look at."

"The Passion Pit?"

"The what? What did you call it?"

"Passion Pit. It's what we called it in high school. It's where the kids went to…you know."

"I can guess. I suppose you know the place well?"

Mary punched him in the arm. "I went there once. I was a sophomore and the football team's captain asked me out. I was so flattered I didn't think why this hunky guy would ask a gawky tenth grader for a date."

"I can't picture you as a gawky anything."

"Well, I was. You should see my high school year book. I was a nerd, first class."

Blake looked out of the corner of his eye at the beautiful woman beside him and decided she was being modest. No one that gorgeous could ever have been described as a nerd, much less gawky.

"So what happened?"

"You don't want to know. Let's just say it's a long, long walk from that park back to where I lived, especially in heels. Why do you want to go to the Pit?"

"Well initially I just wanted to look at some things that have me worried, but now, well…"

"Don't get any funny ideas. I'm not a sophomore anymore."

"But I was the captain of my high school football team. I want to show you that all of us hunks are not alike."

"Sorry, captain, not today…at least not in the Pit. I can think of better venues for what you have in mind."

"Okay. The real reason I want to see it has to do with this." He handed her the report and filled her in on his conversation at the school. "You remember the kid with the cross, the satanic avatar. Well, Lanny mentioned it to the principal, who called me in and told me, in no uncertain terms, I was to keep my opinions about evil, sin, and everlasting perdition to myself."

"He said that?"

"He thought that. What he said was, and I quote, 'I know your kind would like us to quiver in our boots at the thought of some old codger in a red union suit carrying a pitchfork taking over our lives, but this is the twentieth century—'"

"He said twentieth?"

"He did. And he went on at length about the enlightenment that has visited the country, the state, the county and, most importantly, the school board."

"Roger DiComo is an idiot."

"You know him?"

"You could say. We went to school together. You two have something in common."

"I doubt it. What could we have in common?"

"You were both captain of your football team."

"Ah. And we both want to take you to the Pit."

"I'm wearing my running shoes, so don't get any ideas."

They pulled up in the graveled parking area and walked to the sinkhole. Blake had to steady Mary on the rock crossing at the stream. They stood at the edge. Mary turned to go.

"This place gives me the creeps. I'll wait for you in the car."

"Bad memories?"

"No, not that. Looking back on that night, I remember it as funny rather than scary. No, there is something else, something not quite right, about this place. It gives me goose bumps."

Blake pointed to the stone construction at the bottom. "Was any of this here when you—"

"I don't think so. Is that where they found the blood? It looks like an altar, doesn't it? A shabby, lopsided altar."

"An altar, of course. And the fires don't form a pentagon… you connect them to make a star—a pentagram. Six and two-thirds yards is six-point-six-six yards."

Chapter Fifteen

Ike rose early and once again savored the salt air blowing in from the ocean. He could get used to that. He spread out his road map and planned the day. Innumerable inlets and creeks would make it impossible to move directly from one point to another. He would have to travel down one road, backtrack and drive down another. The aroma of fresh brewed coffee pulled him back to the moment. He drowned a biscotti in his cup, scarfed it down, and headed for the car. He snatched the jockey shorts from the ceiling fan. He assumed the surveillance system had been shut down, but you never knew, so he gave the camera a quick one-fingered salute on the way out. He expected the equipment would be gone, or perhaps repositioned, when he returned.

He left the main highway just east of the Bay Bridge and turned south. The local names, Chesapeake, Matapeake, Mattapex, Romancoke—native American names—juxtaposed against neighboring towns with old English names: Wye, Kent, Cambridge, Oxford. A lot of colonial history tangled up in that mix. He passed by the Bay Bridge airstrip. He'd seen it on the aeronautical map but not up close. He tucked the visual away against some possible future use. His marine chart showed a pier of some size at Romancoke. From it he'd have an unobstructed view of Eastern Bay looking north, south, and east. By day's end, he hoped to be in Claiborne, where he'd have the reverse view of the same shoreline. It would also put him close to that oddly positioned duck blind. He passed another airstrip. He nearly missed it. Only the Day-Glo windsock and a small sign announced its presence. Kentmoor Airpark.

At Romancoke the road dead-ended at the pier. Ike strolled its length and took in the expanse of Eastern Bay. Charlie had sent him a digital camera with a telescopic lens.

"It's the least I can do," he'd said.

"You're just feeling guilty for the snooping your playmates are doing in my cottage. You know, if I get any action, I'll have to book into a motel."

"When have you ever sought or received any 'action'? You wouldn't know a hottie if she danced naked in your hot tub."

"You're the one to talk. Besides, I don't have a hot tub, but thanks for the camera."

"Any time. Ike, find out what happened to the kid."

"You were fond of him, weren't you?"

"My niece needs to know."

"I'll do what I can, Charlie."

"If anybody can do it, you can."

Charlie wasn't one for sentimentality or compliments. That was as close as Ike had ever heard him come to either.

Through the camera's lens, the shoreline looked lush and green. The myriad inlets and creeks that cut in from the main part of the bay were effectively masked by trees and shrubbery. Unless you looked straight up one, you'd miss it. He swung the camera slowly in an arc snapping pictures. He hoped they would augment the satellite images he'd received from the CIA techs. The last was a long shot to capture the duck blind. He'd take a closer shot of that later.

He trained the lens at the beach where the tail section washed up. He could make out the workboat at the pier, *The J. Millard Tawes*. It didn't seem to have moved. Wouldn't a boat like that be on the bay fishing, or crabbing, or oystering? September had an R in it. Oysters were in season. He ran off a half-dozen shots with close-ups. A careful scan still revealed no signs of the tail section. He had had only the biscotti for breakfast. His watch said eleven; his stomach said lunch.

He wanted to have a look at the larger Chesapeake Bay, so he turned in at the second air strip he'd seen. The road led west toward the Chesapeake but then turned abruptly south close to the shore. Ike found himself at a dead end and the Kentmoor Restaurant, which had the view he wanted. Two birds with one stone.

"Yes, sir, what can I get you to drink?" The waitress looked to be about seventeen. She wore her hair in a ponytail and smelled of soap. His mother would have described her as "perky." She laid a menu on the table in front of him.

"Iced tea, thanks."

Ike watched her "perky" backside as she retreated to the kitchen to fill his drink order and then shifted his gaze to the menu. Seafood mostly, but with the obligatory burger section as well. She returned and placed his tea at his right hand.

"You have soft-shell crabs today?"

"Yes, sir, we do."

"Are they the really big ones? I can't remember what they were called…"

"Whales?"

"Whales…right. Do you have any of those?"

"Lord, I haven't seen any of those in years." Ike wondered how many years she could possibly have experienced—with or without whales.

"No?"

"No, not them and not even any pretty big ones either."

"Why not?"

"Like they've cut the crab harvesting way back and most watermen have had to get other jobs or try their luck down in Virginia waters, and that don't sit too well with them, I can tell you."

"New wars like the oyster wars?"

In the 1880s, Maryland mounted an Oyster Navy to enforce the boundaries between Virginia and Maryland. Shots were exchanged and some deaths recorded as watermen worked the beds hard. The fleet lasted well unto the twentieth century. While it seemed to manage the territorial disputes, it had no effect on the dwindling harvest, and now the bay, which once produced fifteen million bushels of oysters a year, has harvests of a paltry fifty thousand or so. Aquaculture and management techniques had thus far failed, and the famous Chesapeake oysters have been displaced by those shipped in from Louisiana and New England and as far away as Washington State.

"I don't know about that, but what with the limits on the harvest and all, the watermen are up in arms. It's a shame. It seems like the bay is just dying a slow death."

"The soft shells on the menu?"

"We ship them in from someplace. That's why they're so expensive."

She left to fill his order, and he turned his attention to the view across the bay. To the north, the twin spans of the Bay Bridge arced gracefully to Anne Arundel County. To the south, a half-dozen container ships rode at anchor waiting for a bay pilot to take them into Baltimore harbor. From the ground, they seemed enormous. The images on his satellite pictures made them seem Lilliputian. But from twenty-two miles up, he guessed they would.

His soft shells arrived. They were small but cooked perfectly, requiring only a touch of tartar sauce. He poured a puddle of catsup on his plate for dipping his fries and, good as it probably was, ignored the coleslaw.

The waitress checked his progress, refilled his iced tea. Before she left, Ike pointed out the window at the ships in the channel.

"Waiting for a bay pilot?"

"Yeah, mostly. Sometimes they're just waiting for word from their owners, like, maybe they have to backtrack to Norfolk or Port of Richmond, but mostly, yeah, waiting for a pilot."

"Were you here on the Fourth of July?"

"You mean here in the restaurant, or here, like, in the area?"

"Either."

"No, not here at the Kentmoor, but over near Grasonville. That's where I live."

"How were the fireworks?"

"Not much to see this year."

"No?"

"No. See, most times we all go out on the water, like all the people who live around it; well not all, but lots. We get in our boats, raft up, party, and watch in all directions. Usually there's some beer or wine and stuff to eat. We share around. It's real friendly."

"But not this year?"

"No, we all got out there and then the fog just rolled in and you couldn't see nothing, so we went home and watched it on the TV."

"Fog. Was that unusual?"

"The fog? Well, for the Fourth it was, I think…don't ever remember it that bad on the Fourth of July, but we get fog all the time down here. Like, where some schools have snow days, we have fog days."

"So everybody went home."

"Yeah, pretty much except those people who got murdered."

"Murdered? On the Fourth of July? This past Fourth?"

"Yeah. They sailed over from Annapolis, or some place like that, in a thirty-two-footer. Nice boat. And when the fog rolled in they, like, couldn't go home. So, anyway they were found two days after that, drifting off Hampton Roads, I think. Somebody shot them and cut their anchor, I guess. It was in all the papers. Like how they were naked as jaybirds with bullet holes everywhere."

"Who were they?" This opened a completely new chapter.

"Some guy from D.C. they said. He had a boat with a funny name. *Opium*, I think."

"*Opium*. Like that?"

"Yeah, well sort of. I think it was spelled without all the letters or something, but people called it that."

"He came here often?"

"There's lots of day sailors and overnighters that anchors in the Bay. He's been here before, sure. He was hard to miss."

"How so?"

"Well," the girl blushed slightly, "he mostly brought young women and some of them were into sun-bathing in the buff. Seems like the sporting goods store sold out of binoculars this year."

"So, what happened?"

"One story was he was in some shady financial thing and mixed up with, you know, like, the Mafia or something. They think it must have been a hit." She spoke as if Mafia hit-men on the Eastern Shore were as common as flies. "The woman with him wasn't his wife, either, so they were looking at his missus for the murder, too."

"And...?"

"Don't know. Like, it was news for a day and then something else, I forget what, pushed it off."

"You said one story...what was the other?"

"Some locals said they were undercover bay police out to check on them. It don't seem likely, but the old-timers, well, they see police behind every tree. I guess one of them could have done it.

"You think so?"

"No. One of the dead people was this woman and...well it don't seem likely."

Ike paid his bill, added a more than generous tip, and left. As he drove north he wondered why nude people were described as "naked as a jay bird." The only jays he knew had blue plumage and a crest. He tried to imagine one plucked and devoid of feathers. He'd seen enough naked bodies in his time to know that the simile didn't work.

As he turned east on the highway it hit him...Opium but no what? Letters? Vowels? O P something M...O P M...Other People's Money. He'd need to check that out. Three deaths on the Fourth in the Eastern Bay. Anchor line cut. The odds said they were connected.

Chapter Sixteen

It had turned dark by the time Blake and Mary finally came down out of the mountains. They'd stayed longer than either had planned. The fall colors were gorgeous and the weather fine, but unfortunately, or perhaps fortunately, a matter of point of view, the scenic pull-offs were also numerous and, in the middle of the week, private. Like a pair of fifties-generation teenagers, they took advantage of the time and place and would have still been there except they both realized to do so would take them somewhere they had earlier agreed not to go. The descent from the heights, both actual and metaphorical came as a relief and a disappointment.

Mary passed on his dinner invitation when he dropped her off. "We need to talk," she said and straightened her blouse.

"We could talk over dinner."

"If I invite you in, in the shape I'm in right now, there won't be any dinner."

"We could go to a restaurant."

"I need a little space and, I'm guessing, you could use a cold shower."

Blake grinned, "Football captains—we're all the same."

"Not all." She turned to go and added, "Call me."

He drove to the office. He lived next door to the church in the Rectory, and since he'd neglected his duties past the time he'd planned, he thought he had better check his desk for messages before shutting down for the evening. Mary was dead right; they needed to talk—seriously.

A pink while-you-were out slip lay front and center on Blake's desk. Gloria, his secretary, had printed the message in large bold letters, underlined them, and added three exclamation points, just in case he might have missed their importance.

<u>The Bishop Wants You To Call
Him—Urgent—ASAP</u>!!!

The bishop never called. The only conversation they'd ever had occurred when he'd first arrived in the diocese the previous year and he'd made the customary, expected, and wholly perfunctory, call at the diocesan house. Like most Episcopal bishops, this one seemed preoccupied with the ongoing turmoil in the church at large, and a few of his parishes in particular. At the time Blake had been cautiously noncommittal when queried about his stand on the several issues that seemed to obsess the church. He had to. At the time he stood on the brink of unemployment in the church and the only job offer he had was in Picketsville, a place he'd neither sought, nor desired, but loomed as his only, however unattractive, choice.

Blake called Gloria at home.

"What did the bishop want?"

"It was his secretary that called. I asked her the same question. All she could, or maybe, would say is that the bishop had a call from someone in the parish complaining about you and you needed to call him. Actually, she said you should make an appointment. I reminded her of how far you'd have to drive to see the bishop and then she said you should call him and see…"

"Someone from the parish called and complained?"

"That's what she said."

"Any idea who?'

"She didn't say, and when I asked, she clammed up. Is she, you know, normal?"

"No idea. Bishop's secretaries tend to take on themselves responsibilities not in their job description. Once I announced

I was planning to do a full immersion baptism at a local swimming pool during our annual parish picnic and a few matriarchs called the bishop's office to see if that were allowable. The bishop's secretary said I need to ask permission. I pointed out to the ladies, when they announced their findings, that the *Book of Common Prayer* clearly states that immersion is the preferred method, sprinkling a second best, and I did not need anyone's permission."

"What happened?"

"They boycotted the picnic." Blake scanned the note a second time. "I guess I'll call the bishop tomorrow. His office will be closed by now."

He hung up. The last time someone complained to a bishop about him was in Philadelphia. It was a bogus complaint but still, it nearly ended his career. He didn't want to go through that again. He called Phillip Bournet, the Rector of the sponsoring parish of his little mission church.

"If he said it was urgent, Blake, you could call him at home."

"You're kidding, right?"

"Actually, yes I am. When the Episcopate says it's urgent, they assume you will take him at his word and appear hat in hand and heart in throat. Ignore it."

Blake could almost see the twinkle in his friend's eye. "You want me fired, is that it?"

"He can't fire you. That's the point. As the vicar of Stonewall Jackson Memorial, the only parochial mission in the diocese, as you know, you work for me, remember?"

That much was true. The church's arcane polity made him answerable first to Philip, the rector of the parish in Roanoke that sponsored, indeed subsidized, his little church. Blake hoped to end that dependency but the numbers weren't there yet.

"He'll have to ask me to fire you, and I won't—unless you've committed a felony, abused a child or, worse, have become a disciple of Jack Spong."

"Not guilty on all counts. I just got a message he wanted to talk to me. He indicated it was urgent—underlined."

"As I said, you should ignore it. He knows, or should have known, that if he wanted to talk to my vicar, he should have called me first, told me what was wrong, and had me deal with it. So, don't call. Let me call him in the morning, remind him of protocol—politely, of course, and then I'll let you know what's up."

"He won't be angry?"

"Who cares? He's on thin ice as it is. He has bigger fish to fry than to worry about some obscure vicar in the boondocks."

"Thanks a lot, I think."

"How's that beautiful organist I sent you getting along?"

"Wonderfully."

"Anything I can report to my wife, the matchmaker?"

"Give me a week or two and then ask again."

"Really? She'll be delighted."

"No, no, nothing yet, Philip. Don't jump the gun...but..."

"I'll keep Christmas Eve open for a wedding."

"No, wait...Philip..." But Bournet had already rung off.

He decided to take his advice and ignore the bishop's call. If it were truly important, he'd call again, but it seemed equally likely that the urgency stemmed from an inflated sense of importance on the part of his secretary. There was, after all, protocol. Ordinarily, Blake had no use for the ins and outs of ecclesiastical maneuvering, but his instincts told him this would be a good time to buy in. He locked up and went across the parking lot to the rectory and let himself in. He was hungry and some sort of supper was in order. The phone was ringing.

"You were supposed to call me."

"I was in the office. While I was admiring God's splendid fall colors—among other things—the bishop called and said I should report in ASAP."

"Did you?"

"No, I called Philip, and he said I should wait until he had a chance to speak to the Right Reverend."

"Are you in trouble?" He could hear the worry in her voice.

"I don't know. I could be unemployed by week's end."

"You'll be fine. You're too good to toss out. Did he say anything else?"

"Who, the bishop or Philip?"

"Philip."

Blake considered how best to answer.

"What are you doing on Christmas Eve?"

Ike stopped at the Avenue Restaurant for dinner. He'd made the circuit around Eastern Bay, and, as he'd expected, it had taken him all day. The light had been fading when he found the duck blind. The camera Charlie provided had, however, enough light-gathering capacity in its lens to produce a sharp picture in spite of it. As he sat drinking his second cup of coffee and contemplating whether he had earned a slice of apple pie, he clicked through the digital images on the camera's back. They were small, but he knew if he blew them up he'd be able to make out whatever details he needed. The duck blind seemed odd to him. Not just its location out from the shore and facing deep water—there was something else. Tomorrow, he decided, he'd charter a boat, have a look at the area from the water, and check out that shooting platform.

Chapter Seventeen

The next morning, Ike pulled into what must have been a filling station at one time. The pumps were covered with cardboard boxes like those used to ship refrigerators. Scrawled across the face of each, in black marker pen, he read:

NO MORE GAS!

He stepped from the car and walked into the garage bay. He could have found it blindfolded. In fact, in his days with the Company, he'd done just that. The mixture of cleaning solution, used oil, gasoline, and grease smelled the same whether in Bulgaria or on the Eastern Shore of Maryland. A large man in amazingly dirty coveralls bent over the front fender of an elderly Ford 150 pickup that had a mismatched cab and bed. His head and shoulders disappeared in the depths of its motor compartment.

"Good morning," Ike said.

The man extracted his upper body from the truck's inner workings and faced Ike. "We ain't got no gas."

"So I see." Ike nodded at the defunct pumps. "Problems?"

"Big oil companies. Bunch of greedy bastards."

"So I hear."

"Trying to put us indies out of business. Not just trying—doing it, by God. Big oil, big food, big books—all the same, put you out of business. Bunch of greedy bastards."

Ike opened his mouth to respond but the man waved his hand and went on.

"Yep, just plain want us out of business is it. Won't sell me gas except at near retail. Retail! I'd have to charge thirty, forty cents a gallon more than their company store up the road. Who's going to pay that?"

Ike tried again. "Look, I don't—"

"I run a good business here. Honest day's work for an honest day's pay. Never gouged nobody for the gas. Hell, people thought I was getting rich off the stuff, but they didn't know what I had to pay for it. No profit in the gas, not unless you come in here and bought maybe thirty or forty gallons. Then, maybe I'd make a buck or two. No sir, I earned my groceries right in here, in the shop, getting dirt under my nails and burning my hands on hot exhaust pipes, radiator caps; you name it, mister, and I done it."

He must have run out of air, because he paused in his rant. Ike took the opportunity and jumped in.

"Look, I don't need gas right now. I'm lost. I need to get to a house right about here..." He held up the road map and pointed to the approximate spot where he'd seen the work boat. "There's a boat tied up there, the *J. Millard Tawes*, I think is its name, and for the life of me I can't find the right road. I've been driving up and down all morning."

The man wiped his hands on a rag so dark with grease it seemed likely his hands would end up dirtier. He bent his head forward and studied the map. He lifted his gaze to Ike. His mouth formed a tight line.

"You're government, ain't you." A statement not a question.

"Not exactly."

"Why do you want to see Bunky Crispins?"

"I want to ask him a few questions"

"You're government, and he won't talk."

"Look, I understand the watermen are ticked at the restrictions on the harvesting of crabs. I guess it's pretty bad."

"Ticked ain't the word I'd use."

"Whatever. I'm just a cop on vacation. I'm doing a favor for a friend. That's all."

"What kinda cop?"

"A Virginia cop, for crying out loud. Not even local."

"That's worse. Look, Old Bunky, he maybe went south of Tangier Sound a time or two but you can't hardly blame him. He's got a wife and kids and watermen, like, they don't have no fringe packages and stuff. Doctors cost a bundle—bunch of greedy bastards."

"South of Tangier…I haven't a clue what you're talking about. I just want to talk to him about a missing airplane and its pilot."

"You're not from the Virginia Bay Police or whatever they call themselves?"

"I'm the sheriff of Picketsville…over in the Shenandoah Valley. I wouldn't know a crab from a trilobite if it bit me." It was an exaggeration, but Ike sensed the direction the conversation had taken.

"Don't matter. He won't talk to you."

"How about I try? Can you tell me how to find him?"

"You're sure it's Bunky you want?"

"If he's the owner of the *J. Millard Tawes*, he's the one I want."

"Okay, it's your funeral…what in Hell's a trilobite?"

"Prehistoric ancestor of the crab."

◇◇◇

The directions were barely adequate, but a half-hour and a few wrong turns later, he found himself in a graveled cul-de-sac staring at the front side of the house he'd photographed from the back the day before. A Ferguson tractor—it had to be sixty years old—graced a front yard badly in need of mowing. If there were antique tractor collectors out there, if the right buyer happened along, Bunky Crispins had a modest gold mine rusting away in his front yard. Ike pulled in the driveway and opened the driver's side door. He had one foot on the ground and in the process of heaving himself out when someone or something smacked the passenger side door. His instincts made him duck. A man he took to be Bunky Crispins stood a pace back from the door and held a shotgun loosely in his arms.

"You just hop back in that government-issue car and get off my land."

Instead of following his orders, Ike stood and held his hands, palms out, toward the man and the gun.

"It's a personal vehicle and I'm not from the government."

"Harley says different."

"Harley?"

"Up to the garage. He said you were there asking questions and that you're a Virginia police."

"He got that part right. I am, and I was, asking questions, that is. But I'm not here about police business, fishing, crabbing, or any other kind of business. I'm looking for help finding a missing pilot. That's it—the whole bushel."

"Just you step away from the car and put your ID on the hood so I can see it."

Ike did as he was told. The man waved him back and turned his attention to the wallet. The moment his eyes dropped, Ike stepped forward and in one smooth motion took the man's gun and with a leg sweep, dropped him on the ground.

"Ouch." The man rolled over and struggled to place his hands under him. Ike kicked them out so that he landed face down. He broke open the gun's chamber and dumped the shells on the ground, then tossed the piece across the driveway into a clump of grass.

"Your lawn needs mowing. Okay, if I let you get up, do you promise to behave?"

"Cripes, who are you?"

Cripes? What kind of a word was that?

"You going to behave?"

"Yeah, yeah."

"We need to talk about the Fourth of July, and then you need to tell me if I can charter your boat for a spell."

Bunky Crispins eased forward and lurched to his feet. Ike watched as he dusted himself off and then measured the distance between them.

"Don't even think about it, Bunky. I'm here to get some information, and you might not be able to tell me what I want to know if you have a fat lip—or worse."

Ike rarely played tough guy. He didn't have to. Most folks in Picketsville knew him and what he could do. But he was on someone else's turf, and establishing his position seemed required. Also, people who pointed guns at him made him nervous.

Evidently, Bunky got the message. He leaned against the car's hood and picked at the knees of his trousers.

"Cripes. You made me rip my pants."

There was that word again. Coaches at parochial schools used to curse that way. They didn't dare let the nuns hear them take the Lord's name in vain. "Cripes," they'd say, or they'd yell "Cheese and Rice," at some poor kid who dropped an easy pass. Ike never attended a Catholic school but had a roommate in college who had and who spent his freshman year learning how to swear properly.

"Okay, I guess I gotta trust you. Anybody that'll take a loaded twelve-gauge from a guy, I guess don't leave no room for anything else." He paused and took Ike's measure. "But you'd maybe better not try it again."

"Don't plan to, unless that shotgun finds its way back into the conversation. Now, I want you to tell me everything I need to know about this past Fourth of July."

Chapter Eighteen

Blake frittered away most of the next morning waiting for Philip's call. After an hour, he thought he should call him instead. He hesitated. Then, he thought playing procedural games with the diocesan biggies was not such a good idea. Maybe he should disregard Philip's advice and call the bishop himself. He didn't want to risk this job.

He'd evidently annoyed someone, and that someone had the bishop's ear, and that put him on the spot. He guessed he could go back to Philadelphia. His old bishop had offered him a reprieve, but what about Mary—what about all these people he'd come to love? Contemplating the possibility that his tenure at Stonewall Jackson Memorial Church might be ended just when it seemed to be blossoming and Philip's calm assurance not withstanding, he reached for the Diocesan directory.

The phone rang. The unexpectedness of it made him jump. Frank Sutherlin wanted to talk.

"Rev, I got to thinking about what you said in the note you left when you dropped the report off. You didn't have to do that, by the way. It's a copy I made for you. Anyway, I don't know much about that old sinkhole, never did, and I'm sure nothing good is going on out there, what with that bench and those fires, but a satanic cult is a little over the top, don't you think?"

"I didn't say it *was* that, Deputy. I said it looked like that. Five piles of ashes exactly 6.6 yards apart...blood on the...not a bench, an altar I think. I don't know."

"Well, maybe, but I think it's a stretch. I asked my two brothers that are still in town and been here all this time, what they might know about it. Now, they're both a little past the 'Passion Pit' stage, but Billy did say the last he heard, the atmosphere out there had changed a lot in the last couple a years."

"I don't understand—atmosphere? You mean whatever the kids were doing out there in the past has been replaced with something else? Or is he saying the air out there is so full of weed smoke that it smells differently?"

"Um...the first...I think."

"In what way?"

"He couldn't say, so I put Henry on it. He's going to ask around and see what he can find out. Those kids are more likely to talk to him than me or Billy. They know we're police, and town or not, we aren't likely to hear much from them."

Blake recalled Henry, Dorothy's youngest son and episodic congregant. Christmas, Easter, occasional weddings, funerals, and spaghetti dinners accounted for the bulk of Henry's spiritual journey.

"If the kids will open up to anyone, it'll be Henry," Frank added.

"I expect you're right. Any progress in finding my silver? I've notified the insurance company and they are waiting to see if it turns up in a pawn shop or something. Any hits?"

"Nope, and that's a mystery right there. Usually when something worth money goes missing, it's because the guy who stole it needs cash. You know, for drugs, or beer, or to get some girl out of trouble, and it shows up quick. But nothing has turned up in any probable fence sites from Winchester to Roanoke."

"What else would anyone do with a communion set like that if they didn't want money?"

"Maybe they're starting up their own church."

"What?"

"Just a joke Rev. But, you're right, it doesn't make much sense."

Blake replaced the receiver in its cradle and stared out the window. It had started to cloud over. It would rain soon. October, and the rainy season would be on them in a few weeks. Then winter and snow perhaps and then…Christmas Eve. He felt a hollow spot form in the pit of his stomach. Had he overstepped? Was he really ready for that? He took some deep breaths and the feeling eased. It was just that he'd been single and sought-after so many years that a permanent commitment seemed very new, and strange, and not a little scary.

"Get over it," he muttered. The phone rang again.

"So, tell me about this airplane you want to find."

Ike and Bunky Crispins stood shoulder to shoulder staring out into the expanse of Eastern Bay, across the deck of the *J. Millard Tawes*. Ike thought he could just make out the long pier at Romancoke but couldn't be sure. His eyes were more accustomed to the forested, mountainous landscape of the Shenandoah Valley. Flat, wide expanses took some getting used to. He wondered how the people in places like Kansas managed with their endless vistas.

"First tell me about the Fourth. Then, if it makes any sense, I'll talk about the plane."

"For a fellow who wants me to help him and maybe charter my boat, you sure are short."

"Sorry. It comes from staring down the barrel of a double-barreled shotgun. Makes me edgy. Besides, shouldn't you be out oystering or something."

"Not much left for us in that line. Skipjack fleet is about gone. The few that are left and tonging or drudging can just squeeze out a living. Beds are played out, and the limits on us pretty much has put us all on the beach. Government. It takes away your living. Shuts down the whole dinged Bay and they wonder why we don't like them."

"Gotcha. Tell me about the Fourth."

"Okay, okay. Most times on the Fourth of July we take our boats out on the water. Awesome view out there when the fireworks go up. You can see, like, forever. Easton, Cambridge, clean to the Western Shore, Annapolis, all over. I had a party on the boat all lined up and stood to make some money 'til the fog rolled in."

"It wiped out the whole bay?"

"Not all of it but most. By nine or so it sort of retreated up the bay so you could see the displays down toward the south—one especially—like an aerial bomb that misfired or something... heck of a racket...kablam, like that."

"Where was that?"

Bunky pointed toward the bay's southwest edge, beyond the spit of land that formed the bay's southwest border. Beyond that stretch sat an overlarge duck blind and the general area where Ike thought he'd seen the shadow, the suspicious eddy, in the water.

"Over there?"

"Yeah, pretty much."

"What did this misfire look like?"

"You know how them aerial things work. They shoot up, there's a small pop and they separate in, like, a star shell thing, and then, a second or two later, a half dozen go off all over the place—boom, boom, boom—like that. It looked like maybe this one didn't separate and the whole thing, six or so of them bombs, went off all at once. I saw the trail of sparks headed up but there was no, you know, pop and then explosions. There was just this one big kablam. Cripes, what a noise."

"You didn't go to Catholic school by any chance did you, Crispins?"

"What? Catholic? No way. I'm what you'd call Baptist—hardshell Baptist. My old daddy'd whomp me with a gaff 'fore he'd let me inside twenty feet of one of them places. He's dead now, rest his soul. I got some friends that are fish-eaters, though, so I don't share them feelings like he did. Shoot no."

Catholic parochial school or hard-shell Baptist—so much for the fine art of swearing.

"You saw the rocket's upward trail and then an explosion. Anything else?"

"No, not that I can recall."

"No airplane?"

"The flight path over to the BWI, Andrews, and Reagan National airports is all right over this parcel of water one time or another. I reckon I heard a lot of them."

"A small plane."

"I might have. If I did, I didn't take no notice."

Ike let his gaze shift across Crispins' back yard. A weathered shed, which undoubtedly contained boat and fishing gear, stood halfway between the house and the waterfront. A pile of miscellaneous junk leaned against one wall. In the midst of it Ike saw, or thought he saw, something painted camo that could have been the missing tail piece. Ike wondered if Crispins was being dense, or really hadn't made a connection with the bit of wreckage in the pile by the shed, and a missing plane. He decided he'd pursue that later. Right now Crispins' aerial bomb misfire held his complete attention.

"What time did you see that thing go off?"

"Maybe nine-thirty, give or take."

Maybe nine-thirty…it fit.

Chapter Nineteen

Blake picked up the phone on the first ring. Philip had news.

"Am I in trouble?"

"Blake, it seems trouble is your middle name."

"What did the Bishop say?"

"He said several things. Some of them were more or less sensible, some idiotic, and some just inane. First, a member of your congregation, Barbara Starkey to be precise, called him to report that you had excommunicated one of her daughter's friends last Sunday. Then, she said you were on a witch hunt, or more accurately, a devil hunt, and had upset the local high school officialdom, and finally she questioned your mental stability and suggested the bishop order up a series of sessions with a local shrink for you."

"She said all that?"

"He said she said all that. It took him twenty minutes or so to do it, but that's it in a nut shell. I reminded him about the line of accountability that ran from him through me, to you. He wasn't happy about that. He said if you didn't stop preaching superstitious nonsense, by which, I take it, he meant the very existence of the devil, literally or metaphorically, he would assume you had abandoned your orders and could, therefore, no longer serve as a priest in the church."

"What? He can do that?"

"Certainly not. It's just the new double-speak in church leadership circles. Instead of invoking canon law and making an active move that would entitle you to an appeal, a hearing in an ecclesiastical or civil court, they now dump the onus on the victim. If your career is ended or compromised in some way, it would be your doing, not his, you see—sort of passive-aggressive behavior, or something—very popular with the House of Bishops lately. Anyway, I reminded him of that, too, and after a bit more hot air, he let it go with the insistence that I make you promise to apologize to the complainant and smooth things over. He has enough problems with schismatic churches, property squabbles, and theological nit-picking. He doesn't need this."

"Apologize. He wants me to smooth things over. Has he any idea of the seriousness a satanic movement would have on us— especially with kids?"

"I doubt it. It's the twenty-first century. All religions, including the Church of LaVey, or any of its near approximations, are protected under the latest rendering of the Second Amendment. No matter what he thinks or feels, his hands are tied. And, as I said, he has bigger problems to deal with than a small dispute in a, for him, forgettable mission church in the Valley. So, make nice to the unhappy lady, and move on."

"Philip, this is not a trifle."

"How sure are you of this satanic business?"

"Pretty sure…I think."

"Be very sure before you do anything else. You might have a cache of money tucked away somewhere, but I don't, and we both would be liable in a law suit."

"We can be sued?"

"Absolutely, and a civil court will be hard-pressed to find in our—your—favor in the matter of the Devil vs. the State, if you follow me. I don't want to go there, Blake. No matter what we believe, we're in an untenable position in a secular court. If I remember Mrs. Starkey correctly, she is descended from one of the original founders of your church. People like her assume a proprietary interest in churches that has little or nothing to do with spirituality. In addition, her husband is a funding source for various diocesan feel-good projects. So, have a chat with the lady."

"I'll try."

"One more thing—keep this in perspective."

"Meaning?"

"Kids do all sorts of crazy things. They try behaviors, eat, drink, inhale, do drugs, they drive too fast, and take risks. It's the nature of the age. In the end, most of them come home, so to speak. You were right to ask the boy to remove himself and his pendant from the church. Church, after all, is our turf. Pushing into the schools is dicier. You see what I mean?"

Blake said he thought so, but wasn't that sure. He hung up and groaned. He wondered if it were too late to enroll in Washington and Lee's Law School up the road. Would Mary be happy married to a lawyer, to a shark rather than an angel fish? He decided he needed coffee, strong coffee. He didn't dare go for booze. That road could only end in disaster.

He stood and walked to the outer office. Gloria was gathering her things prior to leaving.

"You off?"

"Remember, I mentioned I had a dentist appointment?" He'd forgotten. "And while you were on the phone, Ashley Starkey asked if she could talk to you after school."

"Ashley? Is she the—"

"No, not the girl with the boyfriend last Sunday. She's the younger sister."

"What did she want?"

"She didn't say. I told her tomorrow would work better and she said okay. She'll be here at four-thirty."

"Tomorrow? Why tomorrow? I have this afternoon free."

Gloria paused and shook her head. "I think I should be here when she comes. Kids get funny ideas sometimes."

"I'm not sure I…" Blake stopped in midsentence. He'd had a bad experience in Philadelphia that nearly ruined him. Cleared of all counts, but people might know enough details to harbor small lingering doubts. "You don't think…?"

"Like I said, kids have funny ideas. Why take a chance?"

Why, indeed.

◇◇◇

Ike arranged with Bunky Crispins to charter his boat the following day and for the week following. He didn't know what
he'd find—wasn't even sure what he was looking for, but a boat
seemed the next logical step. They'd haggled over the price, and
even though he knew it was too much, Ike agreed to it. Now,
he needed to let Charlie Garland know the price for his little
favor had just gone up. He returned to his cottage, scoured it
thoroughly for bugs, wiretaps, and cameras. He found none,
but he also knew that since he'd left the CIA technology had far
outstripped his data bank, and he couldn't be sure. The equipment they used now would scare the pants off George Orwell.
Charlie answered on the first ring. He never did that.

"Charlie, just checking, is all your spookware out of this
cottage or must I move?"

"Not mine, Ike, but yes, it's all gone. The Agency is not
interested in you anymore, and they've shut my, I should say
our, little project down as well."

"What do you mean?"

"I had to 'fess up as to what you were doing and they were…
let's say…annoyed. I may be billed for your airplane. You're not
grounded anymore, by the way, but that doesn't matter, because
I can't pay for any more hours in the air. We're going to have to
let this go. I'm afraid."

"I don't think that's a good idea. There's some weird and, I
think, important, things going on down here. Now is not the
time to pull out."

"It can't be helped. I don't know what I'll tell my niece."

"How about I work it on my own for a while, then? I'll still
need some help from the photo-techs."

"Ike, I appreciate the offer, but all hell is breaking loose around
here, and I can't even help you, much less ask the techs."

"What's up?"

"You know the drill—"

"Right, if you told me, you'd have to kill me, I know. Still, give me a minute." Ike could hear Charlie exhale on the other end. "A quick guess—somebody down the bowels of the puzzle palace found something in some obscure intel report that involves possible terrorist activity, and Homeland Security is on your case."

"Not bad, but not my case, Fugarelli's butt is in a sling. I'm just a recruit."

"I remember Fugarelli. He's okay. Give me another minute."

"Ike, I have to report back to the pooh-bahs for instruction."

"Hang on. What if we can tie what I'm doing to what they're stressed about?"

"Ike, I don't think I should put my personal—"

"No, listen to me. You got the call from Nick. It was directed to you, not some more obvious agency he'd call if he was having plane trouble. He wanted to tell you something, and it was really important."

"Okay. So what?"

"Charlie, we both agreed he saw something that worried him—something that belonged in your area. I think he saw someone or something being off-loaded from a boat of some sort in the bay. It was a moonless night. Everybody's home or at some event looking at the sky and fireworks, and down here there was a fog bank."

"What did he see?"

"I don't know, but I'll bet it could be tied to your problem. Maybe he saw a zodiac full of people, a boatload of bad guys carrying a suitcase bomb, hardware, I don't know. I could produce a better guess if I knew what the flap's about. People? Hardware? Give me a hint."

"Your guess is in the ballpark. That's all I can say. You think he saw something and…?"

"He got blown out of the sky. Shot down."

"Not possible."

"Shot down with a surface-to-air missile. Charlie, it's a guess but a damned good one. I'd bet a month's pay on it."

"They don't pay you enough for me to take that bet. You feel pretty confident about a SAM-like thing?"

"You heard me."

"I'll have a talk with Fugarelli; he always liked you. Expect a call. In the meantime, okay, keep digging. If the agency doesn't come through, we'll do it together. You have access to some funds, I think."

"There are ways. Since my assets, so to speak, are really the Company's anyway, why not use them? I'm going to poke around in a chartered boat tomorrow, fly the course once more on Friday, and then Monday I'm on the water again, I think. I need to get out to where I thought I saw something. Do they have underwater metal detectors, and if so, can you lay your hands on one for me?"

"You'll have to wait for Fugarelli on that one. In the meantime, make a list of what you need and put together an ops plan. You do remember how to do that?"

"I'm not with the Company anymore, Charlie."

"If I can convince Fugarelli, you soon will be."

"Not interested. In the meantime, since we're on our dime for the moment, can you at least find me a depth finder and a GPS unit? "

"I'll do what I can."

"I'll need them tonight, Charlie. I sail at dawn, as the old song goes."

"What old song?"

"I don't know. There must be an old song about sailing at dawn. If there isn't, there ought to be."

"I'll look around and messenger the stuff to you ASAP, and keep your cell phone on."

"Cripes." Ike caught himself in Bunky mode.

Chapter Twenty

Tony Fugarelli had come in from the field to occupy a desk at Langley ten years previously. Once in a great while he missed the edginess of covert work, but since the Cold War's end, the agency's work had changed. Young kids, fluent in Arabic in its several dialects and God only knew how many in Chinese, did the job now. And then, there were his three grandchildren to think about. Field work had destroyed his marriage and permanently warped him for another. But he wasn't about to lose the grandchildren.

He thought of himself as a plugger rather than a genius, and he'd risen up the ranks to a position where he believed he could finally do something. This latest flap he took as a needless distraction. Soviet Cold-War hardware went missing all the time. Big deal. Enough years had passed, and newer technology appeared to make most, if not all of it, obsolete. But he was bound to do his duty, and if the wonks on the top floor wanted to go hunting for a few bits of antique weaponry, he'd do it. He did wonder at the apparent urgency. Beyond the nuisance factor, there wouldn't be much they could do.

His intercom buzzed. His secretary announced that Charlie Garland wanted to talk to him. He told her to tell Garland to call back, and settled in to read the Dailies.

"He's pretty insistent," she said. He could hear voices in the background. Fugarelli knew that Garland's title and place in the organizational chart at the CIA put him outside the loop for any but trivial public relations tasks. He also knew that Garland had the highest security clearance and a budget that belied his job description.

The door burst open and Garland pushed in, with the secretary protesting and apologizing.

"Tony, I just got off the phone with someone, and he's on to something that could tie in to the mess the basement turned up."

"Who?"

"You remember Ike Schwartz?"

"Bailed out a few years back, didn't he?"

"Yeah, with cause."

"Yeah, right. So, what's he got?" Fugarelli was always skeptical of input from exes—the drop-outs, the wash-outs, quitters, and burn-outs. He didn't know Ike's story—why he'd left— but he remembered what he'd been, and so he decided to accept "with cause" for the moment and listen.

Charlie filled him in on what he'd set Ike to do and what he'd found, or thought he'd found. Fugarelli's eyebrows climbed a half inch when the possibility of a SAM was mentioned.

"I didn't know Schwartz that well. How far do you think he can be trusted?"

Charlie dropped a thick file on Fugarelli's desk. "This is his personnel file. Read it yourself. Oh, and note that even though he's officially a civilian, the Director insisted we keep him active as if he were merely on an extended, unpaid, leave."

Fugarelli's eyebrows completed the full inch climb. He'd never heard of that with any former agent. "Schwartz knows this, I assume, and we can call him in?"

"No, not exactly. Read the file. Then call me or the Director or, if you're satisfied, call Ike. I think you should touch base with me first, though. Ike can be a little prickly at times."

"But he'll talk to you? Why?"

"Long story…best left for another day. His cell number is on the overleaf. If he doesn't answer there are a series of numbers following that in the order of likelihood he'll pick up."

Fugarelli scanned the list. "Sheriff's Office, Picketsville? What the hell is that all about?"

"Read the file. I'll be in my office. The Director flies to Burundi this afternoon, so if you want him, you'll need to call before five." Garland left abruptly, leaving the secretary agape and Fugarelli puzzled. He realized he needed to do some internal intel on the Agency's employees, particularly Garland. PR flaks didn't talk that way to an EX II. He put the sheaf of reports, surmises, and flat-out guesses that composed the daily intelligence briefing document, the Dailies, aside and opened Ike Schwartz's folder. He was still reading an hour later. He no longer thought of the new crisis as a needless distraction. He called Charlie Garland.

"Go over it all again."

"What part?"

"Okay, tell me about the plane and why you thought you could use Agency assets to look for it."

Charlie started at the beginning. He had only the sketchiest knowledge about the details Ike had uncovered but he filled in as best he could.

"The thing is, Ike thinks the plane was shot down because Nick, that's the pilot's name, saw something. Ike thinks possibly an attempt to introduce personnel into the country."

"But you think it's part of this new thing?"

"Remember, it's a moonless night. In the pitch black, someone in a plane, concentrating on navigating over water, even flying close to the water, isn't going to see anything at the surface. If people were being dropped off a ship, there would be no need to turn on any lights. They'd just slip over the side on a cargo net and into a boat. You wouldn't even need to come very close to shore. Hell, on the Fourth of July, you could motor into Annapolis' harbor. It would be just one more party boat cruising up to the marina. I doubt anyone would notice."

"Point taken. So your guess is?"

"They, someone, whoever, had to turn on their lights for some reason. Whatever they were up to, they had to be careful, and they were on long enough for the pilot, for Nick, to see what was being off-loaded. That, in my mind means some thing, not some body. You follow?"

"How would the pilot know what he was looking at? And why would he think to try to connect to you?"

"The first part is easy. He was a Naval Academy graduate and had four years in submarines."

"The second part?"

"It's hard for people not to guess the connections we have if they hang around long enough. He knew I worked over here. He didn't know exactly what I did—"

"Shit, Garland, I don't know exactly what you do."

"Yes, well there you are. Anyway, he assumed I could at least get the information he had to the right people."

Fugarelli frowned and wished he'd never quit smoking. It was moments like these that a jolt of nicotine to his system always used to help him think. "Anybody talked to the Director yet?"

"Waiting for you. It's your call. If you think there's something out there, tell me and I'll put Ike on notice."

"You said the boss is leaving the country—for…"

"Burundi, yes, at five. You have less than thirty minutes."

"I'll call him, you hold off on the call to Schwartz. I'll need to clear a domestic covert operation with the boss. He's the only one that can order an operation that circumvents the DIA, Homeland Security, and the FBI. Me, I'm too close to my pension to risk it on my own. He's an appointee. Worst case for him is he has to leave and take a five-hundred-thousand-dollar a year job with some fancy Washington firm, selling influence and spreading campaign money around. But…"

"But?"

"I want something substantial, hard data. I need something that says what you suspect is more than just a maybe. I get that, and I'll give it a green light and then, only if the Director says okay, and you can give Schwartz the bad news."

"Bad news?"

"Yeah, that he's one of us again."

Chapter Twenty-one

Ike pulled off the road in front of Bunky Crispins' house just as the dawn lost its golden tinge and grayed into early daylight. Crispins waited for him on the pier. He could hear the little diesel engine turning over in the *J. Millard Tawes*. He removed the box Charlie had messengered down the night before and carried it to the boat. From the corner of his eye he caught a glimpse of the aluminum piece he suspected once belonged to Nick's airplane.

"Did you remember to get yourself some boat shoes and warm clothes? It'll be nippy out on the water this morning."

"I'm layered like I'm going to climb Mont Blanc."

"Climb on who?"

"Figure of speech, Bunky. I'm plenty warm."

"Okay, climb aboard. There's a thermos of coffee and some donuts in the little cabin for'ard. I hope you like your coffee sweet and creamy, 'cause that's the way she's made."

"Sweet will be fine. What can I do?"

"First, you can tell me what's in the box."

"Depth-finder and a global positioning unit."

"What'd you bring them for? I know where I'm at, and I know how deep the water is from here clear down to Smith Island."

"If, and when, we get out over the area where I think the plane went in, I'll turn it on. If I see a blip that shouldn't be there, I'll note the position on the GPU. Later, if I want to go back, I'll be able to find the spot exactly."

Crispins spat over the side to let Ike know what he thought of depth finders and GPUs.

"Whatever. Now, stay out the way 'til I clear that head over there, and then you need to tell me where you want to go. If you want to fish, by the way, there's tackle in the cabin with the donuts, and bait in the cooler. We clear the headland and I'm putting over a line. Rock fish have been running here lately. I'm fixing to catch me some dinner."

He cast off the stern line, pushed the tiller over, levered the engine in reverse, and eased the boat free from the dock. Shifting forward, he put the tiller hard to port and headed out into the chop. Ike stood unsteadily in the workboat's stern as it began to pitch in the gentle swell and concentrated his gaze westward. He wanted a good look at the duck blind, and he wanted to do a grid search over the area where he thought he might have seen something he hoped was the crash point.

"I brought a map."

"Don't need no map. I reckon, man and boy, I been working these waters for thirty years. You just tell me where you want to go and I'm there."

Ike doubted he could deliver on that, but tucked the map away in his windbreaker pocket anyway.

"I want to see that duck blind that sits off the shore down south of the southern mouth of this bay. Then I want to go about a quarter to a half mile west and a little north of it and cruise back and forth to see if I can get a glitch in the bottom with the depth gauge—something, anything that will help me get a fix on that plane."

"That'd put you over some deep water, Mister. Chesapeake ain't the Florida coast. You won't see nothing out there."

"I know, but I want to give it a go. I talked to somebody at the Chesapeake Bay Institute, and he said the bay bottom is mostly silt and mud with sea weed holding it together. With the tides, it should be pretty smooth. Anything as big as a single engine airplane should show a blip on the screen. Besides, it'll give you some good trolling for your fish."

"It would do that, for sure. Hey, it's your charter. If'n you want to run in circles or sit and drink, it's all the same with me. I'd like to have me a look-see at that dinged duck blind my own self. Like to blow it to Kingdom Come, I would."

"Why's that?"

"Them people who bought that place got a dredging permit to allow for them to build a dock and bring in a sailboat. Told folks it had a deep keel and needed a twelve-foot deep trench to handle it. Built a bulkhead to hold the spoil and dumped, jiminy, I don't know how many tons behind it. I still ain't yet seen a sign of a boat, or a pier to tie it to, either. All they did was put up that humongous blind. Ruined a perfectly good piece of wetland, they did."

"And that is bad? How?"

"Crabs feed and do their thing in the sea grass. That's where the little ones go to get bigger. That's where they peel, you know, shed their shells so's they can grow. That's where Jimmy crab gets to fertilize the eggs on the sook. A sook is the lady and Jimmy is the gentleman, if you follow me." Ike allowed as how he did. "Trouble with the dinged government is they let all that developer money dazzle their eyes and then let'em kill the bay. Fill in the wetlands, mud from stripping the land to build houses and all. Where you think all them new septic systems are draining to? And then there's all kinds of other run-off, fertilizers, garbage—you name it and them city folks will dump it. Crabs'll be all gone in another couple of years. First it were the arsters, now the blue crabs. It's a sin, what they done."

Ike had researched the bay the night before. Bunky, it seemed, had most of it right. Polluted water, warming temperatures, and overfishing had reduced the crab population to levels many believed to be well below the critical mass needed to survive. The bay's blue crab stock had dropped 70 percent since the 90s, probably due to overfishing and increasing water pollution. Both Virginia and Maryland had imposed steep cuts in the year's harvest of female crabs and hoped to reduce the number of crabs taken by more than a third. That put people like Bunky off the water and even then, it might well be a case of too little, too late.

Bunky swung the boat around Rich Neck and pointed it southwest. The wind picked up. The air, whipped by a steady breeze, seemed fresh and clean with just a hint of damp seaweed from offshore.

"There's beer in the cooler with the bait if you get a thirst," he shouted over his shoulder.

"A little early and a little too chilly for beer just now."

"Suit yourself, but you can hand me up one."

"Thought you were hard-shell."

"Out here I'm whatever the mood strikes me. Back there," he jerked his thumb landward, "I'm as true-blue teetotaler as they come. Yessir."

Ike pulled a can from the cooler, popped the cap, and handed it off to Crispins. The boat chugged southwest. The bay seemed rougher out from the protective headland. Ike caught sight of the blind. On the water it looked considerably larger than it had from the air.

"Slow it down a bit, Bunky, I want to rig this depth-finder."

"What for?"

"You know the depths along here. I want to try it out in this shallow stretch to see if it works before we head for deep water." He set the screen on the motor housing and switched the unit on.

"Okay, I'm all set. That duck blind is a lot farther from the shore than I thought. How about you steer a course behind it."

"You mean between it and the shore?"

"Is the water deep enough here?"

"Shoot, I used to run a trot line along here before they killed off this patch of bottom." Bunky eased the craft toward shore, then bore off and let it run parallel. Ike studied the screen. The bottom looked smooth and undisturbed. He consulted his map and calibrated the findings. Bunky moved behind him and looked over his shoulder. The duck blind passed by on their starboard side. Ike glanced at the structure as it slid by.

"It's really big, isn't it? I don't know anything about hunting waterfowl, but that thing looks like if could hold a football team. Do they make them that big?"

"Never seen one like that, no sir. And it ain't got no floor. Hard to see how them city slicker hunters are going to shoot out of that thing if they ain't got no place to stand."

"Do you suppose they sit in boats?"

"Don't rightly know, but even with a flood tide and standing straight up, they'd be hard put to get a gun over the top of that thing. Probably fixin' to floor it over later." The blind fell off to the stern.

"Swing around and go by again."

Bunky pulled the tiller over and the boat made an easy three-sixty. They cruised by again with the blind on their port side. Bunky concentrated on the tiller and the depth finder. Ike unslung his camera and quick-shot twenty pictures.

"Whoa, up there. You got that dingus plugged in?"

"Yes. It's on and seems to be working okay."

"Well, something's not right." He swung the craft around again and throttled the engine back to slow trolling speed. "Look at the bottom there."

Ike looked. What am I supposed to see?"

"A twelve-foot deep trench for a sailboat. It ain't there at all. If they didn't dredge a trench, where'd all that spoil come from?"

Ike looked to the shore and the new bulkhead. It had been partially decked over but appeared to be completely backfilled with dredged bottom.

Where indeed?

Chapter Twenty-two

Ashley Starkey arrived twenty minutes early for her appointment. Blake found her in the sanctuary staring at the large carved figure of an ascendant Christ fastened to the wooden cross on the wall over the altar.

"Father Blake," she said as he crossed the chancel to her, "How come this Jesus has clothes on and isn't, like, nailed up like the one in the Catholic Church?"

"It's supposed to represent a resurrected Christ. The image you're thinking of is properly called a crucifix. In that configuration, Jesus is dead. It's before he is buried. In this one he is alive—risen."

"Umm…" Ashley seemed to have difficulty getting her mind around the difference.

"Look at it this way. A crucifix shows the Good Friday message, this one is about Easter."

"Down to the Methodist Church the cross is, like, empty."

"That sends a different message, Ashley." Blake realized that iconology and the meaning of sacred symbols were probably lost on a twelve-year-old. "So, you wanted to see me. Come on in the office and have a seat."

Blake ushered the girl through the Sacristy and into his office. Gloria left her desk and joined them.

"Why's she here?" the girl asked, apparently unaware of how rude she sounded. Blake guessed she'd acquired the tone from parents who routinely assumed their heritage and wealth gave them license to assume an air of superiority, a posture others took for arrogance. Gloria received the remark with a thin smile and Blake let it pass. Kids.

"There is a new policy from the Diocese that requires either the door stay open or a secretary sit in when there is a minor in the room with a priest." Blake knew he stretched the truth on that one. The Diocese's chancellor had sent a memo making that only a recommendation, a suggestion. Ashley looked doubtful. "Gloria can sit outside with the door ajar if you'd rather." If Ashley had any plans to compromise Blake in any way, surely, she'd hem and haw, and soon take a powder.

"It's okay, I guess." She said and sat opposite Blake.

"So what's on your mind, Ashley?"

She screwed up her face in what Blake assumed was an expression of earnest concentration. While she gathered her thoughts, he studied the girl. Some preteens, he'd discovered, were consummate liars. Others couldn't dupe an idiot. He would wait and see what this one could do. Ashley sat in a semislouch. She was at that stage when girls are on the brink of turning into swans after their preteen duckling years. She was freckled and gawky. Her teeth seemed too big for her mouth and her feet the same for her legs. Girls, he'd been told by his sister, who'd raised one, grew into their feet. If that were so, Ashley would someday become statuesque. The bone structure and proportions were certainly there. Ashley would break some hearts in a few years. Right now, however, she remained a kid, all elbows and knees.

"It's like this," she said and paused again while she rearranged her face into what Blake guessed was her serious expression. "I have, like, this friend and she might be in trouble."

Blake had become familiar with the teenager circumlocution of "a friend in trouble."

"What kind of trouble would your friend be in?" Blake did not ordinarily refer kids to Planned Parenthood. He didn't feel as strongly about abortion as many of his colleagues, but at the same time, he thought that, in most cases, such an action should involve the families—particularly with girls as young as Ashley. Lord, he thought, this can't be a pregnancy. She's only twelve!

"Well, people are asking her to do weird things, you know?"

Not an abortion. Blake breathed a silent sigh of relief and allowed as how he did not know. "Weird, what do you mean, weird?"

"Like, you know the place where the kids hang out…out in the park?"

"You mean the Pit?"

"Nobody calls it that any more. Jeeze, my mom calls it that. Like, it's the olden times or something."

"But is that where you mean?"

"Yeah, only now they call it the Cauldron. Neat, huh?"

"Very neat. What sort of weird stuff?"

"This guy I know…my friend knows, is into some, like, really strange religious stuff. That's why I thought I should talk to you on account of you know about religion and things."

"Someone is doing weird religious things out in the park, in the Cauldron, is that what you're saying?"

"Yeah, he wants…my friend to…" Ashley paused and seemed to weigh whether she should continue. "There's a rule that you can't tell secrets that people tell you. Is that right?"

"You mean like the seal of the confessional? Yes and no, Ashley. I wouldn't keep a murder from the police, or child abuse. It's not what most people would say, but that's my rule, and I tell people that up-front if they want to confess. But you're not here to confess to anything like that, are you?'

"Confess? Oh, my gawd, no."

"Okay. Then just tell me about your friend, so that I can give you my take on what she should do. It's not like your friend's confessing, is it?"

Ashley turned that over in her mind. Her new expression said confused. "Okay, I guess. Like, there's this kid in school, you know, and he's doing, like, this Satan ceremony out there. He says it's Christian and all, so it's okay."

"Did he call it the Church of LaVey, or something like that?"

"No, I don't think so. But he said lots of movie stars did it. The Cauldron, that's where they meet."

"First thing, Ashley, Christian and Satan worship is an oxymoron."

"He's not a moron, Father Blake, he's like, real smart, only not in school."

"Oxymoron means mutually exclusive. You can't be one if you're the other, you see?" Ashley didn't. "Like jumbo shrimp, or guest host." Still no glimmer of comprehension. "Okay, so what else?"

"Umm, well, they meet in the Cauldron and he's doing this religious thing out there."

"What's the weird part?" Blake didn't really want to hear what he was sure would come next, but he knew he should, and then if what he guessed were true, he had some work ahead of him that would not win him many friends.

"They want some blood."

"What? Blood? What kind of blood?"

"They want me to give them some blood." All pretense of an anonymous friend had disappeared. Gloria shifted in her chair and leaned forward toward the obviously frightened girl.

"Why do they want you to give them some blood, honey?" she said. Her voice was calm and soothing. Blake was grateful for the intervention. His instinct would have been to yell.

"Like, they want to use it…" she turned her eyes on Blake… "like you do."

"Like I do…Like I do what?"

"You know, in the cup on Sunday. You say 'This is my blood.' In confirmation class they said it was, like, Jesus' blood and all. Chad says they do the same thing."

"Chad. That's your sister's boy friend?"

"Yeah. Only he's not the one doing the priesty stuff. He's just into it, you know."

Gloria cut in again. "Why you, Ashley? Do you go to the religious things?"

"Jeeze, no. But my sister does. She…she does stuff out there that is…"

"Is what, Ashley?"

"I can't tell. She'll kill me if I do."

Blake realized Gloria had a much better sense of how to handle the girl than he, and he settled back in his chair to listen.

"What do they want to do with the blood?"

"That's the really weird part. They, like, you know in the communion service? They want to drink it."

Gloria blinked and glanced at Blake, who breathed slowly in and held his breath.

"You did say drink?"

"Yeah. It's gross. Like they mix water or wine or something with it so they don't, like, need a lot. Like you do, Father Blake."

Blake exhaled and started to say something but Gloria went on. "So why not your sister's blood?" Ashley studied the pink laces on her Reeboks and pursed her lips.

"Ashley?"

"Like they said they needed blood from somebody who's, you know…never done it."

"They need it from a virgin, is that what you mean?"

A tear rolled down the girl's cheek. "Yes, ma'am." Gloria sat back and folded her hands.

"You don't want to do that, do you?"

"No. It's too weird."

"Ashley, I'm sure your parents have given you the talk about your right to your body and your right to say no."

"Yeah, but this is different than…you know…it's not like it's sex."

"Actually, it's not different, Ashley. Tattoos, sex, piercings, touching, and even personal sharing are decisions you make. It's your right. And my advice to you is just say no. Father Blake, you agree?"

Blake roused himself from momentary shock and agreed. "And you might alert your parents," he said. The chances that she would were slim at best. He just hoped she could resist the peer pressure that would be put on her by her sister and the boyfriend and hold off giving blood. Gloria handed the girl a tissue and led her out. When she returned she looked at Blake.

"What do you make of that?"

"Do you think she told us the truth?"

"No idea. It's hard to take in, though."

"If she's lying, what is she after? The whole thing is too bizarre. You think she's trying to get her sister and her boyfriend in trouble?"

Gloria shrugged. "But to call that nonsense Christian..."

"Unfortunately, it's not that odd or uncommon. Christian Satanists are people who've been raised Christians. They believe the principles of Christianity, but they choose to worship the figure of Satan rather than Christ. Their primary motivation is rebellion. I gather they make up their worship services as they go along. In this case they're just aping ours. It may or may not lead to something darker, or it may, like most acting out, go away as the kids mature. But this sounds like it's getting dark and dangerous."

"Whew. I don't think she made that story up. Father Blake. I don't know if it's true, but I think she believes it, and she's upset—scared. So, what do you do now, boss man?"

"I wonder if my father's offer to make me a stock broker is still good."

Chapter Twenty-three

Ike couldn't think of any reason to continue to check the depths behind the duck blind. Several runs in front of, and at various locations south and north, failed to turn up the missing trench. The bottom out from the blind did seem unusually deep. Ike checked his map and even allowing for high tide, the depth was well off that indicated. Bunky declared that the maps, being a government product, were probably wrong. He repeated his "man and boy" speech and declared in his remembrance this particular stretch of water had a bit of a shelf. Ike jotted down the readings anyway and then asked him to cruise the area where he thought he'd seen the disturbance in the Bay's surface. Once Bunky got the idea of running a grid pattern, he managed very well.

Ike started with a quarter-mile square and then increased it another two hundred yards. He nearly gave up in despair after two more hours of motoring back and forth. Bunky, meanwhile, contented himself with navigating the back and forth and tending to his fishing rod. He hooked three big rockfish which took the place of some by-now empty beer cans. He said he figured his day a complete success, even if Ike didn't. On the last pass through the square, the depth-finder showed a disturbance of some sort on the bottom. Thirty seconds later it indicated a second, smaller one. He had Bunky crisscross the area eight times from different compass points, and each time he logged the coordinates into the GPU. Satisfied he'd done all he could, he told Bunky to head for home. The sun glowed on the western horizon. Bunky pointed toward it.

"That there what you see sticking up in the sun is the dome on the state capitol. Maybe the oldest in the country. Well, I ain't sure about it being the oldest, but pert near. Old George Washington gave up his commission in there. Historical is what it is. And that's where today's politicians gave up the Bay to the developers. I'd like to blow it to Kingdom Come along with that dinged duck blind."

Ike settled on the motor housing and packed away his equipment. Tomorrow he'd fly to Martin State and take the GPU along. He wanted to see what that particular stretch of water looked like from the air and, using the GPU, planned to fly over the same spot. He'd turned his phone off early in the morning. Now, relaxing in the boat with the sun setting at his back, he toggled it on. "One missed call," the face announced. He pushed View and read "Unknown Caller." Charlie. He ignored it and called his office in Picketsville instead. He hadn't checked in for days. He didn't think he'd be missed, but you never knew. Frank Sutherlin picked up.

"Frank, what's up in God's country?"

"Ike? Ho. Well, not much to tell the truth. You picked a good time to go off. We had a dust-up at Gary's Grill. Coupla locals took exception to some visitors from Washington and Lee who came over to date some Callend girls. But nobody got hurt and they all left."

"Sounds familiar."

"The women were field hockey players who finished practice early. Can't imagine what the coach is going to think about them out drinking on a week night. Hey, do you think that now Callend is gone coed, they'll put together a football team?"

"I wouldn't count on it. The male students are coming from a business school. Not too many offensive tackles in an MBA program. Anything else?"

"Well, the Reverend down at the Stonewall Jackson church is missing some silver, and Esther Peepers lost her cat. That's pretty much it."

"What about the silver? Someone took it from the church?"

"Yeah, seems like. No sign anybody broke in, and nothing turned up in the reports from pawn shops and jewelry stores. Don't know what to make of it."

"No sign of a break-in means whoever took the things had a key and the combination to the safe. I know there are probably two or three dozen keys in circulation, but there can't be that many people who have the combination to the safe."

"Yeah, you'd think so, but it turns out there's a problem with that, too. My ma helps out down there and she says the combination is written in pencil on the back side of the closet door in the room that has the safe. They didn't figure a thief would look there, and the ladies had trouble remembering it. So, it narrows the field down to the ladies who volunteer, those who have volunteered, the people who sit on the vestry, who sat on it at one time or another, and…well we're back to about three dozen."

"Don't they change the combination?"

"Ma said they did—yesterday. And then wrote the new one up in the same closet. I tell you, if that church's insurance agent gets wind of this, they're out of luck collecting."

"Still, I expect between you, your mother, and the Reverend, you can narrow it down pretty good."

"Yeah, I reckon. How well do you know the Reverend?"

"Not well. He had a shooting in that church a year ago, and that's when I came to know him. Seems okay for someone from Philadelphia. Why do you ask?"

"He's got a bee in his bonnet about devil worship. Caused a ruckus up at the school and has the Starkeys all bent out of shape. They've been calling around."

"You did say 'devil worship'?"

"Yep."

"Well, stay on it, Frank. From what I know about Fisher, he's not the type to get hysterical. It might be worth a minute to hear him out."

"Okay, Ike, will do. How's the vacation going?"

"Great. Sun, sand, and nothing to do all day."

"Oh, I almost forgot, Billy and Essie say 'hi,' and I should tell you Essie is in the family way."

"Well, that's just grand. We're going to need a substitute dispatcher in a few months, it seems. Back to Fisher, you might ask Sam to do a search on the topic. She's as good as they come in finding out things. Ask her to Google Satanism. Um…you might have her add something about kids and Satanism or… juvenile. Like that."

Ike closed the phone and thought about missing silverware, Esther Peepers' missing cat, and the devil. At this remove, he couldn't know, but he'd bet a dollar they were connected somehow. The boat cleared the northern tip of Rich Point and turned east. Ike pulled up the message from Charlie and connected. He answered on the second ring.

"Where are you, Ike? You were supposed to keep your phone on."

"Been out in a boat looking for your airplane."

"Any luck?"

"It's promising. Say, can any of your contacts…doesn't have to be Company assets, maybe your Baltimore friends would know…I need to find out something about duck blinds, one in particular."

"You did say 'duck'?"

"Duck, as in 'quack, quack,' yes."

"Do I need to know why?"

"I don't know. There's one of them in the area that isn't quite right, and there's a channel that doesn't exist, and too much dredge spoil behind a bulkhead that ruined Bunky Crispin's trot line. I want to know why."

"You want to run that by me again? I lost you after channel that doesn't exist."

"Later, but I want to know everything about blinds."

"What's your plan? Assuming I can get you the latest on blinds, duck, Venetian, Texas hold'em poker, whatever."

"I'm flying tomorrow—one more time over the area. I need to see the surface we combed today from the air. If anybody complains and wants me grounded again, you know what to do, right? I should have the rest of my options down by the weekend, say Sunday night."

"You don't work weekends?"

"How will it look, Charlie? The trick to a covert operation is it can't attract attention, right?"

"I remember the lecture. It's just…time, you know?"

"Charlie, it really would help me if I knew what's on the collective mind of your buddies in the Company. You're not thinking another 9-11?"

"Ike…"

"Okay, okay. I'll stay with a generic bad thing going to happen, possibly including something that goes bump in the night."

"Close enough."

"Then, if I have more or less guessed what you guys are worried about and that you suppose it's true, then doesn't it seem likely an anniversary of some sort would be the time to do it? What's on the calendar?"

"It's a thought. Okay, Labor Day and September 11 have come and gone. The month is nearly done, Ike."

"October has Halloween. November? Thanksgiving Day, that'd be a possibility. December we get Christmas—another possibility. And I haven't heard from Fugarelli yet."

"He's waiting for something hard before he…he's kind of cautious these days."

"So, there's not much I can do, anyway. I'll work up a plan and we can talk Sunday."

"Do what you can, Ike. It really is…crucial."

"Wow, crucial. Okay, I'll work on crucial for now. But if I'm going to be scared out of my wits, I'd really like to wait until after the weekend."

"Maybe the satellite pictures will turn up something."

"Your guys would have found it already if it was there, unless there's a hole in the dike. You check all those guys out?"

"We're working on it."

"Talk to me Sunday night or first thing Monday."

Chapter Twenty-four

Blake usually sequestered himself in his office Fridays and spent the morning reviewing his sermon notes. Gloria had strict instructions that he not be disturbed until eleven unless she judged it an emergency. So it came as a mild surprise when, after only a half hour, she poked her head in the door.

"Call for you. It's Frank Sutherlin."

"Did he find our silver?"

"I don't think so. He sounded worried."

Blake picked up, punched the line button, and Frank came on the line.

"Reverend Blake," he said without bothering with the usual hello, "I think I need you to go over that devil business again."

"Go over? I'm not sure I know what you want. I told you that the sinkhole out there in the park looked like it could have been used for some sort of cultic service. My guess, it had something to do with Satanism."

"And that would mean what, exactly?"

"Well, for most people in this day and age, nothing, unless it ratcheted up into physical abuse of some sort. For people like me, however, it is a nonstarter, to say the least." Blake debated with himself whether he should tell Frank about Ashley Starkey.

"I don't think I understand. What kind of abuse?"

"Okay, look, Frank, I am no expert on this and I freely admit my bias. There is no law that says people can't practice Satanism.

Quite the contrary, the current reading of the Constitution specifically protects people who do. If, however, it included public sexual lewdness or behavior, especially with a minor, or battery…that's the actual physical part, right? If those things were to be part of their activity, then the law can step in and stop it, I suppose."

"People do those kinds of things at their…meetings? What do they call them anyway?"

"I only know what I read. And even that depends on what and who, but yes, theoretically. I'm not sure what they're called." The phone remained silent while Frank turned that over in his mind. "I had a young woman in here yesterday…I can't say who, you understand…and she claims to have been solicited by some kids active in that cult for some blood."

"Blood? You don't mean her blood?"

"Exactly."

"What for?"

"She said they mixed it with wine or water and were going to drink it."

"You're kidding. Jesus…pardon me, Reverend, just slipped out. You don't think she might be having you on?"

"She might. Kids have peculiar ideas about what constitutes a joke, but she was frightened. I think there's better than an even chance she's wasn't lying."

"Whew. What'll I do with that, I wonder?"

"There's another thing we ought to think about. When she talked to me she mentioned a cup. She meant a chalice. She said, 'like I do,' meaning the people at the event go through some sort of take-off of a Eucharist, a communion service. To do that, they use a chalice of some sort. What if it's my missing chalice? What if that is where the silver has gone? You said yourself the other day, maybe the thieves were starting a church. You meant it as a joke but you might have hit the nail on the head."

"Jeez…pardon. What do you think we ought to do next? Unless there is some hard evidence of theft, or the blood thing, my hands are tied. Just to look for the silver, I'd need a search warrant, and I haven't a clue where it might be. All we have is the word of a young girl. No judge is going to issue a warrant on something as thin as that."

"I think before you do anything, you ought to consult the Commonwealth's attorney and see if you have any latitude to investigate the cult, if indeed there is one. Right now all we have, as you say, is the story from a prepubescent girl and some fire pits. That's a long stretch to probable cause."

"I'll call the attorney and go one more step. I'll talk to my brother Henry again. He has connections into the weird end of local culture. I'm guessing the kids aren't acting completely alone, or if they are, someone else knows, and Henry will find them. I'll have me a spy to infiltrate the business and find out if I have a problem or not."

"Of course, if they have the silver, you won't need to go into the behavior to make some arrests, and that will create exposure and, hopefully, give some parents a heads-up. With any luck, that'll be all we need. Oh, and by the way, the sinkhole, you know, that used to be called the Passion Pit is now referred to as the Cauldron."

"Didn't know that. Is it important?"

"Maybe yes, maybe no…it's all new territory for me."

Blake hung up and picked up his notes again but did not look at them. His mind wandered back to something else Ashley Starkey had hinted at. She said her sister did something at the gatherings, and she couldn't say what because her sister would kill her if she told. Blake did not have a particularly graphic imagination, but after what he'd read on the Internet, it didn't take much to picture the possibilities.

Charlie had Ike's grounding lifted, and he could fly again. The girl behind the counter looked at him curiously as he signed out the plane. Neither she, nor any of the staff had ever seen a grounding order reversed so quickly. She handled his Government Issue credit card with new respect. Preflight check completed, he ran up the engine and taxied away. He put on his recently acquired aviator-style glasses, adjusted his headset, and took off for Martin State. He wanted to grill Fonts again. Charlie's hinting at Armageddon concerned him enough to want to go over everything Fonts and Nick had said the night he disappeared.

The weather was perfect for flying, and Ike let his mind wander over the possibilities Charlie had avoided saying. Something, not somebody. What thing would have the CIA in a double swivet? In the past, his instincts had served him well. He'd trust them this time. Something, somewhere, was creating major static in the system. Something was out of place, something important. It had to be buried deep but it existed. He increased his airspeed.

He landed without incident and spent two hours with Trent Fonts. Satisfied Trent had nothing new to add, they took off for Eastern Bay. They flew to the area on the Bay where Ike had recorded the irregularities in the bottom. Fonts flew from the left seat while Ike used the GPU to locate the spot. As he hoped, the coordinates corresponded to the point where he'd seen the eddy the previous week. He hoped that at altitude, he might be able to penetrate the Bay's waters and see into its depths. No luck. Unlike the tropics, where the bottom can be viewed through crystal clear water, the Chesapeake Bay remained murky and inscrutable. He told Trent to head for home.

Chapter Twenty-five

Ike taxied up to the hangar and cut the engine. He'd need to refuel before he could fly to Georgetown. Thank goodness Charlie was paying for the gas. Folks driving cars thought gas prices were out of sight—they should check out the cost of a gallon of 100-octane Avgas. Trent opened the cockpit door, waited until the prop shuddered to a halt, and called out to him.

"You finished for the day, or you going out again? The ramp guys will want to go home."

"We've done what we can for the time being. I'll be in touch."

Fonts clambered down and sauntered away with an over-the-shoulder wave. Ike looked at his watch. The refuelers and tow men were off duty in twenty minutes. A skeleton crew would work the night shift, one refueler and a supervisor. He asked for a top-off on the tanks and then watched as the truck drew up to the plane and the ramp crew went to work.

He retrieved his cell phone and powered it up. He'd missed four calls. Before he could retrieve any of them, his phone chirped.

"Where are you?" Ruth's voice seemed far away. Ike looked at the signal indicator on the phone's face—low.

"Around…here and there…thither and yon, as Hardy would say to Laurel."

"Who? Never mind, I've been calling you for hours and all I get is a transfer to your voice mail."

"Phone's been off. I told you it might be."

"Great. I have to get in line to talk to you? I repeat, where have you been? You haven't been out on the sand romping with some beach bunny, have you?"

"I never romp. Besides, the temperature at the beach is in the high fifties and the wind is blowing at ten knots. There are no bunnies, beach or otherwise, in sight. The only people out there are old guys in windbreakers, swinging metal detectors around."

"Doing what?"

"Metal detectors. They walk up and down the beach and when it beeps or lights up or does whatever the gizmo does, they dig in the sand to find out what caused the beep, light, or whatever. Treasure hunting on the beach. Last week one guy told me he found six quarters, a penny, and a wrist watch. Apparently he had a good day."

"A wrist watch?"

"Timex. He said it still read the correct time. 'Takes a licking, keeps on ticking.'"

"You still haven't answered my question."

"Which was?"

"Arrgh...Don't go dense on me, Schwartz. You're up to something. I recognize the symptoms. What are you doing?"

"Not much, really. I got a call from Charlie and I'm doing him a favor, that's all."

"A favor...for Charlie Garland? I don't like the sound of that. Every time you get mixed up with Charlie, people get hurt."

"I only promised I'd look into something."

"He can't do it himself?"

"Well, he's CIA and the local constabularies, not to mention the Bureau, take a dim view of Agency people poking around on their turf."

"I see. So what kind of favor are you doing?"

"Looking for a missing person."

"The police can't do that?"

"They already have."

"And?"

"They think the person is dead."

"And you and Charlie don't?"

"No, we think he's dead, too. It's just we want to know how it happened."

"What do the police think, or doesn't it matter?"

"It matters, but not the way you think. The missing guy, his name is Nick, was flying from Baltimore to Cambridge and dropped off the radar. They think he packed it in the Chesapeake Bay. Death spiral."

"What's a death spiral? It sounds gruesome."

"The kid was a baby pilot, very little experience. It was a dark, moonless night and he was not that familiar with instrument flying. It happens often—too often."

"So, okay, what's a death...thing?"

"Imagine it's pitch black. You're flying blind, so to speak. You lose your sense of position in the dark and don't pay attention to what your instruments are telling you—flying by the seat of your pants, they call it. Add to that, in this case, the fog—a double whammy. Anyway, what happened...see, sometimes the plane's wing will tip and the plane goes into a slow turn. When a plane does that, it tends to slide down a little—lose some altitude. If you're not careful, if you're not watching your compass heading and you don't check your horizon...in the pitch black you can't do that...you may compensate for the altitude loss by pulling back on the stick in an effort to climb, you see?"

"No. Hold on a minute there's some idiot trying to cut me off...Watch where you're going you moron...Yeah? The same to you! What a jerk. Okay, what's a stick?"

"In old planes, that's what they called the device that steered the plane. Push it forward, dive, pull it back and climb. Right or left to turn. The apparatus is more complicated now. It looks like a steering wheel with the top sawed off, but it still pivots forward and back. So, he's looking at his altimeter...that's—"

"I know what an altimeter is."

"But not a stick? Interesting. Your moron safely past? Okay, so the altimeter says he's losing altitude, he pulls back on the stick to climb not realizing he's in a turn. All that will do is make the turn tighter. The wing heels over some more and he loses more altitude, he pulls back harder and maybe increases power. That makes things even worse, and when the wing reaches a critical angle, the plane just plummets to earth, or in this case, the bay."

"Is that what happened?"

"Maybe, but at this point, we don't think so."

"Why?"

"Can't find the body. Can't find the plane. If he crashed, there ought to be something."

"That's not all, is it?"

"What do you mean?"

"I know you, Ike. You wouldn't be poking around looking for a disappearing airplane if there weren't something else. Charlie wouldn't have dragged you into this unless he believed something else happened and it involved more than a baby pilot."

"The kid was supposed to marry his niece. It's personal."

"Not good enough. There's something else."

Silence.

"Ike, answer me."

"Okay, maybe something else."

"That's it? 'Okay, maybe something else.' That's your answer?"

"It's just a maybe, Ruth, that's all. Nothing definite."

"Sheesh. Well, I guess you can take the boy out of the Agency, but you can't get the Agency out of the boy. Where are you now?"

"At Martin State Airport, outside Baltimore."

"Baltimore? You're not at the beach?"

"Not at the moment. As I said—"

"I heard you. What are you doing there, for crying out loud?"

"Um…"

"I was planning on joining you at the beach this weekend. I went to a heap of trouble to make that happen. I've been driving for hours, the road is full of moronic drivers, I'm starving, and now you tell me you're not there."

"Where are you, exactly?"

"In my car headed east on route 50 approaching the Chesapeake Bay Bridge. It's Friday and the traffic is moving at a snail's pace. I can't very well make a U-turn in the highway. Hell, it's a divided highway anyway."

"Keep going. I'll join you. If you get there before I do, I've hidden a key so you can get in and make us some coffee."

"How long will it take you to come down from Baltimore?"

"An hour and a half maybe. I might beat you there."

"An hour and a half? Not in this traffic not even if you plan on breaking some speed limits."

"I'm not driving, flying."

"You're flying…an airplane?"

"Yep."

"By yourself?"

"Yep."

"You're a pilot too? Is there anything else about you I don't know? Don't give me another 'yep.' I'll find out when I see you. We need to talk, lover."

"How long can you stay?"

"I have to leave Sunday afternoon."

"See you soon. Wait. You're coming across Route 50 to the 404, right?"

"There's another way?"

"There is, but that's not the point. Listen, drive to Georgetown and pull in at the Georgetown Air Services facility. I'll meet you there. They have a nice little restaurant. We can have dinner and then you can follow me to the cottage."

"Georgetown on the 404? Okay, I got it. See you soon. Well, probably not soon. This traffic is insane."

Ike snapped his phone shut and gazed across the tarmac. Frank reappeared at his elbow.

"You're refueled and good to go."

"Frank. If we fly the route again, it'll have to be later. I'm booked for the weekend. And early next week I need to be back on the water. I've seen enough from the air for now."

"Roger that. You okay flying at night?"

"I'll manage. Sun's still not yet set. There should be enough light to keep me honest."

"Okay, be careful. You know what happened to Nick."

Ike wished he did.

Chapter Twenty-six

By the time Ike and Ruth managed a quick dinner and the drive from Georgetown to Dewey Beach, it was nearly ten-thirty. Ruth dragged her overnight bag into the bedroom and flopped on the duvet.

"You'd better make your move quick, lover. I'm whipped and expect to be fast asleep in about ten seconds—just as soon as I can get out of this dress. What in God's name possessed me to drive all that distance in a dress in the first place? I came straight from a faculty council meeting. I couldn't have been that anxious to see you."

"Admit it, I'm irresistible."

"So is gravity, but I don't dress up for it."

"Personal magnetism, that's me."

"Bullshit. Help me out of this thing." She reached behind her and fumbled for the zipper.

"Not so fast. Let me check for intruders."

"Excuse me. Intruders? Like who, or is it whom? I never did figure that out. You have goblins hiding under the bed?"

"You're close. Charlie's higher-ups took exception to his lavishing money on me, so to find out what I was doing, put a surveillance system in here earlier. He said they took it out, but you never know."

"Oh great. You're off playing 007 and I'm about to star in an adult porn movie as your Bond girl."

"Nothing adult about you, babe, if you know what I mean."

"I don't, and resent the inference. These bugs…do they call them bugs? They do in books and things. What do real spies call them?"

"No idea. I'm not now, never have been, hope never to be one."

"Again, bullshit. You spent your youth traipsing around the world causing trouble for innocent people and saving the world for God, country, and Big Oil. You probably killed people, too." Her expression shifted as she realized that the remark, meant to be flippant, might have the ring of truth to it.

Ike said nothing but circled the room, peering into air ducts crevices and over the tops of furniture. He dismantled the phone and ran his hand along the dresser's drawer bottoms, night stand, and even peered under the bed.

"Did you?"

"Did I what?"

"Kill people? We've never really talked about that part of your life."

"That was a long time ago—another life. It's over and done with."

"You're sure? If some bad people burst through that door, what would you do?"

"Call 9-1-1."

"You don't have time. They have guns and knives and broken bottles—"

"Machetes, hand grenades, and vials of bubonic plague?"

"Okay, okay. You know what I mean. I'm serious. I need to know."

Ike drifted into the bathroom and checked the mirrors, faucets, and shower head. "I'd do whatever I had to do to keep you and me alive."

"You'd kill?"

Ike, his normally soft eyes turned to flint, stared at her. "I'd do whatever I had to do to keep us both alive."

Ruth shivered and hugged herself.

"I think we're clean. Hey, what's wrong with being the star in a porn flick?"

"Not until I drop ten pounds."

"I don't think anybody would notice."

"Your friends have no taste."

"True, too true. I'll have a go at that zipper now."

"Turn off the lights…just in case."

They lounged on the porch and watched the sun climb up from the ocean. Salty air carrying just the smallest hint of damp seaweed mingled with the more familiar aroma of fresh brewed coffee. Ruth stretched her arms above her head and yawned. "This is nice. We should do it more often."

"We could retire and move to the beach. Then we could do it every day."

She gathered her bathrobe around her and folded her arms. "Mmmm. Dream on, sweetie."

"I could manage it…financially, I mean."

"How? Not on your sheriff's salary, you couldn't."

"I have assets. I don't work for the money."

"That's the other reason you'd never do it. You'd be bored silly after three days of just sitting and watching waves." Ruth gave him a knowing look, which he dismissed with a smile. "What assets? Are you holding out on me? How much have you stashed away?"

"Enough."

"That's not an answer."

"Nope."

"Sheesh, here we go again…yep, nope. You could be a side-man in one of those old movie Westerns you collect. 'Howdy Hopalong, you fixin' to catch them there bank robbers?' 'Yep.' 'Today?' 'Nope.' Come on Ike, I'm your main squeeze, you can tell me."

"You're my what? Where'd you learn to talk like that? You're a college president. Shame on you."

"I learned it from a book, I think, maybe a TV show. It means I'm the honey in your Honey Bunches of Oats, so how much?"

"You'll know the day you—"

"No fair. I have too much on my plate right now. You know that, and besides we had a deal."

"Speaking of your plate, are you hungry? I could fry us an egg or something…toast, marmalade, bowl of Honey Bunches of Oats?"

"Had enough of them last night. Well, maybe not enough, but sufficient. If your friends were still tuned in they may not have seen anything but they sure got an earful. By the way, when did you become a top gun?"

"Excuse me, a what?"

"You never told me you could fly an airplane."

"Never seemed important."

"Listen, hotshot, if you and I are going to continue in our roles as the scandal of Picketsville, you'd better level with me. What other secrets are you keeping under your hat?"

"Don't wear hats, as you surely know. Well, except when I have to put on that ridiculous 'Smokey the Bear' uniform hat."

"I like your Smokey hat. You should wear it more often. It's very fetching."

"I'll wear it to bed tonight."

"Never mind. You haven't answered my question. What other secrets?"

"I once won a gold medal in the Olympics."

"Ike—"

"Checkers. I am an Olympic-level checker player. Never lost. Won the freestyle, alternating jump, and total kingings, all in the same year."

"I give up. But understand this, you will tell me someday soon, or else. Now, tell me about what you're up to with Garland."

"I told you about the plane and his niece's fiancé. Here's the problem. He went off the air leaving a message for Charlie—not his intended, not the cops, or the Coast Guard, and not the usual places you'd call in an emergency. There was no call for help on the plane's radio. That would be the logical and easiest thing to do if he were in trouble. Why fool with a phone when he could simply toggle his radio on and ask for help, you see?"

"I guess. Would it mean he'd seen or heard something that he thought the CIA needed to hear?"

"Probably, and the call didn't sound like a man who thought he was in trouble."

"So, why didn't the authorities figure this out?"

Ike shrugged. "We think we know why they never found the wreck."

Ike filled her in on his week, the flying, the boat, Bunky Crispins, and the suspicious blips on the depth finder. Since he couldn't see the significance of it, he left out the missing channel and the sudden and mysterious appearance of a duck blind.

"But with all that, it still could be the…whatchamacallit, death thing."

"Yes, it could be. Unless the Company connects the disappearance to whatever is turning their wine into vinegar, we may never know."

"The CIA is worried about this? Oh, yeah, that's right, they're bugging our love nest. Do you think we might be blackmailed into giving up government secrets? That's what they do in the movies, don't they?"

"Not in the good ones they don't. Besides we had the lights off."

"They could have those night vision goggley gizmos on the camera. Remind me to lose the ten pounds. My coffee's gone cold." She placed the mug on the porch railing and cinched her robe more tightly around her waist. "What could he have seen that would warrant a call to his only CIA contact?"

"No idea. Possibly people in a boat without papers, something scary, who knows?"

"So what do you do now?"

"Either the CIA decides there's a connection, or I return to contemplating sunrises every morning."

"You don't believe that, do you?"

"No, I guess not. Charlie and I will find a way to at least finish what we started—find the plane, maybe retrieve the body."

"You know something, Schwartz, you're just a superannuated Boy Scout."

"With assets. Don't forget the assets."

"We're back to that. You're referring to some dollars you have squirreled away in offshore bank accounts, I assume."

"Actually, I was thinking about my personal magnetism."

"Forget it. You're a hunk, but Hollywood is not on your radar screen."

"Breakfast. Get dressed. We're going to Rehoboth, and after that I want to show you a little park up in the dunes—a well preserved wetland—and then we can go to Lewes for lunch."

"What's Lewes?"

"Cute little town on the Delaware River. You need to see it. We may retire there in umpty-ump years."

"Woo-hoo, sounds exciting. You sure you don't want to put in a little adult porn time first?"

Chapter Twenty-seven

Ike watched the tail lights of Ruth's car as she drove away. She'd intended to leave that afternoon. But they had lingered. It had been a while since they'd had a chance to be together without either townspeople or university faculty serving as omnipresent chaperones. So, time had slipped by, and they, reluctant to end their moments together, had put off her departure. Two hours after dinner, Ruth finally packed and pulled away. Next time, he'd suggested, he'd rent a plane and fly her up from Roanoke. She just gave him a look. As she turned the corner onto the Ocean Highway, his cell phone vibrated.

Charlie talked a blue streak. Ike listened. Finally, after what seemed like ten minutes but was probably no more than two, he managed to wedge his way into Charlie's rapid-fire monologue.

"Sorry, Charlie, but no dice. I am done with you and yours, professionally or otherwise. I said I'd help you look for an airplane. That's it. International intrigue, snooping, guns and glory and all the crap that goes with it are not on my dance card any more. I am currently the sheriff of a small town in a remote part of the planet. I aim to stay there and prosper, and incidentally, stay alive. Also, I am on vacation. I said I'd help you find out what happened to your would-be nephew. I said three and a half weeks. I didn't sign on for anything more and certainly not another hitch in the spook brigade or, worse, contract work for Uncle Sammy. That's it—period."

"Ike, you may not have a choice in the matter."

"Excuse me? You're planning to conscript me?"

"If we have to, yes. Ike, please listen to me. It's a matter of National Securi—"

"Security? Don't even say it, Charlie. Too much political dissembling and chicanery prowls behind that door. I don't want to hear it. You have assets galore up there on the farm. You don't need me. Send down a team and I'll brief them. Then I'll go back to the beach, to drinking coffee on my porch in the morning, contemplating early retirement, and watching the dolphins. They frolic by almost every morning, heading south along the coast toward Ocean City. You should join me."

"They're porpoises, not dolphins. Ike, the problem is if we do as you suggest, it'd be a domestic operation and a violation of our charter. Theoretically, our hands are tied."

"I'm glad you had the decency to say 'theoretically.' I know you guys and I know that launching a domestic operation never bothered you all before—that is, as long as you weren't caught. Besides, what's the problem with turning this over to the FBI?"

Silence.

"Look, you guys are going to have to learn to live together. They're nice people."

"Yeah, yeah. But interagency rivalry is only a small part of this, Ike."

"What's the big part?"

"They won't give a rip about Nick or the airplane. They will barge in like a SWAT team and we'll lose all the intel that got us this far."

"You have sources that you can't compromise. Is that it?"

"In a nut shell."

"Tell Fugarelli to call me, and if he can convince me that only Ike Schwartz, dashing sheriff and raconteur, can prevent the 'end of civilization as we know it,' I might reconsider. And they are dolphins—I looked it up.'"

"This is serious, Ike, and being facetious isn't making it any easier. The truth is—it's quite possible that the fate of the world et cetera…is at risk."

"Time for a little truth in advertising here. What's this really all about, Charlie?"

Ike stared at the phone and waited for what Charlie might say or, more accurately, might not say.

"As God is my witness, Ike, it really could be a matter of National Security—the real stuff...Ike?"

"I'm still not with you, Charlie, but we go back, so, okay, what do you want me to do?"

"Find that airplane, maybe find out what Nick saw and come in. The Agency is sufficiently persuaded that Nick's disappearance and our latest intel crisis could be connected to give us a green light."

Ike stared out the window at the surf breaking on the beach. Contemplating the ocean and the waves should have been relaxing. But he knew the ocean could be as fickle as international politics and, like international politics, could turn dangerous in an instant. One day the breeze blew in zephyr-like. The next, hurricane-force winds would roar across the ocean, destroy the beach and everything near it. One zealous fanatic with the wrong materiel could destroy a civilization. Unlike some of his higher-ups, Charlie had never been guilty of overstating the seriousness of anything. If he said it was serious, it was serious.

"Ruth is going to kill me when she finds out. Okay, you win. I'll make the list. I'll need divers. I'll need equipment. I'll need access to your satellite photo techs. They can start right now and see what they can turn up in Eastern Bay for the last year—every day and as often each day as they can. There has to be a connection with the bay and whatever happened on the Fourth of July. I don't know what that is, but there has to be. Tell them to study ship movements. Maybe there's something there. Hell, I don't know. I haven't done this for years. Focus in on the piece of land near that duck blind. By the way, you were supposed to run some G2 on duck blinds. What did you learn?"

"Duck blinds? Oh, yeah, not much. You need either a license or permission to hunt from them. It varies from county to county. In the case of the one you charted, you could only use it if the property owner said you could. That any help?"

"I don't know. Perhaps there's a connection. I'd planned to go on the water again tomorrow. If you can dig up that metal detector I asked for, with any luck I'll have the precise location where the plane went down. It will take you that much time to get your game plan together. We'll start Tuesday or Wednesday in earnest. We can send the divers down and maybe we'll have some hard facts for you. I gather you will be out of sight on this one—providing backup and muscle if I need it."

"You know it has to look civilian for as long as possible. If we need a raid, we'll call the FBI. But you're the point on this, Buddy."

"Is your boy Fugarelli okay on this?"

"He doesn't get a choice."

"Wonderful. Get me divers."

"You have a suggestion on that? Divers-Я-Us is not in my Rolodex."

"Try Little Creek, Virginia. It's the Navy SEAL base for the even numbered teams. The SEALs are used to working with you people. See what you can do. I'll try to get a name and number."

"Not you, Ike, us."

"Three weeks, Charlie. No more, and get whatever is left of that surveillance junk out of my bedroom."

"It's all gone, I promise."

Ike hung up and called Frank Sutherlin.

"Frank, your brother, Danny, is a Navy SEAL, right?"

"Last I heard, yep. You need to talk to him?"

"What team?"

"Four. But I never know if he's there or not. Those guys come and go, you know. Danny said he'd report some days for duty in the morning like nothing was going on, and the next thing you know he'd be in Afghanistan or Somalia or some other not-so-nice place."

"I need to contact him about a small job."

"You want to contact the Navy SEALs about a small job? With respect, you know, Ike, that doesn't make a whole lot of sense. It's like getting out your shotgun to solve a small problem with a pesky fly."

"I can't talk about it, Frank, but it's pretty important."

"You say so, it's so. I'll get the number."

Ike wrote down the headquarters number and left it on Charlie's voice mail, with a reminder to ship him the metal detector. Then he called Bunky Crispins and arranged for a week's charter.

Tony Fugarelli did not look happy. Against his advice, the director had ordered him to take Charlie Garland's lead on the missing airplane. It wasn't as if he begrudged the expenditures. It just galled him to divert assets on a wild goose chase using a burned-out ex-agent. It seemed a colossal waste. Garland was on the phone, his secretary said. With a small groan, he picked up.

"What?"

"Schwartz is on board and will be at the wreck site tomorrow."

"You mean the presumed site. He doesn't know for sure where that plane went down, and even if he finds it, what the hell do we do with it?"

"You need to relax, Fugarelli. Listen, if it will make your day easier, I will be more than happy to assume the operation's overall direction. I'm in the book. You can check."

Fugarelli already knew that Garland, the putative PR flak, was, in fact, authorized to run an operation. How and why, eluded him, but in his years with the Agency he'd learned not to be surprised at anything.

"My ass in the sling on this one, Garland. You screw up and it's my pension."

"I can have that changed."

"How can you do that? Never mind, I don't want to know. You put it in writing, and the business is yours and yours alone."

He slammed the phone down and opened the second file on his desk—the one describing his retirement benefits. He only had to survive one more year.

Chapter Twenty-eight

Monday it rained. Early fall, and the Mid-Atlantic states mimic Seattle for a few months. It rained a steady downpour up and down the coast from the Appalachians to the Atlantic. The first day would be bearable. After a week, area dwellers were ready to move to Arizona, where, they'd been led to believe, it never rained. Bunky Crispins, his slicker gleaming, greeted Ike with a grin and a surfeit of enthusiasm.

"Great day for fishing," he called and started the *J. Millard Tawes'* antiquated diesel. Ike grunted a reply which, had he heard it, would have offended Bunky's hard-shell sensibilities. He heaved a duffel bag containing the depth-finder, metal detector, and GPU onto the deck and slogged back through the deluge to his car for a second duffel. In it, embedded in a stainless steel case, packed in multiple layers of bubble wrap, lay an underwater television camera complete with its own light source, battery pack, and monitor, another present from Charlie. If a plane wreck lay in the muddy bottom of Eastern Bay, where the depth finder hinted it might be, they'd know it for certain by day's end.

He pulled his rain gear tighter around him, and watched the shore fade into the rain and mist as Bunky cast off and headed the workboat out into the bay. Bunky sang an off-key, tooth-grinding rendition of "Somewhere over the Rainbow." Water ran down Ike's shirt collar and then down his back. He quietly cursed Charlie Garland, the CIA, the law enforcement profession in general, and every known terrorist group he could think of. He threw in a few prominent Washington politicians for good measure. He was not happy.

Samantha Ryder signed on as a deputy in the Picketsville Sheriff's department just over a year before. She had the distinction, then, of being "the rookie" and received all the grief that goes with the designation. She took it happily, because Ike Schwartz and Picketsville had been the only law enforcement program in the country that would ignore her physical limitations. It was not a matter of a handicap. On the contrary, she'd excelled in both her studies and athletics at college. It happened, however that she'd grown too tall and become too reliant on strong contact lenses to pass most police departmental, FBI, and other security agency physicals. Ike did not care. He hired her because he recognized her keen intelligence, enthusiasm for police work, and extraordinary Internet skills. The department routinely referred all searches of that electronic phenomenon to her.

When Frank Sutherlin left the state police for a slot in the Picketsville Sheriff's Department and moved home, he soon learned that his new office relied on her for anything referred to as "geek work."

She reported to him in the morning, her hair still damp from the rain. She towered over his desk. Frank stood an inch short of six feet. He found her six-three intimidating. He riffled through the papers she'd laid on his desk. Printouts from, who knows how many, web sites.

"So, how have you been, Sam? Any news from Karl?"

"Nothing lately. The Bureau reassigned him or something. Since the election, things are different, he says."

"Really? How?"

"I don't know, he just said that the FBI is getting with the times. Whatever that means. You know how he is. Anyway it's all on the Q.T., so I have to wait and see, I guess."

Frank shoved the papers on his desk into an untidy pile. "You found all this by Googling Satanism?"

"I don't Google, Frank. I have my own search engines. I didn't stop at Satanism. I asked for peripheral hits as well. Then I put in 'The Cauldron.' That turned out to be an interesting exercise. I hoped the people you are interested in would have their own Web site. They did, do, but their webmaster spelled cauldron with a K and misspelled the rest, Kaldrun. It took a while, but I managed to pull up this" She laid another sheet on the desk entitled "The Kaldrun."

Frank thumbed through the papers. "Holy cow, Sam, I'll never be able to read all this."

"Take your time. Most of the posts on Satanism are repetitive. They're either a severe condemnation promising all sorts of heavy consequences or a carefully constructed apologetic for it as an authentic religion."

"Makes you wonder."

"It's not my place to judge. What people do or believe on their own time is their business, as long as they don't impinge on the rights of, or person of, others. What concerns me, though, is what happens when kids get mixed up in this stuff."

"You think the business out at the park is dangerous? You agree with the Reverend?"

"I won't say dangerous in the sense you mean it. But kids are naïve. As nearly as I can make out, they have no real commitment to the practice as a religion or belief set. They are acting out— being on the edge, taking risks. They think that this is relatively harmless because they don't really believe, you see?"

"Don't believe? Then what are they doing?"

"Being cool. They are, at the same time, shallow and sophisticated. They can construct an elaborate website, complete with a forum page and streaming video, but can't spell cauldron. They think their parents are electronic morons, so they post pictures of themselves and their friends in compromising situations. You want to see teen sex, drunkenness, and wild parties? Go to the Internet. They can take pictures with their cell phones anywhere, in the locker room, ladies room, at parties, and God knows where else. And they post them—to brag, to embarrass their friends, to humiliate their enemies, or just for the hell of it. The pictures and comments used to show up on the better known sites like Facebook and U-Tube, but those sites are monitored more carefully now. So they build their own. They assume the adults will never see them and, worse, there'd be no consequences for what they post—pictures, words, whatever."

"So, you have some data on the park site. That's what's in this pile of paper?"

"They have chronicled their activities over time. Like the Rotary or the Lions Club or, God forbid, the Police Benevolent Association, they have recorded their meetings, they have a chat room, a message board, and even video."

"Kids did this? High-school kids know how to do all that?"

"That and more. Frank, you need to see this. Is your laptop on?" Frank nodded. She turned it to face her and plugged a jump drive into one of its USB ports. "One of the kids you're interested in is named Peachy, right?" Frank nodded again and wondered where all this was headed. Sam moved the cursor around, clicked a few times, and turned the lap top back so he could see the screen.

The picture was dim and slightly out of focus. Peachy Starkey appeared encased in a shimmering cloak of some sort. Frank couldn't be sure, but she seemed to be under the influence of something. Her eyes were wide and glassy. Next to her stood a boy, a young man, dressed in a black robe crudely embroidered with silver symbols. The both smiled into the lens of what must have been a hand-held camera. In the background other, out of focus, figures seemed to gyrate, their faces smeared with paint or makeup.

"So what—"

"Watch."

Peachy shrugged out of the robe. Her smile turned manic and she danced away from the camera. Whirling and staggering, she bumped into a stone bench, lost her balance, and sat down. Frank recognized the place. The Cauldron. Peachy flopped backward. The robed figure moved to her and crouched between her legs.

"Is this going where I think it's going?"

"This particular bit ends here, but there are other postings and I'm guessing it doesn't get any better."

"She's on something."

"Satanism, at most levels, is about drugs. It's a *quid pro quo*."

"Christ Almighty, what do we do now?"

Sam shrugged. "If it were my kid, I'd want someone to tell me about it before something really scary happened."

"They're just kids acting stupid."

"That's for sure, but that is not a good place to be if you're going to be stupid."

Frank drummed his fingers on the desk. "The problem is we live in this open democracy and one man's goose is another man's gander."

"Frank, I'm not saying anything really bad will come of this. She's obviously high on something, and that's not good. But she's not the first or last kid who's experimented with drugs. It's the proximity of good and bad that is worrisome. Look, not everyone who smokes marijuana will graduate to heroin, not everyone who has a drink will become an alcoholic, and in the same way, not everyone who dabbles in the occult will become a Satanist, nor will all the Satanists then become stone killers like Charlie Manson or Berkowitz and their friends. It's the possibilities that worry me, not the probabilities."

"In the show, or whatever this is, do they do, like, a communion service?"

"They do. I didn't download that bit. I thought this was the part we should react to first."

"You're right about that, but I'd be interested in seeing the other parts of the service as well. If I'm right, we could kill two birds with one stone. Download whatever you can find, make me a copy, and tell me when you're done. I think the Reverend needs to see this too."

"You want the whole ceremony?"

"As much as you can reconstruct, every bit of it…They really post this stuff on the Internet?"

It wasn't a question.

Chapter Twenty-nine

The rain pelted the boat and churned the Chesapeake Bay into dappled gray-green soup. It soaked the deck and drenched Ike. His windbreaker, its Scotchgard overwhelmed by the elements, became plastered across his back and water sieved through to his already soaking shirt. His mood worsened. Water sluiced across the decking and into the scuppers. Bunky set the bilge pump to automatic and seemed blissfully unconcerned. He'd left off singing and turned his attention to fishing. He baited a hook, tossed it overboard, and locked his rod in a socket on the boat's gunwale.

"You want me to rig you a line, too, Mr. Policeman? The blues are running. They don't cook up as good as a rockfish, but you throw a dab of bacon grease in the pan and fry you a fillet and, with a little corn bread and fresh tomatoes, it's a meal."

"No, thanks, Bunky. I just want to keep from drowning. How long is this rain going to last?"

Bunky scanned the horizon. Dark clouds stretched westward as far as the eye could see.

"Won't end today, I reckon. Maybe tomorrow."

Disgusted, Ike shook his head, which released a small cascade from his hat brim. He unpacked the GPU and set it up, out of the rain, in the boat's cramped cabin.

"Let's get to work, Bunky. I want you to put us on top of the wreck sites, assuming that's what we have. How tightly can you maneuver this boat?"

"How tight do you need?"

"Can you hold it steady over the wreck so I can send down the metal detector and, if it turns out the way I think it will, then the television camera and inspect it?"

Bunky scratched the stubble on his chin and considered the request. "Well, sir, it'll be tricky in this storm, but I'm pretty good at holding a position. The hard part is I gotta calc'late on the tide and current, and in this here rain it's hard to get a fix on the shore. But I'll give her a go."

"Okay, take it slow over the first spot." Ike stared at the GPU and directed Bunky with hand signals. "Stop here."

Bunky throttled back and held the boat steady. Ike dropped the metal detector over the side. He was rewarded with a series of beeps. "Let's try the smaller site."

They cruised fifty yards to the second site. Again, Ike positioned the boat over the second set of GPU coordinates and lowered the metal detector. More beeps. He hauled in the equipment, stowed it, and unpacked the television unit. It took him a few minutes to assemble the components and power up the camera and monitor. To Ike's annoyance, Bunky had a strike on his fishing rod and allowed the boat to fall off into the current while he reeled it in.

"Wooee, that's a beauty," Bunky held up a large bluefish by the gills. He disengaged the hook and dropped the fish in his cooler, and rebaited,

"Bunky, I chartered this boat to do some work, not to provide you with a fishing trip. I think I paid you enough to supply you with groceries for a month, so I'd appreciate it if the work comes before the damned fish."

Bunky seemed a bit taken aback by Ike's outburst. But he stowed the rod and resumed his place at the tiller. "Cripes, no reason to cuss me," he muttered.

Ike lowered the camera, switched on its light boom and studied the monitor. Seaweed and an occasional cousin to Bunky's dinner drifted by. The camera seemed to be facing in the wrong direction.

"Hold it steady." Ike rifled through the instruction manual. He needed to know how to pivot the camera in the direction he wanted. He'd assumed it would swing and when something came into view he could lock it in place. The manual seemed to say so when he read it in the early morning hours. He found the place in the manual, and that is how it worked. He'd missed the method. Apparently small servo motors on the edges of the light boom positioned it on command. By alternating the direction of each, he could rotate the camera, move it forward and back. Once he had his field in focus, he could press Lock On, and the servos would hold the camera on the object. Amazing.

He manipulated the motor controls to rotate the apparatus. Still nothing. He checked the GPU. The *J. Millard Tawes* had yawed off the mark.

"Bunky, we're drifting. Pull her back to the coordinates."

Crispins made a face. "Whyn't you bring that doodad back here so's I can see it. You play with your toys and I'll keep her in place."

Ike kicked himself for not thinking of that. Of course, once Bunky figured how to read the screen, he could manage locating the boat. Ike carried the GPU aft and positioned it in on the thwart. The rain made the screen immediately unreadable.

"You sure picked a beaut of a day to play what's-his-name... Captain Cousteau."

"Can't be helped. If we're lucky we'll have divers aboard tomorrow or Wednesday."

"Divers? Shoot, you're real serious about this, ain't you?"

Ike nodded and went back to his camera, just in time to keep it from being buried in the mud on the bottom. Bunky wiped the GPU's screen and held the corner of his slicker over it. It took a few minutes of trial and error, but he got the hang of maneuvering the boat using the GPU instead of dead reckoning.

"Hey, this here is slicker than an eel. How much do one of these cost?"

"Tell you what, Bunky, you hold this boat steady, help me with the divers, and forget about fishing for the next four days, and I'll have an accident—lose that thing overboard so you can salvage it."

"You wouldn't really pitch this overboard, would you?" Ike cocked his head to one side and gave Bunky the look. "Oh, right, I get it. You'd do that?"

"Just get me over those two sites and hold this boat steady."

Bunky repositioned the *J. Millard* over the second site. Ike lowered the camera and rotated it. "Ease it off a little." Bunky let the boat slip. The plane's tail section came into view. The picture was blurry and jumped in and out of focus as the boat pitched at the surface. The plane's rear section had torn away from the rest of the fuselage and settled in the mud at an acute angle. Ike could just make out its N number. No doubt about it. They had the spot and they had the plane. He raised the camera up toward the boat.

"Okay. Now take her back the first spot."

Bunky punched up the coordinates Ike had saved into the GPU's memory and worked the boat farther out into the bay. He waved to Ike, who lowered his camera down again. It took five minutes before he had the plane in view. Except for the missing tail section, the plane rested on the bottom as though it had made a perfect three-point landing. He directed Bunky to reposition the boat so he could view the cockpit's interior over the motor cowling. He thought he could make out a body. He was in the process of adjusting the focus when the boat pitched and the camera's tether became entangled in the wing strut. Ike worked it back and forth. The boat pitched again.

"Hold it steady, Bunky," he yelled.

"Trying to, boss, but we just caught a wake."

Ike looked up. Sure enough, a large yacht had crossed within twenty feet of their stern, and the wake had pushed the *J. Millard* forward. The camera was now hopelessly entangled with the plane and stretched to its limit. The monitor started to slide off the cowling. Ike unplugged the tether and let it fall over the side.

"You done lost your cable and camera thing there, Mister."

"The divers can retrieve it when we send them down. We have what we came for. Take her home, Bunky."

"You don't mind if I throw over my fishing line on the way home?"

"Knock yourself out."

"You get the registration on that dinged yacht? If I didn't know better, I'd think he tried to swamp us."

"Too busy with the camera to notice. Did you?"

"Same problem as you. Are you sure you don't want me to put a line over for you?"

"No, thanks anyway. Cooking is not on my to-do list this month. I'm on vacation."

"Funny durned way to take a vacation, if you ask me."

Chapter Thirty

Except for a parishioner with a hacking cough at the eight o'clock and a crying baby at ten-thirty, the Sunday services had proceeded without a hitch. Blake had noticed the Starkey family, without the boyfriend in tow, remained in their pew during Communion and left during the recessional, thus sparing him another confrontation. How much longer he would be able to avoid one was another matter. Ashley's problem had to be addressed, but he felt unsure as to what he should or could do. Mary had no advice for him at dinner Saturday night. Now, on a rainy Monday afternoon, he sat at his desk looking across the parking lot and watched as gallons of water cascaded from the Rectory's eaves. The downspouts emptied on asphalt and formed freshets that separated fallen leaves into microcanyons. He half expected to see salmon swimming upstream to spawn.

At noon, Gloria had poked her head in the door to announce she was off to lunch and asked if he wanted her to bring him anything back. He'd refused and thanked her, saying he had some work to do and he'd grab something later. In point of fact, he had nothing much to do: some paper work, update the books and attendance statistics, read the accumulated mail from the weekend. No one had been hospitalized, and there'd been no requests for a visit. He worried a little about Esther Peeper's cat and thought he ought to call her, but decided it could wait. Who knew, maybe it would turn up after all. Tomcats were not known for their stay-at-home qualities. The rain streamed across the windowpanes and filled the areaway below. It depressed him. It never stopped, never slackened. He felt damp just looking at it through the window, and he most certainly did not want to go out in it, even to dash across the parking lot to the rectory to eat.

After Gloria left, he'd raided the church refrigerator. He found some leftover veggies and fruit, a gesture by a parishioner toward healthy snacking and an alternative to the cookies and donut holes that usually weighed down the refreshment table during post-service coffee hour. He ate some limp celery, found a jar of peanut butter in the Sunday school's cupboard, which he opened and spread on the rest of the stalks. Only way to eat celery, as any six-year-old could tell you. He finished off his lunch with a cold, week-old slice of pizza and cup of coffee, reheated in the microwave. He treated himself to a handful of oatmeal and raisin cookies for dessert. He felt fed but not cheered.

On dreary rainy days, the sun did not set. Things just got darker and then it was night. As soon as the rain eased, he thought, he'd make a run for the rectory, heat a couple of hot-dogs, and find a good movie on the TV. Maybe two movies. Better yet, he'd invite Mary over and they'd have a film festival. The phone rang. He checked the clock on the wall. It read four-fifty. The office officially closed at five. He debated whether to answer. On the fourth ring, the answering machine picked up and he listened as Frank Sutherlin started to leave a message.

"Reverend Fisher, um, Father Blake, I had a deputy search the Internet, and she found some things you should probably see. Give me a call."

Blake hesitated. His idea of a film festival with Mary, had grown in his mind from a fantasy to a plan. Images of a crackling fire, a flickering television, and an appropriate film to set the mood had displaced any thoughts of earnest work. Why couldn't Frank have called earlier? He had frittered away the entire day with mindless busy work, he had his evening planned, and now a call to duty. He exhaled in frustration. Christmas Eve notwithstanding, Mary would have probably begged off anyway.

She had funny ideas about spending time alone with him in his house—or hers, either, for that matter.

He picked up and called Frank Sutherlin back.

"Frank. Sorry, I was on my way out the door and didn't pick up in time. What have you found?"

"Can you come to the office? I have some things you need to see."

<>\<>\<>

Ike stowed his equipment back into their duffels and slogged to his car. His shoes squished as he walked, and he wondered if there had ever been a time when he'd been wetter. Once, in Paris, years ago, he'd spent an uncomfortable night in their famous sewers, but that was another time, another life. At least this soaking didn't smell bad. As he passed Bunky's shed he noticed the pile of miscellaneous items, including the presumptive tail piece, were missing.

"What happened to all that junk you had piled up next to your shed?"

"Aw, there wasn't nothing there to see. Once a month I collect all the trash that floats up on my little beach and haul it over to the landfill. You won't believe what washes up here."

"Anything in particular?" Ike would probe a bit. He felt sure he could trust Bunky, well almost, but the bit of missing airplane needed an explanation.

"Shoot, bottles, condoms, Styrofoam cups—I tell you, I got me a list of people who I'm nominating for a quick trip to Hades, and the inventor of the dinged Styrofoam cup is near the top of my list, along with the morons who run the government, of course. Who's on your list?"

Ike had never thought about a list of people he'd happily condemn to the fiery furnace. "I haven't thought about it, but I think the guy who came up with blister packaging would be right up there. I asked about the trash, because I thought I saw a piece of aluminum in there that could have been a piece of our airplane."

"You think?" Bunky studied the mud puddle at his feet. "Well, now, maybe it coulda' been, now that you mention it. Now, a piece off a boat I'd right away know, but airplanes is not something I know a lot about." He kept his eyes down. Ike pushed.

"It's in the landfill?"

"Yup." Ike could usually tell if someone was stretching the truth, and his instincts said Bunky had something to hide. He squished his way to the shed.

"Okay if I store my gear here overnight?"

"Golly, I think she's full up. Maybe up on the porch'd be better."

Ike pulled the shed door open and peered inside. The shed seemed cluttered but not full. The piece of tail section leaned against the far wall. He turned to see Bunky's reaction. He, in turn, had the decency to look embarrassed.

"Look, lemme explain," he said. "It didn't seem likely to me you'd be out here looking for an airplane that just had somebody's nephew, or whoever, in it. I mean you must have ten or fifteen thousand dollars worth of equipment in them bags. That's not counting the camera and cable you let slip overboard. Seems to me like somebody's mighty interested in that airplane, that's for sure. I figured there musta' been a pretty important person in that wreck. Come on, who's out there? A movie star, or a government big shot, or a gangster maybe? I'm figuring it has to be somebody big to get all that attention. I just reckoned when the story about it hit the papers and TV, I'd put that piece of whatsis on E-Bay and collect me some money."

"Bunky, I promise you, the person in that plane is most definitely not famous or important, and the story will never—I repeat, never—appear on the TV, in the papers, or anywhere else. But you can keep it if you want. However, in the unlikely event the FAA or NTSB needs it, you may have to give it up."

Bunky looked crestfallen. "It ain't worth nothing?"

"It's worth something as scrap. But, if you want to post something on the Internet, you ought to consider that old Ferguson tractor in your front yard. What year is it, anyway?"

"Forty-eight or '49, I think. Why?"

"Does it run?"

"Last time I tried her, she did."

"How are you at restoring machinery?"

"Not me, but my boy can. He's down to the Vo-Tech learning auto mechanics, body work, you know, all that mechanical stuff. He could do it."

"Put him to work on it. You should lop down the weeds in front, take some decent pictures, and post it for sale on Craig's List. If you can get that thing running and fixed up, you're looking at a couple of thousand, at least."

"No. Really?"

"Wouldn't be surprised. Help me put these bags away. I don't know about tomorrow. I hope to have some divers with me, but I can't be sure when."

"You paid for a week. You get a week. If you ain't here, I'll have a look at working on that tractor. It's really worth some money?"

Chapter Thirty-one

Ike drove east toward the beach through the rain which, by this time, had slacked off. He took that as a mercy. Still, every time he switched his foot from accelerator to brake, his sodden socks reminded him of his afternoon on the water, as if he needed a reminder. Hungry, wet, and squinting through the glare of a seemingly endless stream of approaching headlights, he took a stab at summarizing his day. Wet and weary? Close. Successful but suggestive? Better, a neater précis, but still not quite right. Beyond surmising that the Cessna had been shot down, a stretch at best, he still didn't know how Nick Reynolds ended up in the reedy bottom of Eastern Bay. Who packs a surface-to-air missile on their person or their boat? But more important, who would have the temerity to fire one on the Fourth of July, even if they did have one?

Now, if a malfunction had developed in the fuel line, an explosion could explain the plane in two pieces and Nick in the drink. But what had he seen that prompted him to call and ask for Charlie? Frustrated and still hungry, Ike pulled into a restaurant that advertised it served breakfast twenty-four hours. At least one thing remained certain in an uncertain world—Denny's did breakfast.

Settled in a booth and warmed by a cup of coffee, Ike dragged out his cell phone and punched in Charlie's number. He answered on the first ring.

"Where have you been? I expected a call hours ago."

"Sorry, Dad, I lost track of the time. Am I grounded?"

"Cut the crap, Ike, I thought you'd have something sooner and I started to wonder—"

"Aw, were you worried about me? I'm touched, Charlie. No worries. We, that is Bunky Crispins and I, have found your airplane."

"I guess I'm happy about that."

"You guess? Charlie that's the whole point of this exercise, or did I miss something?"

"Yes, yes, of course. But now I have to tell my niece and... What can you tell me?"

"I understand, closure can be painful, even though everyone involved knew the worst all along. It's the finality of the thing. Anyway, the plane is in two pieces, separated by at least fifty yards. I think you can safely scratch death spiral off your list of probables. I will need those divers if I'm to tell you more than that. Have you requisitioned some for me?"

"We have contacted a SEAL team, number four, I think, and their commanding officer is okay with the idea of releasing some personnel from the group's dive locker but needs authorization from higher up. We're working on that now. I can't have them much before Wednesday. Tell me, was there—"

"A body? Yes. The water out there is murky, and the camera ended up tangled in the aircraft's wing struts, so I couldn't maneuver around and have a better look after that. You will need to supply the divers with a body bag, I guess."

"Yes, will do. What did you do about the camera?"

"I left it in the drink. The divers can retrieve it later. That reminds me, I lost your fancy GPU overboard."

"What, when, how?"

"I think it will slip overboard sometime later in the week."

"What—later in the week?"

"Or maybe next week, I can't be sure just yet. Consider it an insurance policy or a performance bonus for Captain Bunky. I want him on the job and steady and, equally important, silent when we finish."

"How will a GPU do that? I don't begrudge you the unit. We lose stuff all the time, money, weapons, watches, and…you know."

"It has *Property of the United States Government* stamped on it, a traceable serial number. If Bunky decides to be indiscreet, we'll have him arrested for possession of stolen goods. He'll dummy up. Besides he seems pretty straight."

"Why would he say anything? It's okay to gift it to him, I guess but…what did you say his name was?"

"Bunky. He's a waterman and he hates the government, you see?"

"See what? Everybody hates the government. It's an American tradition. We call it democracy—the inherent right to despise the government at any and all levels. Only we despise everyone else's government even more than we do ours. That keeps us secure when we elect a really bad President."

"Charlie, you've become a cynic. Shame on you."

"Go to hell. What else have you found?"

"Precious little. Some niggling thoughts, some maybes, some what-ifs, that's all. What have your satellite guys turned up?"

"Nothing yet. They don't know what they're looking for. And nothing has jumped out as odd or suspicious. I'll call you when the divers are approved."

Ike snapped the phone shut and greeted his waitress who laid out an American Slam. Ike tucked in. He felt better already.

◇◇◇

Charlie Garland closed his phone and turned to Tony Fugarelli. "You heard?"

"What are you two, old fraternity buddies? Yeah, I heard. How much do you think he knows?"

"Ike is no fool. He knows it's something big and sooner or later he'll figure it out."

"That can't happen, Garland. He's not with the Company anymore."

"Actually, he is. The director made it clear. We treat him like one of us. Besides, he agrees with you; he would rather not be. But for the purposes of working out this puzzle we need—"

"All right, already, but I'm still not convinced what the guys in Counterterrorism are freaking out about, and your missing airplane may not have anything more in common with it than a coincidence of timing."

"I hope you're right. Frankly I can't see how they mesh either. But the boss says look and so we look. What do we know for sure?"

"Since the last time we talked, nothing new. We can trace the hardware, years back, from Russia to China. That was easy. All the old Soviet apparatchiks faced some hard choices when the wall came down. Go to work for the Russian mafia or sell out-of-date intelligence to the West. Once the goods were in China, they lingered until the Chinese ramped up their own manufacturing capacity and started making newer, better copies. Then they dumped the old junk on the Arab arms market. We can trace them to Iran and then, *Bupkis, bupkis mit kuduchas* even."

"Very colorful. That would be Sicilian Yiddish?"

"What can I tell you; I grew up in Yonkers. How do you want to handle the plane?"

"For now, I think we should leave it. We'll put divers in the water, pull the body out, grab what we can, then wait and see. If we haul a crane and a tug down there, every TV station in the area will be on it. If we have to, we'll pull it up later. Right now I want to get the body out and go through Nick's things."

"What do you think you're going to find? Come on—he makes a call and then, pow, he's gone. And he'll have been in the water for nearly three months. Autopsy won't be worth anything."

"As you say, *bupkis*, I know. Maybe we'll find trace explosives."

"You don't buy Schwartz's idea of a SAM, do you?"

"I'll buy anything right now. I've two problems to solve, yours and my niece's. I'm working on both at the moment."

"Right, but for the record, I remember Schwartz from the old days. That was then, this is now, and I don't care about him beyond what he can do for us in the short run, and, in the unlikely event we tie this all together, I'd have no problem terminating him if it seemed necessary. I want you to know that, Garland. We need to be clear on it. The director may have a soft spot in his heart, if indeed he actually has a heart, for this guy, but I can't. If the protocol calls for it, he'll have an accident on his way home to whatever that burg he lives in down there in Hicksville."

Charlie measured Fugarelli like an undertaker would a corpse. "Fugarelli, as I said before, Ike is no fool. You will have to get up early in the morning to do anything to him. When he first walked away, couple of years back, some idiot, your predecessor I think, tried to arrange something like that."

"What happened?"

"Nobody knows. The guy went out and never came back. No trace. So, good luck with your moronic protocol. My advice? Walk away."

Chapter Thirty-two

Blake studied the dark and blurry figures gyrating across the computer's screen. Sam Ryder had enhanced the image as much as she could, but he could not distinguish faces.

"I can't see anything," he said and leaned closer to the screen.

"Sorry, the picture isn't much. I think whoever recorded it must have used a cell phone. See, it jumps around, starts and stops, as if they turned it off and on. In a minute you'll see some clearer pictures. I'm guessing they were shot from a different phone."

"No hand-held video cam?"

"Doesn't look like it."

"And you think more than one person contributed to this thing?"

"That'd be my guess. Here, this part is better. That's Peachy Starkey and Chad what's-his-name, the Goth kid."

"I recognize the pendant. I won't call it a cross. What's she up to? She looks wasted. It looks like drugs and dancing don't mix too well. Any idea what she's on, Frank?"

"Hard to say. My take would be some prescription drugs from her parent's medicine cabinet and maybe a dose of ecstasy."

"You can tell?"

"Just a professional guess. When I was with the Highway Patrol I stopped kids all the time who were on one thing or another. She looks like *X plus*, as we used to say."

"Oh, oh, they're not going to—"

"We don't know for sure. I hope not."

The image blanked out at the point where Peachy flopped down on the altar and picked up again some moments later.

"This is the ritual part of the business. I'm sorry, Blake, but we can't see any details of the cup or anything else that might lead us to believe they've got their hands on your silverware." Frank seemed genuinely disappointed. "There's no way I can muscle in there on probable cause and I surer'n hell, pardon Rev, I surely can't get a search warrant for it either."

"I guess that's it, then. All I can do is talk to the Starkeys and show them this video. They won't appreciate the gesture, but at least we'll call some attention to this nonsense."

"And maybe shut it down."

"Sam, is this everything?"

"I downloaded everything I could find. I'm guessing they add and subtract from time to time, but they haven't lately. They're due to update their site soon, I think."

"Well, since we don't know when that might be, it wouldn't be wise to wait."

Sam frowned and then brightened. "Actually, we may know when they'll have their next go at this. Give me a minute." She dashed out and returned with a calendar. "The date stamp on this bit of video was the seventeenth of this month. That was the last full moon. My guess is they only do this on the full, so they will be at it on the fifteenth of next month."

"So we have to wait another two weeks?" Frank sounded annoyed.

"Not necessarily." Blake took the calendar from Sam and scrutinized it. "We could have some activity by Friday."

"Friday? Why so soon?" Frank said.

"It's a moon thing again, and it depends on how sophisticated, you should pardon the expression, these kids are when it comes to being Satanists, or witches, or whatever they are playing at. This Friday night, we will have a black moon."

Puzzled, Sam and Frank waited for an explanation. "A what moon?"

"You've heard of a blue moon, right?" Frank and Sam nodded uncertainly. "People say, 'once in a blue moon,' and mean rarely, or not very often. When you have two full moons in the same month it's called a blue moon. Since the moon's cycle is twenty-eight days, every now and then it will wax full twice in the same month. Well, the same phenomenon produces two crescent moons in the same month as well. That's called a black moon, also rare. A black moon is a witch's moon and if these kids are up on their reading, they'll dance on Friday night."

"Or Thursday," said Sam.

"Why Thursday?"

"Stroke of midnight, the witching hour. Friday begins at midnight Thursday."

Frank had been listening to the two and finally broke in. "You've lost me. You think something will happen on Thursday or Friday night, have I got that right?"

Sam and Blake both nodded.

"Which?"

"Given they're kids and school's in session, I'll go with Friday but it wouldn't hurt to keep an eye peeled on Thursday."

"And you think we should do what, exactly?"

Sam ticked off the possibilities. "A raid would be appropriate."

"On what grounds, Sam? We can't just barge in there because we think they might have some silver."

"I'm thinking, disturbing the peace, creating a public nuisance, unauthorized use of state park property, littering, any and all of the above, and if Peachy doesn't behave herself, public lewdness. And if we're seeing this activity right, we include possession and use of controlled substances."

Blake laid the calendar on Frank's desk. "If we're right about this, what we witnessed in that last bit of video could be considerably starker and more dangerous the next time. It's not my call, Frank, but I think this should be nipped in the bud."

Frank looked dubious. "Frank, if you had a daughter, and if you caught her doing what Peachy seemed to be doing in this video and may be doing a good deal more of soon, what would you want the local cops to do?"

"I guess I'd want someone to stop it. Damn! I hate being Buford T. Justice, but you're right. This isn't just an alternative to a Boy Scouts camping trip or a kegger in the woods, is it? What ever happened to sock hops and hay rides?"

"Went out with fins on cars. Frank, you can't be that old."

"I try."

◇◇◇

Ike finished a half-hour hot shower and wrapped in terry cloth that still carried Ruth's scent from the weekend. He had started sipping a stiff bourbon, a decision he deemed as a necessary preventative against the pneumonia he'd surely contracted on the bay that afternoon, when Ruth called.

"I need you back here, Ike."

"I'm pretty busy right now. What's up? Are you missing my personal magnetism already?"

"In your dreams, Schwartz. No, our mutual friend and Callend's biggest booster, not to mention donor, M. Armand Dillon, is due in town to survey his handiwork, and he asked for you especially."

"I'm flattered."

"You should be. Since you saved his art collection last year, he thinks you hung the moon. He thinks you are a cop's cop. He would probably fund you if you wanted to run for president."

"As I said, personal magnetism."

"Then you're not interested in a run for the presidency?"

"Tell him to talk to my father. He still thinks I should run for attorney general."

"Why don't you?"

"And lose close proximity to my main squeeze? Never. When do you want me to appear before the great man?"

"Friday night. I'm throwing a soirée in his honor. All Picketsville's big shots, town and gown, will be there. He wants you as well."

"I'm not a big shot, town and gown-wise?"

"You're the sheriff. Isn't that enough?"

"You want me to park cars, is that it?"

"Stop it. Can you come?"

"There's a little private landing strip on Hooper's farm. I'll call him and arrange for the strip to be mowed. There are no lights, so I'll have to fly down Friday late, but before dark, stay overnight, and fly back here early Saturday morning. If I'm tied up here late and it looks like I can't get to you before dark—"

"You won't come? Ike I need you here."

"If that happens, I was about to say, I'd fly to the airport at Weyer's Cave and rent a car. I might be late, but I'll be there. Will that do?"

"Yes. Thank you. Do you have a black tie?"

"The one I wear with my uniform is black."

"Don't get smart with me, Schwartz. You know what I mean. This is a black-tie affair. Food will be catered, entertainment provided. The works."

"I think I can dig up a monkey suit. It will probably smell of moth balls, though."

"It will have to do. Where will you stay Friday night?"

"I'll leave those arrangements up to you."

Chapter Thirty-three

Ike had the sports section of the *Washington Post's* bulldog edition open and his second cup of the day creamed and sweetened, when his phone vibrated like a miniature jackhammer on the table. He glanced at the caller ID and frowned. He almost didn't recognize it and would have canceled the call, except Harley's Garage sounded familiar. Then he remembered the stop at the former gas station he'd made to ask directions to Bunky Crispins'. Bunky was on the other end. He sounded hysterical.

"Who in tarnation are you, Mister?"

"Excuse me, who am I? Bunky, what happened? Why are you calling from Harley's?"

"My dinged phone were on the *J. Millard* is why. I thought you said whoever was in that plane was nobody. You said, like, nothing important. Now look what you done."

"Done? Wait, slow down and back up. What happened?"

"Somebody torched my boat."

"*The J. Millard Tawes?*"

"I ain't got no other boat. 'Course the *J. Millard*."

"When, how?"

"Shoot, I come home after getting me some groceries and when I turned onto the road I seen a glow and there she was 'bout burned to the waterline. Then a wave come and swamped her. Now I ain't got nothing."

Ike clenched his jaw. He certainly did not expect this. Somehow, though, it came as no surprise. He'd had a feeling, a bad feeling ever since he'd seen the shattered airplane, and heard the evasion in Charlie's voice, that this adventure would go sour and soon.

"Bunky, I don't know why your boat was burned, trust me, but I will find out. In the meantime, don't touch anything. Go back to your property, get out that shotgun of yours and guard the area. I'll get some people and be there as soon as I can. If someone makes an attempt to do anything else, you know what to do."

"What'll you do? Heck, the boat's gone. That's pert near the end to me and mine."

"I'm not sure what I'll do, Bunky, but this isn't the end to anything. Now go get that gun and sit tight."

Ike closed the phone and stared at his scrambled eggs. He wasn't hungry anymore. Someone, or some people, had been frightened by the two of them scouting the bay over the wreck. That could only mean they had a hand in its downing. But since they burned the boat and nothing else, they probably hadn't figured out that the people out over the wreck were anything more than coincidental curiosity seekers. If they'd connected Bunky to anything more, they would have done something to him as well. They still could. He called Charlie.

"Ike? What?"

"Time to spring for the muscle, my friend."

He told him what had happened and what he thought it meant. "Either take the locals into your confidence, or get me some anonymous gorillas down here pronto. We're on someone's radar screen, and if we were to put divers out on the site tomorrow, bad things could happen. I want someone watching my back. Also, send some crime scene techs if you can. And do it now, Charlie."

Charlie's line went silent.

"Charlie, did you hear me?"

"Sorry, Ike, I had to confer. It's a little risky, you understand. Local jurisdictional conflicts and all—"

"I don't care about all that crap. We have a serious problem that needs solving, and it needs solving now."

"Okay, okay, I'm with you. I'm thinking, that's all." Another pause. Ike could hear muffled voices in the background. "We'll send a group down. We will want to insert them as unobtrusively as possible. Any suggestions?"

"These people down here are suspicious. No, make that disdainful of governmental types, so no official-looking black SUVs, no suits, nothing that would set them off from real people, if you follow me. Come in a pickup or a van and dress like locals, watermen or maybe firemen, out to inspect the burn scene."

"Got it. What else?"

"I have a really long list, are you taking this down? Okay. I'm guessing the people who sank your boat are not fools, and the folks in the area are not our friends, at least not yet. The latter will try to stop you from getting to wherever you want to go. The former could cause some major grief. Also, I expect we'll be under surveillance. Put someone on the pier at Romancoke with a long lens. See if they can find out whom and where. I don't think they'll be toward the wreck because—"

"Whoa, slow down. What's a Romancoke? And who are they?"

"Romancoke is a little settlement on the Eastern Bay. It has a pier that sticks out into the water and faces the place where the boat was torched. You can see across it to the pier where I'll be. Anybody who wants to watch us will have to be somewhere in the bay. The location of the downed aircraft is around a spit of land. To see us from near there, they'd have to be out in the open, so look for a boat anchored in the bay. A sailboat, power boat, something with a cabin to hide in and watch."

"I thought you said you were rusty and couldn't do this anymore."

"I said I was rusty and said didn't *want* to do this anymore. There's a difference. Besides, Bunky Crispins deserves better."

"Bunky, right. What else?"

"If I knew what you guys were worrying about, I might be more specific."

"Hang on." Ike heard more muffled voices. It sounded like an argument. "I had a chat with Tony Fugarelli. He thinks you should be brought up to speed. Are you sitting down?"

"I am, or was, eating breakfast. Something tells me I'm about to lose what's left of my appetite. What have you children been up to now?"

The phone went silent again. Ike imagined he could hear the wheels in Charlie's brain grinding out a suitable answer. It must really be serious. Finally Charlie, voice lowered said, "What do you know about the Sunburn?"

"Am I to assume you are not talking about overexposure at the beach?"

"Come on, Ike, of course."

"Not much, I'm afraid. It is, or more properly, it was an anti-ship cruise missile developed by the Russians years ago. Nifty piece of 1980s-'90s hardware that created a major problem for the boys in naval antimissile warfare for a while. I think they solved that puzzle, though. It flies at a very low altitude, nap of the earth, and at mach 1 or so."

"It's a little faster, mach 2 plus and has a range of a hundred miles. As you said, it flies under the radar."

"I hate to ask, but this is connected to me, how, exactly?"

"Those old missiles were sold to the Chinese and then by them to the Iranians, and then some of them disappeared into the international arms market. We can't find a half dozen of them."

"Okay. So your field guys can't find a bunch of old ship-to-ship cruise missiles."

"Did you hear me? I said they have a range of one hundred miles."

"I heard you."

"Draw a circle with one hundred mile radius from where we think Nick's plane went down. What's in it?"

"Jesus! Washington, Baltimore, Norfolk, Philadelphia —"

"Patuxent Naval Air Station, Andrews AFB, Dover AFB, and on and on. The Sunburn is capable of carrying a small nuclear warhead. Can you imagine a nuclear strike on DC? Nick saw something important that night, but I don't think it was people without green cards."

"You think he saw a Sunburn?"

"Don't know. We'll need something hard, but two acts of violence must mean something."

"Three acts of violence. You should check out the police reports on a boat found off Hampton Roads a day or two after the plane went down. It's a murder scene, and as far as I know the case is still active. Witnesses place the boat in the bay on the Fourth of July. The forensics might be interesting. Or not. Hell, Charlie, I don't know, but this is really getting scary."

"We're sending in the cavalry. Sit tight. Do you need anything else?"

"Like what?"

"A weapon."

"I have my duty belt and S and W. That should be sufficient. Oh, wait. I'll need another boat, preferably one painted black that can sneak out to that site in the dark and not be seen from shore."

"You want a boat."

"Yes, and it should have one of those super-quiet engines with a jet drive for shallow water. I think we will have to dive at night. The moon is on the wane and that will help. With any luck it will rain again on Wednesday. Underwater lights, generator on board, the works."

"I'm on it."

"One more thing. If you are right about the Sunburns, and I sure hope you're wrong, think about how they would be deployed normally."

"You mean from ships?"

"That too, but armament...the warhead?"

"We don't think they're nuclear. Intel would have that."

"You're sure. It's a risk if you're wrong."

"I'll double-check. What about the ships?"

"I don't know. It just seems important. Put some of the big brains you have over there to work on it. After, all your middle name is Intelligence."

"Now I wish you really were rusty. And Ike?"

"Yeah?"

"Be careful."

Chapter Thirty-four

Ike pulled into Bunky's driveway just after eleven. Bunky and five hard-eyed men stood at the entrance. Bunky had his shotgun slung over his arm. There were two other long guns, deer rifles by the look of them, in hand as well. Bunky had taken Ike's advice seriously. Ike recognized Harley from the non-gas station. The other men could have been interchangeable. Watermen with grim faces barely concealing rock-solid anger. Ike slid out of his car with his hands in plain view. Bunky signaled to his posse to lower their weapons, but he didn't look happy doing it.

"You need to talk to me, Mister," he said.

"In good time, but first you can send these guys home. We'll have some professionals here in an hour or so." No one budged.

"They ain't going nowhere 'til you give us some answers. What're you doing?"

"I told you—"

"I know what you told me. It don't wash no more. My boat is sitting on the bottom and there ain't no reason in the world except I was helping you find an airplane. So you need to be a tad more to the point."

The men had gathered around him as he spoke. Their faces tightened when he described the boat's fate, and the barrels of the guns swayed upward.

"What I told you hasn't changed. I hired your boat to find a downed plane. We found it. What I did not know then, but do now, is that plane crash was probably not an accident. The people who made it happen, it seems, got a look at us out over the site and decided to make sure you wouldn't go there anymore."

Bunky shook his head. "Nothing's that simple."

"The world is full of complicated ideas that are the inevitable end result of people disbelieving that things can be made simple. What I've told you is the truth. Now, whether you want to accept it or not is up to you. I have to tell you, however, that your boat going up in flames has set a series of events in motion that neither you, nor I, nor your friends here, can stop. My advice to you is, go with this. I promise you it's important beyond belief, and the events will occur, as I said, with you or without you."

The men shuffled their feet and looked at Bunky. He stared at Ike for a full minute and then relaxed. "You're square with me, Ike?" It was the first time he'd called Ike by his first name. A good sign.

"Straight as a string, Bunky."

"I guess I don't have no other choice but to play this one out, but I tell you true, if you ain't right on this, me and these good men will have something to say about it." The men nodded but relaxed a bit. "I reckon they'll hang around a spell 'til your people come, though."

"Fair enough. I also should tell you that we are probably being watched right now. No, no, don't look around. You won't see them. But in a few hours I might ask some of your friends here to have an accident with a boat out in the bay. Not a bad accident, mind you. I don't want you to hole the boat and send it to the bottom, just bad enough to force it to head home. I want to see where it goes."

"Which boat would that be?" Harley asked. He glanced toward the bay and looked ready to set out immediately.

"I don't know yet Harley. There's a yacht out there that looks familiar, but I can't be sure. We'll have our own surveillance going soon, and then I'll let you know."

"Why'd they be watching us?" a tall man in camo pants asked.

"They're unsure what, or who, we are. So far they think Bunky and I are curiosity seekers, but they can't know exactly. See, last week I flew over that area very low."

"So that was you," the man said. "I wondered who the idiot was that was flying over the bay."

"I'm the idiot. Anyway, they're nervous."

"Why'd they be nervous?"

Ike considered his options. He had to be straightforward with this group but there were some things he couldn't talk about. "Hard to say. People are funny, you know?" then he added, "They might be Virginia watermen out to see who from up here has been poaching their crabs down in Tangier Sound." It didn't make any sense, but Ike counted on their chronic anti-government paranoia to cloud the illogic of the statement. Nodding, they bought it. A temporary stay.

"Let's go look at your boat." As they made their way toward the water, Ike glanced at the shed with his equipment in it. "Did they go for the shed?"

Bunky shook his head. "Near as I can make it out, they sailed in from the bay, sloshed gasoline over my boat's gunwales and tossed a match. 'Course the gas went into the bilge and spread stem to stern. No way could I save her. I tried. I holed her out to sink her, but 'bout time the wave took her down that so it didn't do no good. The *J. Millard Tawes* is history, and I'm done working the Bay."

"When I drove over here a week or two ago, I stopped at the Kent narrows for lunch and saw several work boats for sale. It's not like it can't be replaced."

"How am I going to find the money to do that?"

"No insurance?"

"I'm an independent operator. When the crabs don't run, I don't eat. Insurance lapsed last year."

"Stick with me, Bunky, we'll get you back on the water, one way or another."

The work boat sat on the bottom with only the charred remains of its small cabin above water. An oil slick trailed from it out into the bay and away. The tide was at ebb.

"How do you mean, stick with you?"

"I still need you to pilot my boat."

"You have a boat? Where'd you get a boat? If you had one, why'd you use mine? Cripes, I mighta' had my boat still."

"It's not mine. Belongs to the folks that'll be arriving soon. You familiar with bigger, faster boats?"

"I did my time in the U. S. of A. Navy on PBRs and FPCs—you know, river boats, swift boats. Yeah, I can handle something bigger and faster, and before you ask, no, I never met what's-his-name who ran for president and drove one of them. Didn't vote for him, neither."

"Wasn't going to ask. We'll be working at night. You okay navigating in the dark?"

"Is the Pope Catholic?"

As they walked back to the house, a van and two battered pickups drove into the yard.

"Now who in the heck is that?"

"That would be the folks I mentioned. Have your pals mix and mingle. They don't have to make nice, just seem to. In an hour or so they will pull out and, hopefully, so will some of your guys. Not all will go. Four or five will slip into the shed and the bushes over there. They will be here for the duration. I don't want the people who sank your boat to get any ideas about putting you under the water too." Bunky swallowed. Ike's phone chirped. Charlie.

"Hello, Charlie. The troops just arrived. What else do you have for me?"

"We have the spotter in place off the pier in Romancoke. Tonight a boat will be berthed at the Kent Narrows. Tomorrow evening two SEALs and two divers will join the crew with their equipment. They'll be ready to do some night diving. The crew is not that familiar with the waters around where you are. Can your guy help them?"

"What kind of boat?"

"A PBR, surplus Navy riverine patrol boat. We borrowed it from the ATF. They use it for interdiction and had it sprayed flat black. Your man?"

"Oh yeah, he can drive it. We'll be ready." Ike turned to Bunky. "Get plenty of rest today and tomorrow. We're going out there," he waved toward the crash site, "tomorrow night, and you'll be steering. Meet me at the Narrows at dusk. You can't miss the boat. It'll be painted black." He turned back toward Eastern Bay. Its waters, usually inviting to sailors, hunters, and fishermen, now seemed ominous and forbidding. "Charlie, don't you think it's time to call in the locals or the FBI?"

"Can't do it, Ike. Upstairs doesn't want the embarrassment if we're wrong."

"What embarrassment would that be, Charlie? We're on a hunt for what could be a major disaster that could make 9–11 seem like a missed dental, and they're worried about looking bad?"

"How would it look, Ike? We go to the bureau and say Garland's niece's fiancé disappeared over the bay and since we lost track of some Sunburn missiles somewhere around Iran, we want you to tear the Eastern Shore of Maryland apart looking for them?"

"It's more than that."

"Okay, yes, there's more, but you know the drill."

"I do. That's why I don't work there anymore. Say, what did you tell Fugarelli about me? Some of these clowns he sent down here are giving me a look."

"A look? What kind of a look?"

"I don't know, exactly, like I'm off the reservation somehow."

"Oh, that. Well, Tony has funny ideas about what we do to nonagency personnel to make sure they don't talk after an operation. You remember the rumor that made the rounds after Hawkins took a walk?"

"They sent someone to terminate him and the guy never returned?"

"Yeah. I just told him it was you, not Alex Hawkins. Scared the you-know-what out of him, and his boys apparently got the word, too. You're a dangerous man, Ike."

"Thanks for nothing. Okay, we go tomorrow night." Ike turned back to Bunky, who studied him with something between fear and admiration in his eyes. "You folks don't mess around, do you?"

"Can't afford to. More than anything else in the world, Bunky, I wish this will turn out to be the wildest of all wild goose chases."

"But you don't think so."

"No, I don't think so."

Chapter Thirty-five

Frank Sutherlin had a problem. He'd agreed with Blake Fisher about the potential danger the sinkhole activities held and with the need to shut them down, but in the hard light of morning, he wasn't so sure. If he stormed into the site and found nothing more than a group of kids partying, there'd be some angry parents to deal with. If he were to do nothing, that wouldn't happen, but then other consequences might rebound to him. He did not think of himself as a coward, but he also didn't believe in rushing in without something substantial in hand. He didn't need a warrant to mount the raid, he knew, but he wished he did. That would give him an out, one way or the other.

Essie and Billy strolled in to announce they were taking off for lunch. Frank had the feeling that since Ike left for vacation, his deputies were stretching the limits of what he took to be standard procedure.

"Whoa up, you two. Since when did the department start having a lunch hour?"

Billy waved vaguely toward the clock on the wall. "Shoot, Frank, I'd be pulling off patrol to grab me a bite anyway, and Essie always has an hour, so I figured we'd just combine, like."

Frank gave them a sour look. "Before you go, I need to ask you a question. You saw the video of the kids in the park. The Rev wants us to stage a raid and pull them in. He thinks that crazy devil stuff they're doing is dangerous. Sam agrees. What do you think I should do?"

"When you planning on doing it?" Billy asked. Essie sat and cradled her belly with her hands. It was flat, showing no signs of her nascent pregnancy, but she sat, a Mona Lisa smile on her lips, as though she held the future of the world in her hands. Frank's mother had laughed when she saw her do it the night before. "First-timer," she'd said. "By the third you just plow ahead like the *Titanic*."

"That's part of the problem. We don't know when they'll be out there again. Sam and the Reverend think Friday night or, possibly, Thursday. I'd hate to set up a big operation and then have to send everybody home. You know, I'd have to get some county help to pull it off."

"I saw the dancing, and it's pretty clear they're doing drugs out there." Essie said and shifted in her chair.

"Lord, Essie, if we busted every party in this town where we thought there might be drugs, half the population of Picketsville under the age of thirty-five would be in the slammer—including you two."

"Not no more, Frank," Essie said patting her nonexistent bump, "we got to think of this here baby. Ain't that right, Billy?" Billy looked less sure.

"You still didn't answer my question. What do you think I should do?"

"You know something, Frank, if Ike were here we wouldn't be having this confab." Billy said.

"What do you mean?"

"Ole Ike, he'd just make up his mind and do it, or not. I don't think we ever voted on whether we should, or should not, do this or that."

"This isn't a vote, Billy, I'm asking for advice."

"Well, I ain't got any for you. Come on, Essie, my lunch break is dwindling down to take-out."

"You should do it," Essie said, and stood to follow Billy out the door. "I think the Reverend is right. That business can lead to no good. That's what Ma says."

"You talked to Ma?"

"Sure I did."

"Times they are a-changing. We never brought work home to Ma before."

"Sometimes I think all you Sutherlin boys are thick as sticks. You think she didn't know every detail of what you were up to twenty-four seven? Come on Billy, I'm hungry. Remember, I'm eating for two."

They left the office. Frank drummed his fingers on the desk. His brother and sister-in-law had been no help at all, and the suggestion that Ike would have simply acted without consultation galled him. Ike had his ways, Frank had his. He shuffled through the papers on his desk. He picked up the phone and called the county. He still did not like the prospect of facing a roomful of angry parents, but he guessed, on the whole, the operation made sense.

Ike hung around Bunky Crispins' place for the rest of the afternoon. A call from the spotter at Romancoke identified the yacht Ike had indicated earlier as having a man with binoculars watching them.

Bunky dispatched Harley and the guy in the camo pants, who turned out to be the brother-in-law of the waitress who'd served Ike lunch over in Kentmor the previous week. The shore provided an up-front look at how a closed society worked. Ike thought for a moment he was back in Picketsville. Everybody knows everybody and is probably related to them as well. The plan Harley hatched involved the two watermen accusing the watcher of spying for the Virginia authorities. Camo pants would wave his deer rifle around and with any luck chase the yacht off. An hour later, Harley's battered Boston Whaler smacked the yacht amidships, and an argument ensued that Ike could hear, even though the boats and their occupants were a mile away. The yacht hauled anchor and left. Ike had instructed the two men to follow at a distance to see where it went. It ended its flight at a marina south of Kent Narrows.

When he returned, Harley said that three men who "looked like foreigners" drove off in an old Pontiac with DC plates. He also reported he'd written "Watermen Rock" on the boat with a Sharpie. He allowed it would be a while before the message wore off or could be cleaned. Ike was impressed. About the same time, a spotter on the opposite shore reported he saw a vehicle answering the description of Harley's Pontiac entering the property that had the duck blind. Ike wrote down the plate number and called Charlie.

"Charlie, do a trace on a yacht in the marina south of the narrows with a North Carolina registry. I don't have the number but there can't be that many North Carolina yachts in the area, and it has "Watermen Rock" scrawled across the port side near the waterline. Also find out what you can about a Pontiac with DC plates." Ike consulted his notebook and gave Charlie the number.

"Yes, sir, Chief. Anything else?"

"When is your guy going to show up and run this operation so I can get back to doing nothing?"

"He still wants something solid."

"He's dreaming. Look, I'm good until Friday. Then I'm out of here."

"Ike, you know what's at stake here. You can't walk away now."

"I should, I can, and I will. This business is way over my head. I have no creds here, Charlie. If anything goes bad, I'm standing here with my pants down. This is your deal. You do it."

"Ike—"

"I mean it. The risks are huge and even if you're right about the Sunburn, it's a job for the real cops, not an on-vacation, off-duty Smokey from the Valley. You get someone with authority on board, and then get their ass down here pronto."

"Ike—"

"That's it, over and out, and goodbye." Ike turned the phone off and snapped it shut. "Enough is enough," he muttered, to no one in particular.

Chapter Thirty-six

Wednesday dragged. Ike tried, but failed, to sleep in. It started to rain. Again. His mood began to match the weather. Gray and bleak, the hours ticked away. He took a stab at sorting through the satellite pictures scattered across his kitchen table. He didn't see anything new. He studied the duck blind-barge again. As far as he could see there was no connection, one to the other. The barge seemed to be occupied solely in the dredging process. Ike didn't know anything about dredging but, then, what was there to know. Suck up the mud, dump the mud somewhere, in this case, behind the bulkhead. He jotted a note to have the company that had been contracted to do it checked out. He didn't know where that might lead, but when you have zero, anything is something.

He rifled through the pictures a second time, searching for the yacht. If it was in the area, that might mean something. After an hour and a half of fruitless searching, he stacked the pictures in a pile and surrendered to his frustration. A rainy day at the beach is a downer under any circumstance. He tried the television, nothing on but soap operas and reruns of game shows. The cable channel had been disconnected for the off-season. Ruth's line was busy. His father didn't pick up. He left a message for both to call if they could. He left the cottage and went in search of lunch. The Avenue had a special on tilapia. He wondered about the state of the world when a seafood restaurant situated on the Atlantic Ocean had to resort to frozen fare from some aquaculture establishment in Alabama. Where were the rockfish, the croaker, the red snapper? He settled for a second breakfast.

Charlie called him in the afternoon. He sounded hesitant.

"You still there, Ike?"

"I'm here." Ike felt a little guilty for snapping at Charlie the day before. He hadn't changed his mind, but they had been through some things together and…"Where's the ops director? Is Fugarelli going to show up and earn his salary or not?"

"Out sick today. But, listen, what's on the agenda is simple enough. Just get those divers out over the plane tonight, extract the body and anything else you can find, and come in. We'll take it from there. Okay?"

"One more day. That's it, Charlie. Then either Tony Fugarelli shows, or you do, or somebody with important-looking paper in his pocket does, or the operation ends."

"One more day may be all we need. Have you any thoughts for me? I could use something—anything."

"I went through the photos this morning and…I couldn't see anything except ships, freighters coming and going up and down the Bay. And a gazillion sailboats. Even in late September there are sailboats out on the Bay. Oh, and powerboats, yachts. Speaking of which, have you run the trace on the yacht and the Pontiac?"

"We have, but there's not much to know. They were both leased by one of those corporate entities that bury their owner-ship in layers of holding companies, off-shore and European, and with absolute anonymity. We'll keep looking."

"While you're at it, find out who owns the land adjacent to the duck blind and who did the dredging for them. I don't know why, but I don't like that whole operation. Something's not right."

"Any reason in particular?"

"None whatsoever. I've studied the satellite pictures 'til I'm blue in the face, and I can't see a thing. The barge is there, the dredging ends, the barge is gone. The duck blind appears. No big deal."

"But you don't like it?"

"Not even a little bit."

"I'll trust your hunch and put someone on the property and the dredging. Meantime, rest up."

"With my luck, it will pour out on the bay. I'll get soaked again, and die of pneumonia."

"You're not that lucky, and if it does rain tonight, whoever they are that watch us won't see you, or what you're up to, out on the water. I'll have a doctor on call, and a bottle of brandy put on board."

◇◇◇

Mary did not want a ring. "I will settle for a simple band. I had an engagement ring once before and it didn't work." Blake didn't know if he should be relieved or offended. Diamonds are not, and never have been, cheap, a tribute to the diamond cartel that limits the number of carats on the market to keep the price up and the economies of some African nations afloat. Not having to come up with the cash on a vicar's salary put her decision on the plus side of the equation, but there is something about a ring on your fiancée's finger that was part of the whole experience. How would anyone know?

"That's not the point, Blake. You sound like a rancher who wants to put a brand on one of his cows."

"Oh, come on, Mary. That's not fair. And you will never be mistaken for a cow. I think ranchers herd steer, or do you say steers? It must be like deer, don't you think?" He said, and conceded, in his mind, that she might, in fact, be close to the truth. A ring did give the man a proprietary sense.

"How about we do this. I will buy you a ring instead," she said.

"No, that's..." He wasn't sure what he objected to. Mary never struck him as a radical nonconformist before. Her reluctance confused him. But he was sure that he would not be interested in becoming the wearer of the engagement ring. "Let's go to dinner and figure this out later."

Mary smiled and agreed.

They wandered away from the jewelry store and made their way to a small restaurant off the food court. It boasted an Italian menu, but the food's relationship to Italy was mostly a matter of semantics. It tasted fine, had an obvious acquaintance with oregano, garlic, and tomatoes but probably had a closer connection with a can bearing a picture of a mythic Italian chef on it.

"Tell me where you are with the Starkeys and their offspring," she asked, between bites of her Caesar salad.

"I'm worried where this might lead. We have a tape of some kids from the school, including the older Starkey girl, on tape. Sam, the deputy with the computer skills, downloaded video of their latest gathering. Peachy is clearly featured, and so is her boy friend. We don't have much else, I'm afraid. Except the drugs, of course."

"You're sure about the drugs?"

"Pretty sure, yeah." Were they? The images on the tape were blurred and erratic. One could make a case that the behavior was no more frenetic than that of cheerleaders at a pep rally. If Frank raided the event Friday night, as they had tentatively planned, and they turned up nothing, there could be some serious explaining to do. Blake would not be exempt from a parental backlash either. "I don't know, Mary, what's your take?"

"Are you worried you won't find the silver or drugs? I mean do you think the threat of angry parents is that important?"

"Well, if the cops go charging in there and there's nothing except some kids acting out…"

"That should be a problem for the police. It should not be a problem for you."

"How's that?"

"Blake, the police need to worry about the niceties of the law, not you. They need probable cause or something. They need to feel sure about stolen goods, or drugs, or some other activity on the part of the kids that will justify their time and effort. The business needs to be certifiably illegal, and if not felonious, at least it should be a misdemeanor. If they simply break up a party, they may be able to explain it away as disturbing the peace or something, but they will also put themselves in a bad light and maybe be sued or harassed for false arrest. Is that what they call it?"

"But the Constitution allows any worship under the second amendment."

"The Constitution is their problem, not yours. Your position is, or should be, Satanism is wrong, dangerous, and the parents of kids who are dabbling in it need to know about it. Remember, you're the clergy guy, not the police. They have their priorities and you have yours. It's your job to deal with the occult. The police can take care of the rest."

"You're right, of course. Still, if there isn't some sort of criminality at that event on Friday, assuming we're right about Friday and the black moon, we'll be in hot water with somebody."

"You're worried about the bishop and the Starkeys, aren't you? You shouldn't be. Trust your judgment—trust God. After all, in the end, He's the only one you need to answer to. You just do what you think is right."

Of course, Mary hit it. "Tell you what. We'll compromise."

"On the police action? How?"

"No, on the rings. No engagement ring for you, but a nice wedding band with little diamonds set in it. One for you, one for me."

"A double-ring ceremony, yes, that sounds about right."

Chapter Thirty-seven

The weather worsened as the day wore on. By nightfall, rain-squalls raced along the Delmarva Peninsula and up the Bay. Visibility on, the water dropped to a few hundred yards. The remnants of a waning moon disappeared behind scudding clouds. By the time Ike arrived at the marina, he felt a cold coming on, and he hadn't even set foot out in the storm yet. The divers, SEALs, and crew waited for him aboard the patrol boat. Flat black paint made the craft functionally invisible. Only its running lights flickered in the downpour, and they would be extinguished as soon as they cleared the marina. He tightened his rain gear's fastenings against the wind and climbed aboard. Bunky had settled himself in the stern and was in full teaching mode, describing to the boat's crew how it would have been armed when it served as a Navy boat. He pointed to the now empty gun mounts, fore and aft, and explained the range, use, and accuracy of the twin fifty-caliber machine guns and other exotic armament that once graced them. The crew, all young enough to be his children, or perhaps grandchildren, listened politely. Ike unpacked his GPU, introduced himself to the captain, and sneezed. He really did have a cold. That realization did not improve his mood.

The captain, who looked to Ike to be about twelve years old, gestured toward the unit in Ike's hand. "We have a global positioning unit on board, Mr. Schwartz."

"I'm sure you do, and I'm sure it's a sight better than mine. However, the coordinates we want are locked into this memory chip and Bunky, here, is used to working with this one."

"I see. For my information, sir, who is Bunky?"

"He's the guy who's been lecturing you on the good old days of river patrol-boat command. He knows the Bay like the back of his hand, in the dark or the daytime, and he's going to be your navigator on the way out. He will drive this craft while we're over the site, and he will no doubt bore you to tears about the state of the government, the plight of Chesapeake Bay watermen, and the sex life of crabs. However, if you watch and listen, you will have an exciting night, and will, no doubt, add some useful seamanship tips to your skill set. But it will require a good deal of patience on your part."

"No one said anything about giving the helm over to a civilian."

"Son, you are probably not as familiar with the spook business as you might be. For your edification, this is a civilian undertaking. Your orders, if I understood them correctly, were to do what I ask of you. Is that your understanding, too?"

"Yes, sir, but—"

Ike waved him off. "Start your engines and put this bucket in motion. It's cold, it's wet, and I'm not in a particularly good mood, and certainly not in one ready to dispute the chain of command here."

"Yes, sir." The boat's captain did not look pleased, but he had his orders, and they did say he should follow this man's directives. He glanced at Bunky and shook his head.

"Captain," he said to Bunky, "Will you step up here and chart our course?"

"Sure thing, sonny. You see the green light on that buoy in the gap, there? Well, keep that to starboard 'til I tell you otherwise. Then, you can open her up as soon as we clear it."

The boat eased away from the pier and, its twin Detroit diesels throbbing, and made its way into the channel. Once clear of the marker, Bunky circled one finger in the air and the boat roared south.

Ike positioned himself out of the wind as best he could and huddled with the divers and the two navy SEALs. It would take at least fifteen minutes to reach the dive site. Enough time for him to fill in the gaps of their earlier briefing. Satisfied they knew what he wanted, Ike released them to unpack their gear and suit up. The SEALs took positions at the gun mounts. Ike knew they had weapons under their rain parkas. He prayed they would not be needed. In spite of the snuffling and sneezing that now occupied him, he started to appreciate the weather. It would effectively cover any noise they might make as well as keep other boaters off the water and ashore.

At Bunky's direction, the young captain brought the boat to the approximate site and handed the helm over to him. "You want to drop anchor here?" he asked.

"No anchor. We might have to bug out, and I sure don't want to cut your line."

"How do you plan to hold this position? The divers will need a stationary platform."

"Watch and learn, son, watch and learn. Okay, Mr. Police-man," he shouted into the wind, "we're ten yards, more or less, south of the plane. Tell them divers to go in and swim north by northwest for ten yards, then turn on their lights. They should be dead on it."

The divers gathered their equipment and went over. By holding the boat south of the wreck, any glow the lights might show at the surface would be screened from anyone watching from the shore. It didn't seem likely any sane person would try, but Ike recognized that in the scenario Charlie described, sanity did not play a major role. The divers retrieved the body and bagged it. They filled a basket with miscellaneous items found in the cockpit, shot some pictures of the torn fuselage, and retrieved Ike's television camera. In less than two hours they were back on deck, the body stowed in an over-large ice chest brought for the occasion, the boat turned into the wind, and they were on their way back to the marina.

"That corpse was in really bad shape, Mr. Schwartz."

"I'm not surprised. He'd been in the water nearly three months. Did you see anything interesting down there?"

"That plane did not have an accident, I can tell you for sure."

"Why do you say that?"

"I've done some salvage for Uncle. I've seen what planes look like if they have an explosion on board. This plane was caved in at the break, not pushed out. If I didn't know better, I'd say it took a shot."

"Anything else?"

"His body…well, like I said, it wasn't in good shape. Um… sort of coming apart, like. His ring and watch must have slipped off and were on the floor, along with a cell phone. They're in the basket." Ike opened the wire cage and removed the three items. "Say, is that an Academy ring?"

"Yeah, he was Navy."

"Hey," the diver called to the cadre from Little Creek, "he's one of ours. Some bastard shot him down."

"We don't know that for a fact."

"Maybe you don't, sir, but I do. This ain't the end of this drill."

Bunky set a course to follow home, and handed over the wheel to the captain. "All yours, Skipper. When you see the channel marker remember, it's red, right, returning." The young man scowled but said nothing.

Ike wiped the phone down and pushed the power button. It didn't work. No surprise there. He stuffed the items in an evidence bag and slipped it into his slicker pocket.

"This should be the end of it." His words were carried away by the wind.

Chapter Thirty-eight

Ike sat across from Charlie in the same booth, with the same breakfast before him as he had nearly two weeks previously. The aroma of fried food and coffee filled the air—no change there either. Silverware and china clinked and scraped against the countertop as if nothing had happened during the interim. The plastic bag with Nick Reynolds' ring, watch, and cell phone lay on the table between them. Charlie fiddled with his butter knife. He hadn't touched his food. Ike wondered if Charlie ever ate. He'd never seen him do so. He usually talked and then bolted out the door, leaving a perfectly good meal behind. Ike did not have that problem. He blew his nose and attacked his pancakes. *Starve a fever, feed a cold.*

"Eat, Charlie. I'm buying, so you at least ought to be polite and eat. Didn't your mother tell you it's ungracious to spurn the host's offerings?"

"I'm buying, and my mother had very little to say about gustatory obligations. Tell me about last night."

"We went to the site, retrieved Nick, or what was left of him, and recovered those items from the plane. The divers agree that the plane did not have an accident. It was downed deliberately. I doubt there's much you can get from the phone, but the SIM card may have some photos and messages on it that your technical people can reconstruct. They may help your niece. I don't know. I expect his parents will want the ring and watch."

Charlie pulled the bag to him and poked the items through the plastic with his finger. "Your divers were right about the downing. I had an ME work overtime last night. Nick's back, neck, and arms, were full of bits and pieces of the airplane. It took a hit and blew. It seems incredible that anyone would do that out in the open, and on the Fourth of July."

"No so odd, Charlie. It was a moonless night and all the folks on the bay had gone ashore because of the fog."

"Not all. There was that sailboat you gave me the heads-up about."

"Anything on that?"

"Nothing yet. It's tricky, sometimes, to convince local police to cooperate with us."

"Gee, I wonder why."

Charlie grimaced and swept the bag and its contents into his briefcase. He started to rise as if to leave.

"Sit, Charlie. We are not done here. I want an official release from this mess. I want to arrange for the return of all the junk you've dumped on me, except the GPU, of course. It fell overboard, as you recall. And we need to find Bunky Crispins a new boat."

"What? A new boat? Where did that come from? We can't buy him a boat."

Ike blew his nose again, snuffled, and fixed Charlie with an "I'm not taking any crap from you" stare. "He lost *The J. Millard Tawes* because of us—of you. He was a civilian who simply rented his boat to help me look for a missing pilot. His livelihood was taken from him by the bad guys, whoever they are. By the way, who are they? Never mind. I don't want to know. He never bargained for the loss of his boat. We owe him a new one. Now, you go rooting around in that pile of money you people have squirreled away to fund black operations, and buy him a replacement."

"But…"

"He'd settle for that nifty black PBR we used last night, but I don't guess the ATF would be willing to part with it. Anyway, on your way back to the asylum, stop at the marina at Kent Narrows. There are two or three workboats for sale there. Buy him a nice one. Fix it up and paint *The J. Millard Tawes II* on the transom."

"You're being very uppity, Mr. Schwartz. You know that?"

"Uppity is my middle name."

"Actually, it's not. It's Abraham, after your dad. And I'll see what I can do for your waterman. No promises. You're off the hook, for now, but keep your cell phone on."

"Not a chance. I am in way over my head as it is. Thank you anyway, but I am going back to my little cottage. Drink lots of eighty-proof cold medicine, and tomorrow I will return to Picketsville for a party and a sleepover. I may spend the weekend. You can go now. Don't call us, we'll call you."

"No, I will mind my manners, and eat this gorgeous heart attack breakfast. Then I will go back to the office and try to explain to a committee of my peers what the hell you were doing in the middle of the night on the Chesapeake Bay, on our dime."

"Mazel tov."

"The same to you."

◇◇◇

The sun shone hard and hot, causing evaporating rainwater to rise like steam from the pavement. With his newly acquired sense of freedom, Ike made his way toward the boardwalk. He remembered seeing a gift shop with an end-of-season sale sign in the window. He would buy Ruth a present. One turn around the shop, "shoppe" to be accurate, and he realized that its sales prices were still significantly above what he'd pay for the same item back home, not on sale.

Farther down the boardwalk, an auction house caught his attention. He loved auctions. It would be a nice way to relax and let his breakfast settle. He entered, helped himself to free coffee and Danish, and took a seat at the rear. The item on the block was a Tabriz rug. He liked the colors and the size. He toyed with the notion of bidding on it, hesitated, and a woman with an unlikely up-do bought it before he could act. He considered bidding on several other items. Auctions, as every auctioneer knows, are as addictive as potato chips. Between the first gaveling and the last, otherwise fiscally sane people will, under the influence of a skillful presenter, buy practically anything. Ike, it turned out, was one of those people. By lunchtime he had bid, but lost out, on seven items ranging from a pair of silver candlesticks to a painted Sarouk of dubious vintage. Overall, he felt lucky to have gotten off so easy. Then, just as he was about to leave, he did successfully bid on a one and a half carat, yellow—"canary" the auctioneer called it—diamond in a platinum ring setting. That would put a serious dent in his savings. He'd set out to buy Ruth a present, but this was ridiculous. He tucked the box with the ring in his pocket and left before he ended up buying its matching choker.

He ate lunch in the same booth he had at breakfast. His cell phone, contrary to Charlie's orders, had been turned off. He powered it up. No missed calls. He speed-dialed Ruth. Perhaps, he thought, he should sound her out on the whole ring business before he sprung his purchase on her.

"I'm in the middle of something here, Ike, so make it quick." He could hear voices in the background. "What's up?"

"Just checking on tomorrow, we're still on for the big hoo-hah for Dillon?"

"Yes. I would have called you if it were off. Is that all you wanted to know?"

"That and I have finished with Charlie, so I can stay the weekend, and I could use your sizes."

"My what? Sizes?"

"Yes, you know, dress, hat, ring, that sort of thing."

"I don't wear hats or jewelry, as you must know by now. I maintain my dress size is a four, but six is closer to the truth, and eight is coming at me fast. Are you going to bring me a present? Forget the clothes. You have terrible taste in women's wear. I could use a new blender."

"A blender? What size would that be? And the lady at Victoria's Secret said I had enviable taste."

"She would. I gotta go, bubba. Stay safe, and I'll see you tomorrow. A whole weekend together sounds great. We can go to your little mountain hideaway right after the party." She clicked off.

"I think I handled that well," he said.

His waitress, pad in hand, raised an eyebrow. "Sir?"

Chapter Thirty-nine

Ike flew from Georgetown after lunch on Friday. He'd plotted his flight path to Picketsville, which required him to thread his way past busy airports in and around the Baltimore-Washington corridor and avoid several restricted military areas. Had he been allowed to fly in a straight line, he'd have cut thirty minutes off his transit time. Once clear of urban sprawl, however, Virginia's green piedmont spread out before him like a giant Christmas garden. He cleared the Blue Ridge and turned southwest, following I-81 to Picketsville. He decided he needed to fly more frequently. He should take Ruth up. Perhaps they could travel to more private places on their weekends together. His euphoria over the joys of aviation slipped away when he hit some rough air south of Harrisonburg and the Reuben sandwich he'd wolfed down before takeoff started talking to him.

Ezra Hooper owned not quite one hundred acres of farmland east of Picketsville. The arable land he leased to a factory farmer from Winchester. The wood lots he kept stocked with game. On weekends, during the various hunting seasons, he had congressmen, industrial movers and shakers, and the bevy of sycophants that usually accompany them flown down for a weekend of hunting, drinking, and deal-making. Ike phoned ahead to inform him he'd need to use his private strip. Eager to do a favor for the police that might someday need to be returned, Ezra agreed, and had had the grass mowed the day previously.

Ike made a bumpy landing on the undulating field and taxied to the barn where Hooper hangared his King Air. Frank Sutherlin waited for him in a patrol car.

"Good to see you, Ike. I didn't know you knew how to fly."

"The FAA has a few thoughts on that matter, as well. I learned a few years back. In another life, you could say."

"Well, as long as you're in town, I could use some help."

"Help, as in manpower or help, as in advice?"

"Both, I think, but advice is what I need straightaway. We're going to raid a kid's thing out in the park tonight, and I'm afraid there'll be repercussions from some of their parents."

"What kind of kid thing? Is this about Blake Fisher's satanic stuff you were telling me?"

"Yes. See, we are going in there on a suspicion, at best. All we have is a video of the last time they met, and it certainly looks bad, but we don't have any real reason except we think they'll probably be up to more of the same. And then there's Ashley Starkey's business to account for." He filled Ike in on the conversation the girl had with Blake Fisher.

"Aside from your weak probable cause position, your problem is what?"

"Well, that's pretty much it. If we go and all they're doing is dancing and partying, there will be hell to pay when the parents are called in to pick up the kids."

"You're sure they will be doing whatever they do tonight?"

"Yes, that's confirmed. I had my brother, Henry, you remember him…"

"Who could forget the walking bill board?"

"Yeah. Those tattoos of his are pretty defining, for sure. Anyway, I had him ask around and it checks out. Tonight's the night."

"What did the video show, exactly?"

Frank described the scene they'd watched from the downloaded material Sam had prepared.

"It sounds to me like you need to get out there and break that business up, Frank. Never mind what the parents may or may not say. That is not good, clean fun by anybody's standard.

It needs shutting down. You do it. If there is any flak from the parents, have them talk to me. Say you're working under my direction, or something."

"Ike, don't get me wrong. It's not that I don't want the responsibility, it's just that local policing is still new to me. On the Highway Patrol we didn't do much of this kind of thing."

"I know, Frank, and even though you grew up in Picketsville and you're local, you've been away and so you're still new, sort of. Trust me. It will be fine."

"You're okay with this, then?"

"Protect and serve, Frank. It can't always be about legal niceties. These kids may be on the edge of something bad. Or they may not. Prudence says protect first, apologize later if necessary. That's what local cops do. It's one of the benefits of small town living. Everybody knows everybody and we share responsibility for each other in ways city folks cannot understand. That's why they think we're hicks."

"Right. Okay, you want to help?"

"No can do. I am booked for the evening and most of the weekend. Tell me how it turns out, but for all practical purposes, I'm still on vacation."

Ike caught a lift with one of his deputies to the Callend University campus and made his way down the pathway to the president's house. He'd had too many high-calorie breakfasts at the Crossroads Diner in the past three years, and he'd unable to wedge into his tuxedo. His only suit, however, was dark navy blue and with a white shirt and a subdued tie, he managed to look more or less presentable. A flunky in a brocade waistcoat ushered him in the door. Ruth waved to him from across the room. As Armand Dillon was not a supporter anyone wanted to disappoint, the president's residence had been decorated for the occasion. Fresh flowers in autumnal hues crowded every nook and cranny of the living room, dining room, center hallway, and parlor. Waiters in black tie circulated the rooms with trays of hors d'oeuvres and glasses of wine: red and white, and probably expensive. That was not something Ike would know for he frequently, and truthfully, confessed he had no palate. He ordered a gin and tonic. The waiter, for a brief moment, seemed about to say something, but changed his mind. Ike had become accustomed to the questioning looks from wait-persons, bartenders, and other drink purveyors who believed that gin and tonic, like white shoes, was not acceptable after Labor Day. He didn't care; he knew what he liked and had decided long ago that he had earned the right to be contrary.

Ruth brought Dillon over to him.

"Mr. Dillon asked for you especially, Ike. Try to behave," she said and walked away to greet another guest.

"She's a winner, Sheriff. When are you planning on making an honest woman of her?"

"As usual, your subtlety is lost on me, sir. Just what is it you want to know?"

Dillon laughed and took Ike by the elbow. "I think you ought to lasso that heifer before someone else puts his brand on her, that's all."

"A word of warning, Armand, don't ever let Ruth hear you refer to her, or any other woman, as a cow, young or old. As much as she depends on you for all sorts of things, she can be positively sulfuric about sexist allusions. They may even cause her to become homicidal. Second, she is not the sort to worry over much about the honesty, as you so delicately put it, of her relationships."

"So I hear. Nevertheless, when?"

Ike shrugged and shook his head. "It's a matter under study."

"Okay, I get it. It's none of my business. How's your dad?"

"Not his usual self lately, I'm afraid. My mother died last winter and he's not quite recovered. He's over there." Ike pointed out Abe Schwartz, who, on any other evening, would be working the room like a candidate for office or an insurance salesman. Tonight, he stood staring at a dingy oil portrait of a DIP, deceased important person, probably one of the beneficent Callends.

"I'll go jolly him up a little." Dillon made his way to the elder Schwartz. Within two minutes he had Abe laughing and pointing a finger at Ike.

"Now, what are you two old birds up to?" he muttered.

Ike's cell phone vibrated in his pocket. He made a face and retrieved it. Charlie.

"Charlie, I am at a very nice party, having a cocktail, and being charming to Ruth's friends and a few of her enemies. Don't bother me."

"Ike, charming is not in your toolbox. Anyway, we have a problem."

"Not we, we do not have a problem, Charlie. You. You have the problem."

"Listen, Ike, this is serious. It's about the cell phone you recovered."

"I assume you mean Nick Reynolds' cell phone. What about it? Surely it doesn't still work."

"It had a picture."

Chapter Forty

"A picture? Listen, Charlie, I told you I was done with this project. You asked me to find a plane. I found it. You wanted to know how it ended its flight in the Chesapeake Bay, I found that out, too. I am done, Charlie. What part of *no* don't you understand?"

"Ike, the technicians in the lab were able to restore a bad picture on the cell phone's SIM card. It's amazing what those little phone cameras can capture."

"Hurrah for Japanese technology. I should care about this, how?"

"The picture, Ike, is of a ship close to shore, and it's off-loading a Sunburn missile."

Ike swallowed. This was serious. "So, I was right, you do have a problem. You have a big problem. Operative word is, *you*. Now I intend to rejoin the party."

"Don't hang up on me. We need to talk."

"I'm done, Charlie. Good luck and goodbye." Ike powered down and snapped the phone closed. He stood a moment staring out into the dark, questioning his refusal to help Charlie. No, no, no. Enough is enough. He refused to shoulder any guilt over this. He didn't owe anybody anything. He re-entered the chattering throng of academics and snagged another drink from a passing tray. It wasn't gin but it would do. He made his way to his father and Dillon.

"What are you two plotting? It had better not have anything to do with me."

"What makes you think we were talking about you?" his father asked. "See that, Armand, the boy is all about hisself."

"I know you, old man. You are up to something." Ike retrieved a handkerchief and blew his nose.

"Why do you have to go and be so difficult all the time, Ike?" his father said. "Me and Armand, here, have been doing some figuring, is all. We calculated that if you'd get an early start next spring, we could get you into the Commonwealth's Attorney General's—"

"You remember what happened the last time you plotted my future?"

"Shoot, you're all grown up now. You ain't going to run away from home. Jest listen for a minute."

"Not tonight, Pop, I'm only interested in enjoying this very fine party, having some time with Ruth, and continuing my vacation at the beach."

"Now, that's another thing. You ain't hardly ever to home anymore. You aren't planning on missing Yom Kippur, too?"

"What? What did you say?"

"I said, are you planning on missing Yom Kippur? I know your momma's not around, but we were always together for the high holy days, at least when you weren't gallivanting around the world."

"When?"

"When what? When you was gallivanting? Well—"

"No. no, when is Yom Kippur?"

"Wednesday, of course."

"In five days?"

"Unless the government introduced a new day of the week and I didn't hear about it, yep."

"Oh, my God. Excuse me, I have to make a call."

"Kids now-a-days, always glued to them mobile phones. You got one of them doodads, Armand?"

Ike didn't linger to hear Dillon's answer. He exited the room and stood outside on the wide veranda that surrounded the house on three sides. Its wisteria had long since lost its purple blossoms and its leaves had turned a golden brown. He opened the phone and powered up. The face read One Missed Call. He ignored it and speed dialed Charlie.

"Ike why did you turn off the phone, I wasn't finished."

"Never mind that. Five days, Charlie. You guys have five days to find those missiles."

"What do you mean, we have five days. What's the big deal about five?"

"Yom Kippur. It comes on the ninth day of Tishrei. That's always in late September or early October. We forgot about Yom Kippur."

"You would know that."

"No, that's the point. I don't know that. My father would know that. I missed it."

"Okay, you're haphazard in your faith. What of it?"

"The war, Charlie. They're going to launch those damned missiles on the anniversary of the Yom Kippur war. Don't you see?"

The line fell silent. Then Ike heard Charlie's voice, slightly muffled, speaking to someone at the other end. He heard his name, Yom Kippur, and five days. Ike figured he'd gotten through. He turned the phone over and had his finger on the power button when Charlie came back on the line.

"You have to come in, Ike."

"No way. It's your hot potato."

"Wait, hold on a minute. Don't hang up…okay…here's the director."

Ike had never had a conversation with the Almighty, and didn't expect he ever would, but he was sure that if he did, He'd sound like the director of the CIA.

"Ike, you need to come in."

"Director, absolutely not. I told Charlie no, and I'm telling you the same. This is way out of my league."

"You don't get to choose, son. I'll draft you if I must."

"With all due respect, Director, you can't. More importantly, you don't have to. You have assets all over the place. Flood the Eastern Shore with them, find the damned things, and call me when you're done."

"Ike, please listen to me. It's not a question of assets. You're right. I can call on as many people as necessary. I can borrow from the FBI, the Army, you name it. But you said it."

"I said what?"

"You said we have five days…don't interrupt. I think you're right and I haven't the luxury of time to get anyone else up to speed on this. And flooding the Eastern Shore is not an option. If they get even a sniff we're on to them, you can bet they won't wait five days. You were on the spot. You did the ground work. You must run with this."

"What's happened to Fugarelli?" Ike felt his independence slipping away. He didn't want to inspect the director's analysis for fear it was correct.

"Has pneumonia or something. I think he's losing his nerve and is coddling his retirement plan, but I could be wrong. And before you ask, I can't spare Garland. I need him in place, and if he ran this operation, it would blow his cover."

"What did I do to deserve this?"

"Put it down to bad Karma. I need you here in the morning at seven sharp."

The line went silent for a moment and then Charlie came back on. "You okay, Ike?"

"I'm in Picketsville, Charlie. I had a weekend all planned. I don't even have a car here."

"I'll send one."

"No, don't do that. I'll tell you what, clear me to land at Fort Belvoir and have a car and driver waiting for me. I'll fly out tomorrow morning. I'll call you when I take off. You can figure somewhere around an hour, more or less, for me to get there, and pick me up."

"Done."

Ike looked at his phone. The One Missed Call winked at him. He closed it. Ruth came out onto the veranda.

"There you are. Why aren't you schmoozing my guests?"

Ike stared off into the night.

"Hey, what's up, Doc? You look sick. Bad booze or bad news?"

"I have a cold." He sneezed as if to confirm it.

"Gesundheit. I know. You promised to give it to me this weekend. See the sacrifices I'm willing to make for you?"

"The weekend is off. I'm sorry. Something came up."

"By the looks of you it's something serious. You look terrible and it's not just the cold, is it?"

"You should see me when I've had one of Flora Blevins' pork chops. Anyway the weekend at the A-frame is out. I have to fly to DC tomorrow around six or six-thirty."

"It's bad serious, isn't it."

"Yes."

"You want to tell momma?"

"I'd love to, but—"

"You can't. Damn Charlie Garland anyway. I told you it would end badly."

"Did you? I don't remember."

"I did. You may not have heard me, because I said it in the shower last Sunday. But I said it. Are you okay?"

"Super."

A waiter drifted by with canapés and Ike snagged one. One bite and he was looking for a discreet place to spit it out.

"What on earth is this?"

"Agnes, my secretary—"

"Administrative assistant."

"Give it a rest, Schwartz. She wanted to help and offered to make an hors d'oeuvre. They are her famous, you should pardon the expression, asparagus roll-ups. They're ghastly aren't they?"

"Better keep them away from Dillon. They could cost you some serious cash."

"Right. So you have to go and be a hero. Okay, I know we're agreed that you are the last Boy Scout in town, and you must go save the world from imminent destruct…" She caught sight of Ike's expression and gasped. "It's like that?"

"I can't say. It's important."

"Woof, I am not ready for Armageddon. Are you sure? Don't answer that. We will wind up officially nine-ish, which means everybody will be gone by ten or so. You try to be civilized to all these people. Try not to scare the pants off with dire news—"

"I only have one set of pants in mind—"

"Shut up. And then when the place quiets down, slip upstairs. I'll join you when I can. We'll spend some time exchanging germs and things, and I'll drive you to your airplane in the morning. How about that?"

Ike kissed her lightly on the cheek and nodded. "Youse is a good boy, Denny."

"What?"

"See you later."

Chapter Forty-one

The phone's insistent chirping finally woke him. With just a sliver of moon to light the room, Ike could barely see and, befogged with sleep, couldn't remember where he was either. He tried to think. Ruth huffed and pulled herself up on one elbow to squint at the luminous dial on her alarm clock. Then Ike remembered. He scrabbled to retrieve the phone.

"What time is it?" he mumbled.

"Without my glasses on, or my contacts in, I can only say with any certainty that it's either 12:30 or 6 AM. The hands make a straight line up and down."

"That's firm? No possibility of a three or a four?"

"See for yourself?" Ruth flopped back on the bed and pulled the sheets up over her head.

"Okay, I'll settle for twelve-thirty." Ike flipped the phone open. "Yeah, Schwartz."

"Hi, Ike, I know it's late and you probably have other things on your mind…" The understatement of the week "…and I hate to bother you…this is Frank down at the office."

"What's the problem?" It had to be a problem. Frank would not have called, otherwise.

"We did that raid I told you about, and now I have a room full of upset parents. I'm not used to this."

"You will be. So how did it go?"

"Good, I think. One or two kids managed to slip away but we corralled about a dozen. We confiscated drugs, nearly a pound of weed, a dozen rounds of ecstasy, some prescription pills, you know, oxycodone in several brand names, a few tranquilizers, and some other stuff I haven't identified yet. They were either having, had, or were contemplating having, a pharm party. Judging by their behavior, I'm guessing they'd already had it. Oh, and there was some stolen property."

"What kind of property?"

"Well, the reverend insisted on riding with us, and he identified his silverware. The kids were using it in their ceremony. And there was a video camera with 'Property of Picketsville H. S.' engraved on it. They said they borrowed it. You know how that goes."

"The parents are angry at you, or their kids?"

"A little of both. When I said drugs and stolen property, most of them settled down and started giving their children the dirty eye. A few others are talking attorneys."

"How many others?"

"Actually, just one. Mrs. Starkey is raising bloody you-know-what."

"Put her on." Ike waited while Frank found and brought Barbara Starkey to the phone.

"Okay, here she is…"

"Sheriff—"

"Barbara, it's me, Ike. What's the deal?"

"Frank Sutherlin broke up a little get-together in the park and has all the kids confused. I mean, it was just a party, for goodness sake. I've spoken with Peachy, and she's very upset. I can hardly understand her. I think it's terrible. And Blake Fisher is going on, and on, about Satan and…well, you can imagine. It's all wrong. They're just some kids doing a little acting out, and your deputies come barging in like storm troopers and—"

"Whoa. Stop. Did Frank tell you about the stolen property? Your kids were using the missing silver from the church. Your church, if memory serves. That can't be brushed off with a 'kids acting out.' Then there are the drugs. Peachy is more than upset. I'm willing to bet she's stoned. I'm sorry, Barbara, but Frank is right. As for the devil business, I don't know the ins and outs of it, but I do know that it can't lead to any good. You mix drugs and that sort of occult foolishness and you are bound to have trouble. It may seem like nonsense to you, but it's potentially dangerous."

"But—"

"Look, you put childproof caps on your drugs, and safety catches on the cabinet doors when the kids were young, right? Well, this pre-emptive action by the deputies on what could be bad news is the same thing. I can give you a book or two about it if you like, but it is not something you should take lightly."

"Oh, Ike, really."

"No, you listen. Your daughters—"

"Only Peachy was involved."

"Both of your daughters were involved. You need to talk to Ashley about blood. Is she around?"

"She came to the jail with us, yes. What about blood?"

"Is she sporting a bandage anywhere?"

"Now that you mention it, yes. So what?"

"You need to ask her why. If, and when, she tells you the truth, you will need to go over and apologize to Frank, and thank him for putting the kibosh on what might have turned out to be a small or big disaster down the road."

"You're sure about this?"

"Absolutely. And I think you might think about an apology to Blake Fisher, too."

"I'll talk to Ashley."

"Good. Put Frank back on."

"…Yeah, I'm here. Ike."

"What else can you tell me?"

"Here's something worrisome. There was an adult out there with the kids."

"An adult? Who?"

"New teacher at the high school named Byerson. He teaches English and coaches the drama club, as near as I can tell. He joined the faculty at the end of last year when Susan Meara took maternity leave. Then he hired on full time after she decided to be a stay-at-home mom. He nearly slipped away tonight, but Billy nabbed him back in the dark with a fourteen-year-old girl. Had her blouse off and was going for the rest when Billy spotted him."

"Where is he now?"

"We segregated him from the kids. He's cooling off in a cell."

"What about the fourteen-year-old?"

"She's bawling her eyes out and blaming her absentee dad or something."

"Here's what you should do. Make sure the parents know Byerson was there and suggest—no accusations mind you—just suggest, that he might have been the instigator of the whole business. Then let them pound on their kids a bit, say fifteen minutes or so, and then get their statements. You should be able to tie the whole mess up in an hour."

"What do I do about the kids we pulled in?"

"Release them into the custody of their parents. Byerson stays in a cell. You can hold him for at least twenty-four hours. By then you'll have had time to digest the kid's statements and run a background check on him. You already have him on attempted statutory rape, contributing to the delinquency of a minor, and probably distribution of controlled substances. That bird needs to spend some quality time with adults for a change—in the county lock-up."

Ike hung up and searched for his handkerchief.

"You sounded like the cop I've come to know and admire." Ruth said.

"Don't get smart with me, woman, or I'll get Charlie to release the tape from our weekend at the beach."

"There's no tape…is there?"

"You'll never know."

"I will if I ever get to look your pal in the eye. Men cannot hide things like that. If they've seen you naked, they never look at you the same way again."

"You are wise beyond your years."

"I've been around. What was that all about?"

"Some other time. I need sleep. Do you have anything in your medicine cabinet to make me instantly unconscious?"

"I might. I have some prescription stuff, but if you're going to be Top Gunning tomorrow, you shouldn't use it."

"Top Gunning?"

"You know, like what's-his-name, the hunky guy, who flew the jets in that movie you showed me the last time we were at your place in the mountains."

"Flying a Cessna is along way from driving an F-14 Tomcat."

"That's okay, you're my jet jockey."

"I thought I was the honey in your Honey Bunches of Oats,"

"I like the imagery of a jet jockey better."

"Sleep medicine?"

"I can do better than that, Schwartz. Come over here."

Chapter Forty-two

Blake had not experienced anything approaching a hangover since his freshman year in college. Early Saturday morning he felt as though he'd spent the night at a fraternity party rather than the sheriff's office. He shook his head, a thing he'd been doing since midnight, at the reaction of the parents to their children's arrest in the raid at the Pit, or Cauldron, or whatever it was called. He naively believed that they would be grateful for having their kids snatched back from an event and behaviors that they would never have countenanced in their own youth.

He was wrong.

The complaints and threats leveled at the deputies, at Frank Sutherlin, and at him were shocking. What, he wondered, had happened to society when parents taught their children to distrust and disrespect authority? Schoolteachers, police and clergy were all experiencing the same phenomenon. He'd seen it before, but never as vituperative and open as last night.

He dropped an antacid in a glass of water and watched as it danced and fizzed in a glass. Oddly, it had been Barbara Starkey who, although she came into the station complaining and accusing everyone in sight at the top of her lungs, calmed down the earliest. Her daughter, Ashley, whose presence there seemed a mystery, refused to make eye contact and remained mute when he'd spoken to her. Blake had stayed until the last child had been trundled out the door. Beyerson, the English teacher, had been incarcerated for the night. What would become of him, he wondered. Frank had looked grim when he'd asked. Contributing to the delinquency of a minor is all he would say.

Blake moved to his tiny kitchen and began to fix breakfast, even though his stomach was still doing nip-ups and the thought of coffee made him cringe. He settled for a cup of tea and two pieces of toast. Saturday the church office was closed. If any parents were still on their high horse, they'd have to vent to the answering machine.

There was always the possibility that Barbara Starkey might call to apologize but he doubted it. He knew from past experience, she was as likely to ditch the church as call him. Sadly, he'd learned, people were reluctant to admit an error to their priest, particularly when it involved confrontation—a variation on the "blaming the victim" phenomenon. He guessed.

<> <> <>

Ruth sat in her car and watched Ike's airplane until it disappeared over the mountains. Her eyes were still sandy from sleep. She'd thrown a raincoat over her hastily donned pajamas, slipped into a pair of sneakers, and driven Ike to Hooper's farm. She shivered against the early morning chill. Ike had filled her in on what he was up against, but only briefly. She didn't think he was worried about a security breach. He just wanted to minimize the fright factor. He had failed. If she understood him correctly, he was flying into harm's way. She felt the fear flutter in her stomach. She had so much to learn about this man who could alternately be charming, maddening, serious, and fey. This much she knew: he was fiercely loyal. Loyal to his friends, his family, and to his country.

That was the part that worried her. She came up through academe where cynicism about God and country were *de rigueur*. Ike was an anomaly, a throwback to another era and time.

"You'd kill?" She'd asked him at the beach. His eyes had turned to ice and he'd said, "I'd do whatever I had to do to keep us both alive."

He'd do that for Charlie, and for all those people who'd treated him so badly in the past. Not because he had reconciled himself to what happened, but because he put duty and honor before personal resentment. She loved him for that and she hated him for it. Why hadn't she fallen for a normal man? She smiled. What sort of normal male would dare hook up with her? No, it would have to be someone like Ike Schwartz. Still, she wondered if he wasn't flying into a maelstrom, and if it might destroy him. She rummaged in her purse and extracted her phone. She was about to do something she'd never done before in her life.

<>< ><>

Blake Fisher, his toast half-eaten, stared at the telephone. If the parents grew weary of listening to the service times and requests to leave a message from the church's answering machine, they might soon begin calling him at home. He had just reached for the receiver to take it off the hook and render it inoperative, when it rang. He hesitated. Did he want to listen to another litany of complaints from some kid's parents? He picked up.

"Dr. Fisher." Ruth Harris happened to be the only person in town who acknowledged his doctor of ministry degree. "I have a request. Have you a minute?"

"Certainly." Blake had not spoken with the president of Callend since sometime in the winter, at the Schwartz's Hanukah/Christmas party. No, that wasn't true. He'd said hello at the funeral service for Ike's mother.

"I'm not much for church and praying, sorry about that, but I wonder if you could do some for me."

He heard the anxiety in her voice. Many people who couldn't fit themselves into church for one reason or another seemed singularly uncomfortable asking for help from that sector in times of stress.

"What can I do?"

"I need you, and anyone else who's willing, to pray for the country and for Sheriff Schwartz."

"Is there something special I should know? Is Ike ill or—"

"He's fine now. I don't know about tomorrow. I can't talk, you understand. Oh, Lord, I feel like such a fool. Just put that in your prayer cycle, if that's what it's called. Ike may or may not tell you something about it later. Knowing him he'll make a joke out of it."

"I see." Blake didn't. Obviously something was afoot and Ike had a part in it. "I'd be happy to pray for Ike and the country. We always include the country in our Prayers for the People, anyway."

"Right. Thank you. I'm sorry to have bothered you."

"No bother at all," he said to a dial tone.

Chapter Forty-three

Ike wheeled the Cessna onto the taxiway at Fort Belvoir. A vehicle with FOLLOW ME emblazoned in red on its bumper pulled in front of him. He followed it to a tie-down and cut the engine. While a ramp attendant secured his plane, two steely-eyed MPs escorted him to a waiting SUV. They watched him until he cleared the gate and turned north toward McLean and Langley. Flying in restricted air space had been slightly nerve-wracking. An Army helicopter had shadowed him the last several miles and through his approach. At least he thought it had him in view. He'd never know.

His driver was professionally taciturn. He didn't speak and answered questions with grunts. Ike sat back and read the packet of information that either Charlie or the director had placed in the back seat for him. There wasn't anything new. He studied satellite photos paper clipped to the bundle. They appeared to be some of the ones he'd looked at the week previous. He shoved the materials back in their envelope and stared at the passing northern Virginia countryside, if that's what you called the built-up stretch of real estate in and around Route 1. He wondered what it must have looked like centuries before. George Washington would have ridden this way from Mount Vernon to Foggy Bottom, the future capital of the country.

Something in the pictures jogged his memory. Something he'd seen at the outset, but it hadn't clicked. It still didn't, but he knew there was something in them that he needed to think about. Something about the ships in the bay waiting for a pilot? The barge? He shook his head impatiently. He hated it when a thought nagged at him but would not surface. He knuckled his forehead and tried to concentrate.

◇◇◇

It took ten minutes to clear security at Langley and for him to receive his visitor's pass. The director waited for him in a small conference room. Charlie hovered in the background.

"Sit. You've read the summary?"

"Yes, sir, I have. There is nothing new here, I'm afraid. What exactly do you want me to do? And as a corollary to that, what can it be that any of a half-dozen others in the Agency couldn't do, and do better?"

"You, whether you want to admit it or not, have the chops to make this thing work. If I pull anyone else in they will waste precious hours turning everything over in their mind. You can jump right in."

"I appreciate your confidence, Director, but it may be misplaced, tragically misplaced, if this goes south. Look, at my best, I used to be good at this game, but I was ten years younger and I never had to deal with anything as threatening as this. None of us did. Dealing with massive terrorist plots is new to everyone, and certainly outside my abilities. Five days doesn't leave much time, and I've been away. I don't know the troops, the routine, or the limits."

"You make your own rules. You always did before. What's changed?"

"I'm older, slower, and happily settled in a life I enjoy. No, make that a life I love. Except for latent patriotism, and that grows weaker every time I pick up a newspaper, I am poorly motivated to do this."

"I'll put something in the pot to change that." Ike waited. What could the director possibly offer him to energize him?

"I am aware, Ike, that during the years you were with us, you managed to accumulate substantial sums as a result of unused program funds. They are in your name and in various offshore accounts, and in Switzerland. We never asked for them back. Indeed, until we found a decent tracking system, we had no idea where they were, or how much they were worth. Now we do."

"I've never spent a dime that wasn't due me, or wasn't directly related to the operation and never claimed the money, though, once or twice, I was tempted."

"I know. In that, you may be unique. My proposal is this. We will delete those accounts from our files if you are successful."

"You can't bribe me."

"Don't be offended. You may be the only operative we ever had who either did not overspend his funds, or didn't pay for at least a month in Aruba from them, usually with a spouse or significant other. We always let that slide, as it seemed a small way to compensate them for their efforts. Besides, if you fail, it won't make any difference what we do."

"I'll do it without the bribe, Director."

"Charlie said you'd say that. But we never squared the accounts, so to speak, when you left us. As far as I am concerned, we owe you."

Ike swiveled around in his chair and studied the pictures on the wall, a collection of headshots of people he did not know. He spun back and shook his head.

"I hate this, I really do, but I don't see a way out. I'll give it a go, but remember when this blows up in your face, I told you so. What happens next?"

"It's your op. You tell me."

"Well, first we need to get on the property opposite where the satellite pictures show the ship off-loading the Sunburn. It has to be searched, but whoever lives there cannot know we're doing it. Second, we need to figure out how many, and where, the other Sunburns are, if, in fact there are others. Third…I don't know what's third. I think we need to sit and do some serious thinking. There's something in those photographs that's bugging me and I can't put my finger on it. I need someone to hear me talk it through."

"Talk to Charlie. He's a good listener."

"Hah."

"He's all you have right now." The director stood and left. At the door, he turned and faced the two men.

"I don't have to tell you what's at stake. Give me an update every hour, twenty-four-seven, I want to be in the loop all the way. We have to find those missiles."

The two men sat in silence.

"We could send in a team to the property. Say they were health inspectors or…" Charlie's voice trailed off. "I'm not too good at this."

"We can't do anything remotely suspicious. If they panic, they'll just push the button early. That's assuming there is a button on the property to push."

"What then?"

"We need to look at pictures. Take me to wherever you do photo analysis of the satellite pictures."

Three minutes later they sat in the dark as a projectionist ran through the series of pictures.

"Ask him to put up the pictures from the cell phone"

"Right. We were able to salvage and enhance three, all pretty much the same. The angles are slightly different. Nick must have been circling the ship. They've cleaned them up as much as they can."

A series of images of an old freighter appeared. The photos were dim and blurry, but there could be no doubt what dangled at the end of the midships crane.

"Can you make out the name on the stern?"

"No, we tried. You have to remember, this was shot with a cell phone at night from a moving aircraft."

"Hold that one and go back to the satellite pictures of the day before—the Fourth of July shot." The view of the Chesapeake Bay filled the screen. "Okay, now the next day." The picture changed marginally. "Look, do you see that?"

"See what?"

"There's a ship off to the east of the cluster waiting for a Bay pilot. You see? It's much smaller. On the fourth it is in one location. The next day it is in another. It moved during the night and it must be the one in Nick's picture. Now we know where it went. Can you zoom in on that?"

The ship inflated before their eyes. The distortion was minimal. Soon they could make out the details of the deck and even a few crew members.

"Can you make out the name and registry of it?"

A voice, presumably from the projection booth replied. "It may take a while. We will have to go back to the original tape and work on it."

"If you have trouble with this shot, that ship will be in the next day's surveillance, too. It will be a bit farther east and at a better angle for reading the hull."

"We'll give it a go."

While they waited, Ike turned over the previous week's activities. There was the barge and there was the...what?

"We have it," the voice in the dark announced. "It's the *Saifullah*. Its registry, according to the markings on the stern, is Panama."

"Put the cell-phone picture back up."

Charlie looked at Ike. "Are you okay? What is it?"

"That ship is too close to the shore."

"So?"

"It's something Bunky Crispins said...about the dredging and trot lines."

"About the dredging and trot...Sorry, I'm not with you. You asked me to look up that dredging contract, remember?"

"Yes?"

"I did, and it's interesting."

Chapter Forty-four

"It's the same consortium that leased the car and the yacht."

"Close. The reason it took me so long is that we had some trouble tracking the convoluted lines from the group that signed for the dredging back to the center of the holding company. But the bottom line is this: one of the arms of that octopus did, in fact, order up the equipment."

"Were you able to talk to the people who did the actual work?"

"No, that's the interesting part. They rented the equipment only and provided their own crew. We searched high and low. Whoever they were, they are long gone."

"Bunky said that there was supposed to be a twelve-foot trench from the deeper part of the bay to the bulkhead to accommodate a sailboat's keel. But when we crossed the area, there was no trench. The bottom dropped off precipitously on the other side of the duck blind. Bunky said it might be due to current and tide, but we know better."

"We do?"

"Look at the pictures, Charlie. What do you see? That's no pleasure boat sitting next to the barge, it's a full-sized old freighter. It can't be more than one hundred yards from the shore. They weren't dredging a sailboat slip. They were making channel deep enough to allow that ship to come in from the deeper part of Eastern Bay, drop off its cargo, and return to the Chesapeake afterward."

"What's up with the barge? Besides being part of the dredging operation?"

"I don't think by the time Nick shot that picture, it had anything at all to do with dredging. Look at the pictures taken this month." Ike waited until the more recent films were racked up. "See, no barge."

"That's the duck blind you mentioned. What's it doing there?"

Ike stared at the image on the screen. He closed his eyes. Minutes ticked by. Charlie began to fidget. Finally Ike turned to him.

"Here's what I want you to do. It needs to be done like right away, like yesterday, you understand?"

"Got it. Soonest."

"Even sooner. Get a boat out on the bay opposite the blind. Give it a cover, like, make it a Maryland Department of Natural Resources boat. Have the crew pretend to be taking water or bottom samples, something, anything. Each time they drop a line over, have them slip a lightstick, a twelve-hour lightstick, a big one with a weight on it so it will stay on the bottom even when the tide turns. I want a straight line of them from say, the middle of the bay on a line from the pier at Romancoke, to that blind. I'll need one every twenty feet or so."

"You want to tell me why?"

"Later. Just get on that. How soon can you do that?"

"I don't know. I'll have to make some calls."

"Make them. Then have those divers you found for me last week to report back."

"To do what?"

"I need that boat, the stealth thing from the ATF, again."

"I can borrow it from ATF again. They're happy to work with us. I'll have them deliver back to the marina, by dark. We can put the divers aboard it."

"One more thing. That ship, the *Saifullah*, find out who owns it, and if you can do that, find out if they own any more."

"Ike, I'd really like to know—"

"Get hopping on the divers and the boat. Put your best searchers on the freighter's ownership and then come back and I'll fill you in. I'm playing a hunch, Charlie. If I'm right, we can save time. If I'm wrong, we'll still have time left to sort it out. Oh, and since it's a hunch, I want those two Navy SEALs along for the ride. Oh, and get me an Arabic-speaking agent. He needs to be able to read and maybe write it, too."

Charlie brought Ike a sandwich and coffee and slouched in a chair. The day continued to slip by as the Agency mobilized. They'd not been this frenetic since September 11. Ike and Charlie returned to the conference room, which, by now, had become a war room. Men and women with worried faces came in and out with notes that they placed on the table in front of one or the other of the two men.

"Catch me up. What are you up to, Ike? I need to give the director a report."

"Arrange for a chopper to ferry us to the marina. We'll need some sophisticated underwater communications equipment, too. The SEALs can supply that."

"Okay, but what—"

"Ships, Charlie, ships."

"We're working on it even as we speak. It takes time. The merchant marine is involved. My question is, besides wanting to arrest the crew of the *Saifullah* if we can, why?"

"What is the normal platform used to launch a Sunburn?"

"They were ship-to-ship missiles originally. But they've been launched from submarines and land-based racks, and…oh, I see. Ships."

"You could put one or two of those beauties in the hold of a ship, any reasonably large ship, a ship like the *Saifullah*, for example, and launch anywhere in the world. Any city within seventy or eighty miles of the coast is vulnerable to attack. Even without a nuclear warhead, one or two of them on target in any major city would create a disaster as great as nine-eleven."

Charlie sat frozen in his chair as the enormity of the situation crystallized in his mind. "And they fly under the radar until the last second. A conventional antimissile defense system could not pick them up and therefore couldn't stop them. Lord help us."

"We need to know if they have other ships and where they are, or where they're headed. We have five days, no, make that four and less than a half."

Charlie started to rise, and then slumped back in the chair. "You think that ship, the *Saifullah*, is on its way back to the Chesapeake?"

"No. Remember, it off-loaded a missile. My guess is that it's finished with that venue. It's headed somewhere else with that missile's brother in its hold."

"Where?"

Ike shrugged and pointed at a large map of the United States on the wall.

"Your guess is as good as mine. Look at the possibilities. The hardware has a range of one hundred miles or so. If I were running the operation, I'd want to stay offshore in international waters and away from inspection, so figure the seventy or eighty I mentioned before. What would be your choice?"

"Geez, starting in the northeast, Boston, New York, we already identified the cities in the Baltimore/Washington corridor...um...Miami, New Orleans, Galveston, Houston...in the west, good Lord, San Diego, LA, San Francisco, Seattle—"

"Not Seattle, but Naval bases, airfields, strategic military targets everywhere, and SDI can't stop the launch."

"But Washington—why not launch from a ship?"

"Do the math, Charlie. To stay twelve to twenty miles off shore would put the missile out of range of the choice targets. The Delmarva Peninsula protects DC. It's like a modern Fort McHenry, which protected Baltimore in the War of 1812. The Long Island Sound and Puget Sound in the west do the same for parts of New England and Seattle."

"But why not just sail in on Yom Kippur and shoot?"

"Two reasons. They are well financed, probably by one of our putative Arab allies, and there is a rare skill set involved here. The operation requires people with both a suicide bomber's mind set and the ability to pilot-navigate a ship across two oceans and a crew to run it. There can't be too many fanatics who can do all of those things. So, they will land-launch here from the property. Washington has to be their number-one target and the one that they feel they must be sure to hit. The remainder of the missiles will launch from a ship or several ships elsewhere."

"But, I still don't get why not enter a harbor first."

"Charlie, you're the spymeister. You tell me."

"I can't be sure. I guess if they were carrying nuclear devices, that would be the method of choice. The irony is, we have the capacity to intercept any warship on or under the sea to protect the country, but a commercial ship, boat, or dinghy can sail into any port with a carefully shielded device and before an inspection could be made, detonate a device, and there is nothing we could do about it."

"So?"

"So, this is not good. And you want divers for…?"

"Divers and SEALs. We're playing a hunch and if I'm right, my policy has always been to have back up. You know, this is not a James Bond movie. He can walk into trouble, and the script will get him out. Laser watch, exploding fountain pen, hot dumb babe with a heart of gold, something."

"I'm for the hot dumb babe."

"Of course you are. But, this is the real thing and we don't know what's out there. I want some tough guys on my side. Where are we on all this?"

"You didn't give any of us much time. Like you just said, this is not a movie, and I can't just order up a Maryland DNR boat, and—"

"Time, Charlie. We don't have. Did you get us that chopper?"

"I said I'm working on it."

Chapter Forty-five

Like sand in an hourglass, the day drained away. No windows graced the conference room, but Ike could sense the sun setting. Pulling the whole operation was taking too long. The clock on the wall ticked away. As time dwindled, his frustration grew.

"I wanted to go tonight. What's the hold-up?"

"You said it, Ike: this isn't a movie. I can't produce a Maryland Department of Natural Resources boat, an Arabic-speaking operative, and all the rest of this stuff in a heartbeat. We have your special agent flying in from Dubai. We have a smallish boat in the paint shop being tricked out to look both official and slightly used. That's not easy, by the way. We're piecing it together as fast as we can, but I have to tell you, it ain't happening tonight."

"Five days, Charlie. Now we're down to four."

"What can I say? We are on it, Ike. Come on, you used to do this. You know how it is. Anyway, I do have some news. The *Saifullah* was purchased from an Indian salvage yard. It seems the Indians bought the remnants of a fleet of old freighters and tankers from a Greek company that went belly-up. Before they had dismantled them, a company headquartered in Brussels bought four."

"Just four? Can we account for the remainder of that fleet?"

"Four is the number. We're still checking on it, but four looks firm."

"Any idea where they are?"

"Not yet, Ike. Patience. The ships, cars, yacht, property, are all tangled in a Gordian knot of holding companies, shadow boards, and dead ends. There isn't anything more I can do just now."

"Actually, there is. You can pick the most likely targets, given what we know, or think we know, and send some Navy muscle to the area. SDI can't, but the Navy has the capacity to shoot down Sunburns. Have them put to sea on high alert, tracking radar on, twenty-four seven, and the antimissile system up and unlocked. I don't know the drill, but don't AWACs track missile launches? Better get them up in the air, too."

"What do we tell them?"

"The brass has to have the story, I guess, for the ships' crews. Say it's an exercise to see if they're proficient in antimissile protocols. For all they know, it's a dummy launch."

"You finished, sahib?"

"Almost. Dosimeters, Charlie. If we wander anywhere near a Sunburn and it's nuclear, they'll emit some or a lot of radiation. We need to know."

"Dosimeters? I'm guessing thermoluminescent would be best. Okay. Anything else?

"If there's enough daylight left, I want a flyover and photo shoot of the property."

"Way ahead of you there, Ace. I've had the satellite camera focused in on it all day. We have close-ups of every inch. You want to see them now, or later?"

"Now would be good. Is the director on station?"

"Yes."

"Do you think he'd like to sit in?"

"He thought you'd never ask."

◇◇◇

"Since we have some time, will you fill me and the director in on the business of the light sticks? They were not easy to find, you know. We have just about one of everything in the warehouse, but your light sticks had to be ordered in special."

"Okay. Here's the problem. We don't dare spook these guys. They can't know that we're on to them. Since they burned Crispins' boat, they are obviously skittish. If they get even a hint we're after them, they'll launch early—before we know how many Sunburns they have and, worse, where they are."

"I figured that part out on my own," Charlie said.

"You hear that, Director? Charlie is brighter than we thought."

"Bite me."

"Tsk, tsk. How you talk, Charlie. Did you hear that, Director?"

"Cut it out, you two, and get on with it."

"As soon as it is sufficiently dark, we motor out in the borrowed stealth boat to a point on the line of light sticks. The word in the neighborhood of Eastern Bay is fog is normal and frequent. With any luck, we will have a foggy night or at least a cloudy one. Rain, again, would be good, too. So, either way, we put the divers and SEALs over. They follow the lightsticks to the duck blind. That's a rendezvous point. The water is shallow after that. When they can stand, they unpack headsets and night vision goggles. Are you with me so far?"

The two men nodded. The director jotted notes on a legal pad and studied the blow-up of the property on the screen in front of them.

"Here's the tricky part. If there is a guard watching the bulkhead, we will need to draw him away."

"Why not take just him out?" Charlie asked.

"Same reason we can't let them know we're coming. If one goes down, the others will know something's up."

"Ike you have a big problem on your hands." The Director looked worried.

"I have Bunky Crispins on hold. If we need a diversion, he and some of his watermen friends will arrive at the front gate, ostensibly drunk and rowdy, and accuse the putative property owners of spoiling the crabbing off their property. They did, as a matter of fact, so their anger will not have to be faked. As soon as the coast is clear—I've always wanted to say that. This is the first time I've ever been able to, about a real coast—anyway, the guys will signal us in. We take the rubber dinghy to the bulkhead, climb ashore, and search the property. We cannot, under any circumstances, be discovered."

The director looked up from his notes. "How long will your watermen keep the ruckus up?"

"As long as we want or until the police arrive." Ike stood and went to the screen. "The launchers have to be big. I may have missed it, but I see no evidence of camouflage netting, so it's safe to assume they're in a building. There are two possibilities: the garage, here," he tapped the image on what appeared to be a multibay garage, "or here in this barn. There is a shed closer to the bulkhead. The time-lapse photos show it is a new structure. It is not large enough for a launcher, but since it's new, we need to check it out."

"Why an Arabic-speaking agent?'

"He's a listener. All we have to go on, for identifying these birds as from that part of the world, is the ship's name. *Saifullah,* The Sword of Allah. And the fact the missiles disappeared in Iran. I want someone to listen and, on the off-chance we find something written, to read it and maybe learn something new."

"When you find the launchers, what then?"

"That depends. If we have a bead on the other Sunburns by then, we blow them. If we don't, we sabotage them just enough to slow the launch process down and to allow us to react."

"What if you don't find them?"

"We're screwed."

Chapter Forty-six

As Ike had hoped, clouds closed in and blotted out the scant moonlight over Eastern Bay. The black converted river patrol boat, its engines muffled, ferried them to the bay's center. This time Ike allowed the captain to use his own GPU. With the coordinates he'd determined from the mapping done by the ersatz DNR boat earlier, he put the craft directly over the path of submerged lightsticks.

The divers and SEALs, with call signs Tiger One through Four, signs generated by Charlie, went over the side and disappeared into the inky water. Ike and the agent from Dubai, Tigers Five and Six, dropped into the Zodiac and waited. Ike would have to talk to Charlie later about those dorky call signs.

After what seemed an eternity, they received the all-clear to move to the duck blind. The advance team indicated it would go ashore and scout for guards. Powered by an electric outboard, the Zodiac slipped silently through the wash toward the rendezvous.

Ike could barely make out his hand in front of his face.

"No one so far," rasped one of the SEALs. Ike pointed toward the bulkhead, and the Zodiac moved at a speed just slightly faster than the outgoing tide. When the bow bumped against stones, Ike crawled out and secured the boat to a large boulder. The two men crept forward and waited.

"We're ten yards in and clear so far."

"Spread out. Take the garage first, then the barn. If you see anyone, I mean anyone, freeze. If you have to, bug out."

"Roger that, Tiger Five." Ike shook his head. If he weren't so scared, he'd have laughed. Tiger Five! Charlie, what were you thinking?

Ike signaled to his Arabic speaker to come close. "You make your way to the house and listen. Call me if you need anything or there's something I need to see."

The agent gave him a thumbs-up and melted into the night. Ike worked his way through the underbrush to the shed. He could have moved faster had he taken the gravel path, but he didn't know if it was watched or monitored with cameras and motion detectors.

A light shone through a window at the shed's rear. He edged around to the back. Standing off to one side so that anyone inside would not see him, Ike scanned the left side of the interior. He ducked under the window and repeated the process on the other side. Nobody home. That's good or it's bad. The lights are on. Where are these guys?

He crept to the door and tried the latch. Not surprisingly, the door was locked. He fumbled in his pockets for his lock picks and hoped he would remember how they worked.

"Garage is clear except for a car, an old tractor, and a workshop."

"What kind of tractor, you mean like a farm tractor or a rig that pulls a trailer?"

"Farm—big one, too."

"Anything interesting in the shop?"

"No, sir, nothing unusual. There's some welding apparatus, big air compressor, boxes of tools, things like that."

"Roger," Ike mumbled. "Do the barn."

The lock yielded on his third attempt. I used to be better at this, he thought. The door swung open without a sound. Ike stepped in and searched the area for a surveillance camera. He saw none. He hoped he hadn't missed anything.

A cluttered panel with switches sat against the wall on a table that faced the bay. The identifying marks on it had all been taped over, but he felt sure it was foreign. He removed his camera and photographed the array. He pivoted and took in the rest of the room. A map of the United States was tacked to the wall behind the table. He photographed it. He pulled out a drawer in the table with the console and retrieved a rolled-up paper, thin paper. He spread it out on the edge of the table, and photographed it as well. He froze in place at the sound of footsteps on the gravel path. He quickly replaced the roll, closed the drawer and, moved to the hinge edge of the door so that he'd be behind it, and out of sight, when it opened. He held his breath and waited. If the guy came in and saw him, the game was up.

The door swung back. He heard annoyed muttering. A hand reached into the room and switched off the light. The door snapped shut and the bolt was thrown. He was locked in. He exhaled.

"Nothing in the barn either, Tiger Five. What now?"

"We go home now. Out."

Ike counted to twenty-five, unlocked the shed door and eased out into the darkness. He relocked the door and started toward the water.

"Everybody out," he said, "slow and easy."

He tripped and almost fell headlong into a clump of bushes. He glanced down at his feet and saw what he took to be a tree root. He stepped over it and then looked again. It was too smooth to be a root. He reached down and ran his hand along its length. A sheathed cable that ran from the shed toward the water. He tried to follow it but the underbrush was too thick. He gave up and resumed his trek back to the Zodiac.

"Tiger One on base."

"Tiger Two and Three in, too."

Where are you Four and Six?"

"Four here. I'm about thirty yards out. No sweat."

"Six?"

No answer. Ike made it to the bulkhead and counted noses. Five accounted for.

"Hold your position. I'm going back for Six," he said. "If I'm not back in ten, pull out. It will mean we took another bus home."

The four men looked at each other uneasily. "That's an order. Charlie, are you monitoring this?" Charlie, back at the marina, answered he was. "Okay, give me ten and then blow."

Ike headed back toward the house. At the porch steps he saw Six who held up his hands for Ike to be silent. Enough light filtered through the window next to him for Ike to see the listening device he'd attached to a pane in the corner. Ike held out his hand with five fingers spread. Five minutes.

The agent nodded, detached the device, crept low past the window, and the two men quick-stepped to the boat. The other four were in and casting off when they clambered down the stones and joined them.

In silence they motored to the PBR, and once aboard, sped away to the marina.

They had not located the Sunburns, and Ike started to worry. Tomorrow would be two days down. Only three to go.

Chapter Forty-seven

There was no time to debrief before Charlie, Ike, and Clark Benson, the Arabic expert, boarded the chopper back to Langley. Ike checked the images on his camera, and Benson occupied himself in listening to the tape-recording of the conversations he'd recorded at the house. Charlie looked glum. They landed and hustled back to the conference room. A clutter of papers, photographs, and maps spilled out over the table and onto the floor. Ike thought he'd seen better organized landfills, and he would be the last person anyone would ask to organize a desk. The director waited for them.

"I gather you do not have any good news for me," he said.

"Nothing yet. I still think we should have had radiation sensors, a Geiger counter, anything."

"Ike, we've been over that. No nukes are missing."

"They'd be warheads, Charlie. They might have been riding along with the Sunburns for years. You couldn't possibly know—"

"Okay. We'll send in someone, do a fly-over."

"Get them to us. We're going back, Charlie."

"But we don't have anything."

Benson held up his hand. "It wasn't a complete bust. I have some recorded conversation that is suggestive, and with some time to review and translate it, may give us a lead on the other sites or targets."

"Get on it, then. It may be 3:00 AM, but we haven't time to take any R and R. Charlie, there are a pile of papers on your desk you need to sort through. Ike, what do you have for me?"

Charlie left to retrieve his documents, and Benson put his ear buds in place and began listening to his tape. From time to time he scratched notes in a small notebook.

"Some pictures and an idea." Ike opened his camera and ran through the series of shots of the console map and the rolled paper. "I'll need those blown up."

The director motioned for a young intern to take Ike's camera.

"Get these processed ASAP, Bob, and hustle back here. Okay, Ike, what's your idea?"

"Wait for the pictures to be analyzed. I tripped over a cable in the woods near that shed." Ike pointed to the blow-up. "It seemed to run toward the water. Then, over here," he indicated a second point on the photo, "is a large tank. It's too big to be propane, although I guess it could be, but it's rather far from the house for that."

"And all that means what, exactly?"

Charlie bounced into the room with sheets of paper.

"In a minute, Director. Charlie, the four ships?"

"We have them. They are, names liberally translated, the Sword of God, we know about that one; the *Allahu Akbar*, God is Great; the *Youmud Deen*, Day of Judgment; and the *Alhumdeullah*, Praise be to God. Who'd have thought anything that sounds so lilting in Arabic could be so lethal?"

"Do we know where they are?"

"Not yet, but we do have photographs. Three are old freight-ers like the *Saifullah;* the fourth, *Allahu Akbar*, is a small tanker. The geeks in the satellite surveillance unit say they are good enough for us to get a pattern recognition program set up. We have the Littoral Scan System running dawn to dusk on all our coastlines. If they get within one hundred miles of our shores, we'll know it." Charlie looked pleased.

"Director, can you contact the Navy and put submarines on alert? If they get anywhere near us, we should simply sink them."

"They're not going to like it, but I'll give it a go."

"Tell them about the Sunburns and that one of those ships is responsible for the death of an Academy grad. The Navy is funny about their own."

The messenger, Bob, returned with the developed photos and spread them out on the table. Benson took the buds from his ears and joined them. "That's Arabic," he said pointing to the photo of the rolled document Ike had taken from the drawer.

"What's it say?"

"This is good. The conversation I recorded was mostly about how unhappy these guys are here. The food is bad, blah, blah, blah, and they think the restaurant is serving them pork in their burgers. But then there is a mention to something called 'Choker' and they start sounding, I don't know, pumped."

"And this is related to this document how?" Ike felt his heart beat quicken. He had it.

"This word at the top of this thing, قنتخمل, is *choker*. The other glyphs are the names of the ships Charlie just discovered."

The director studied the document for a moment. "What the hell is all this to do with anything? So, *Choker*, ship names. Now what?"

"Bob," Ike said, "Go back and have these two pictures developed the exact same size. This one," he held out the latter document, "have them print up on transparency film. And hurry."

"What are you up to, Ike?" the director said.

"Charlie, get that SEAL team and that DNR boat back to the marina. Tell the SEALs to bring some UEDs, a bunch of them."

"A bunch of UEDs?"

"Underwater explosive devices. Yes, a bunch. What time is it?"

"Four AM."

"Too early to call Bunky."

"What..."

"You'll see. Where's Bob?"

"Ike, this had better be good," the director muttered.

"Or what, Director? You can't fire me. I don't work here any more. And you're going to like this. Have you called the Navy?"

"At four in the morning? Not likely."

"Call them. Call them now. We have three days to shut this down. Tomorrow we can spike at least one of those missiles, I hope, but the other five…" his voice trailed off.

"The other five?"

"I'm assuming your guys were right that six Sunburns have gone missing. If I'm right, I know where at least one of them is. That means the others are aboard those ships. While you worry about disturbing the beauty rest of the chief of Naval Operations, they are heading toward their targets. The Navy is the only outfit that can effectively stop the ships."

"We don't know where they are and won't until they come into view on the satellites, assuming the pattern recon works."

"We'll narrow it down in a minute."

"How?"

"That document you all saw with the Arabic script was on thin paper. I didn't see the significance at the time but, tracing paper, Director. It was tracing paper. The map on the wall is of the United States. The first has to be an overlay for it. When Bob gets back we'll know for sure. Where the hell is he? We will put one on the other and know where the ships are headed and their probable or potential targets."

Chapter Forty-eight

Ike stared at the photograph of the console, or panel, he'd seen in the shed. "Charlie, what else did those people buy from the Indian salvagers?"

Charlie shuffled through the pile of papers on the table, extracted one, and read, "Miscellaneous hardware thought to have come from a decommissioned Chinese corvette which included large, ten meter long tubes and cables...ah...an instrument panel, also from the corvette."

"That was very careless of them."

"Who?"

"The Chinese. You'd think they'd want to scrap weaponry hardware themselves."

"Maybe they didn't think the Indians would notice."

"Are you kidding? India is on their border and is developing, or has developed, missile capabilities as well."

"What exactly do you think they let go?"

The director re-entered the room. "I talked to the Navy. As I predicted, they are not happy. They said they will put submarines at the ready at 0500 and will wait to hear from us. If we're wrong on this—"

"You mean, if I'm wrong—"

"I said we, I meant *we*, Ike. So what do you have now?"

Bob came in with the two newly developed sheets. Ike laid the clear plastic over the map blow-up.

"There you are boys and girls, your ship positions and, by inference, your possible targets."

The men leaned over the table and looked. The overlay showed the ships in four predictable locations and an oval circled Washington, D.C.

"Okay, now you know where to dispatch the submarines and, as a back-up, put an antimissile team on alert. The damned things will be coming in from the sea and low to the surface from one or all of these points, so it should be easy."

"You are taking a lot for granted, Ike." The director looked disturbed.

"What's our alternative, sir? If we're wrong on the date, no big deal as long as it isn't moved forward. If we're wrong about location, the havoc that will ensue will be so great, no one will care about how we missed the boat, no pun intended, until later when the pooh-bahs in Congress begin posturing and finger pointing. And if the strikes are really successful…well, we're up the proverbial creek anyway."

"I'll call the Navy back."

"What now?" Charlie asked.

"What does this array remind you of?"

"You mean the console thing?"

"Yes."

"I saw something like that twenty years ago. We had pictures of the Russian boomer we raised from the ocean. It was part of the… oh, shit. It was part of the launch system for their missiles."

"It wasn't exactly like this, but close enough."

"I'll pull back the SEALs and dispatch the boat." He moved to the door and then paused. "But in broad daylight? They'll see us and push the button."

"Throw the switch, you mean. That's what Bunky's for. We didn't need him last night, but today, he and his friends will come out to harass us as Department of Natural Resources personnel. They will stay between us and that duck blind and cover the SEAL team's entrance into the water."

"To do what? I don't get it."

"Patience, Charlie, patience."

The director put down the phone and turned to Ike. "I've called in a lot of markers, Ike. Let's hope this is for real."

"Unless one of you has a better idea, it's all we've got right now. We'll know more this afternoon."

"We have one submarine cruising off Guantánamo that's being ordered into the Caribbean off Galveston. It will be there tomorrow—maybe. Two more have been diverted from their return to Bangor, Washington, and sent to the San Diego and L.A. area. And the fourth will sail from Groton, Connecticut, for New York City. They will be in position on time, assuming we have that right. Yom Kippur? You're sure about that?"

"It's a calculated guess, boss. What can I say?"

"I hope you're right. The Navy has also put its entire fleet on high alert in case we're off on the targets. They will try to form a necklace around the country by Wednesday with the antiship missile systems up and running."

"It has to be sooner, but I like the imagery of a necklace to stop a choker."

<>　<>　<>

By eleven they had moved their base of operations from Langley to the Holiday Inn Express on Kent Island. The fake DNR boat had returned to the marina, and the SEALs were back. Ike filled them in on what they'd learned and what he expected to find in the water near the property they'd searched the night before. The SEALs nodded. They placed the five UEDs on the floor of the room and explained to Ike how they would be detonated. Remote, they said, would be risky. The best would be to feed a wire back to the boat and attach a hand detonator to it. Ike didn't like the thought of having to stay out in the bay for hours, maybe overnight. Someone could tumble to them.

"We could borrow a sailboat, sail in, and anchor. Then we transfer the detonator to it. There are a dozens of sailboats on the bay on any given day." Charlie said. He seemed enthusiastic, and Ike thought the idea had merit. More than merit: it would work.

"Okay, Charlie, get us a sailboat and some sailors. You can't have these...," he waved toward the SEALs, "they're going to be hunting for me."

"I will sail the boat."

"Director says you're to stay dark. He needs you in place and this could ruin that. By the way, guys," he said to the SEALs, "you didn't hear any of this."

"I am a well known and acknowledged bay sailor, Ike. I used to own an eighteen-footer and raced it out of Annapolis all the time. Everyone on station knows that. I'm going sailing."

"We'll look for you about 1200 hours or a little later. Take a radio and tack around or whatever you sailors do to pass the time, until we call."

"Just so I don't sound like a complete idiot when the director asks me what you were doing when you blew yourself up—what *are* you doing?"

"These fine gentlemen are going to swim to the duck blind where, unless I am suffering from early dementia, they will find some of that hardware removed from the Chinese corvette, specifically, a launch tube, and...they will use the radiation sensor to tell us if the damn thing is hot."

"Can't be."

"Maybe yes, maybe no. You want to take the chance? And when they find it, they will affix these handy-dandy devices, feed the wire back to you, and you get to blow up a Sunburn when the time comes."

"If they're hot? Blowing them up could be a problem."

"You said they weren't, and anyway they won't have the warhead armed. Perhaps not even in place. They'll wait to do that just before the shoot."

"You hope. And when would that be?"

"As soon as we know the ships with the rest of the damned things are under the waves, we bust this one."

"And if we're wrong?"

"You lose your pension. Mine's from Picketsville, and unless the town is funding the plan with bad mortgages, I'm good to go."

"Ike, there's a problem with the launch mechanism."

Chapter Forty-nine

"What's the problem?"

"They can't launch underwater. Sunburns are air breathers. They have to dry launch."

"Then they've figured out a way to keep them dry, Charlie. They bought launching tubes from a ship. That we know. There's that air compressor and tank. At least one of those tubes is in the water and in compressed air sufficient to keep it dry."

"And maybe the launchers are on the four ships. It would make more sense to mount them in the freighter's hold."

"I hate having to second-guess all the time. Can't your intel people get us some hard data?"

"We're trying, Ike. The problem is we don't have many friends in the area any more, and the ones we do have are given to circumlocutions lately, like they think maybe we aren't going to win and they need to keep an appearance of neutrality."

"Or are playing both sides against the middle. Well, we know our pals across the bay have something. We scoured the place over there and turned up nothing. We have photographs taken over time. Where else could it be? I can't think of any other way, Charlie."

"Okay, but I have a really bad feeling about this."

"Right, but I have no reasonable alternative. Somehow they must have rigged the things to launch from the water. They have a serviceable console and there is a cable running from that shed toward the bay; there is a big tank and an air compressor. It has to be."

"I don't know."

"Neither do I, but without the option of an alternative, we go with the best guess. Go find your sailboat. You will need to be in place as soon as my guys return. Bunky can't keep up the pretense forever."

"I guess we have nothing else to do, but…"

"I know, I know…it isn't clean and I'm missing something important but…"

Charlie left the room to rent a sailboat. Ike studied the series of satellite blow-ups again. What was he missing? Charlie had it right. This batch of obsolete Sunburns were air breathers.

The director called.

"Where are we, Ike?

"We're almost ready to push off. Charlie went to find a boat to sail, and the SEALs are suiting up. Bunky is standing by. I had to promise him a new boat, by the way. Charlie said he'd get him one anyway, so all I did was spoil the surprise."

"I would like a little reassurance, Ike."

"Wouldn't we all. Look, I've spent the last twenty hours or so going over it again and again. I've studied the satellite films. It's the best I can do. If you start with July the fourth as a moonless night, which we know it was, and count back twenty-eight days, the *Saifullah* is in the channel every time, every twenty-eight days starting in May. That ship arrived on moonless nights because that would be the only time it could pull anchor, slip into Eastern Bay, and off-load materiel with any hope of not being detected."

"Do you suppose in all that time, no one saw it? That seems a stretch."

"Watermen might have, but they are so teed off with the government in general and the Chesapeake Bay authorities in particular, they might have decided not to bother reporting it. I don't think there's a law that says a ship can't enter the bay. It's just unusual—rare. And I think at least two people did see the ship and might have reported it if they had lived."

"Who?"

"The couple on a sailboat, the *OPM*, were known to have been in the bay on the fourth, but were found murdered and adrift off Hampton Roads two days later. Charlie has the details."

"What's Charlie doing with a sailboat?"

"I have to go, sir. I'll chat later. It's enough to know we need him in one today."

"I want your radio frequencies, and I want to be kept in the loop. I'll ask Charlie myself. Now get going."

A wind blowing up the bay from the south had raised a chop. Whitecaps punctuated the surface, and the little motor launch, with its Maryland Department of Natural Resources logo, rocked and pitched as it chugged out of the marina and into the rough water.

Ike wiped the spray from his face and scanned the east shore for evidence of Bunky Crispins and his friends. It had taken some persuasion to obtain his cooperation. Bunky had not been called on the previous night and waited until early morning before calling off his friends. But the possibility of a new boat finally swung him around.

Once in position, the crew waited for the watermen to arrive. They went through the motions of taking samples from the bay. Ike stood inside the boat's small cabin with binoculars trained on the shore opposite. He could make out a solitary figure standing just into the tree line. From time to time he spoke into a mike on his shoulder. They were watching.

Bunky and his gang arrived, and the SEALs went over the side. Ike held his breath. In ten minutes, he'd know, and they would have the Sunburn spiked.

"Tiger Five, this is One. We have a problem."

"Tiger One, go."

"We are directly under the duck blind. There is no bottom here."

"What?"

"I can't be sure, but the water under it must be at least twenty, thirty feet deep."

"Move in shore a bit."

"Fine, there is a steep shelf here and now we're looking at mud."

"The tube may be buried up to its top. Look for something resembling a hatch."

"Roger that."

The radio reverted to static. Occasionally Ike thought he could make out a grunt. Bunky waved to him and pointed toward the shore. The rented yacht, with "Watermen Rock" still scrawled across its waterline, rounded the head and turned toward the duck blind.

"Tiger One, heads up. There is a yacht headed your way. Be careful. If they suspect you're down there, there could be trouble."

"Roger, Five. We'll pull back ten yards and wait."

Ike watched as the yacht hove to and dropped anchor. Once the anchor set, the crew moved aft and began setting up some sort of apparatus.

"Director, are you on line?"

"I'm here."

"The sons of bitches are setting up a television camera. They're going to record the shoot."

"Got it. If they are doing it here, they'll be doing it in DC as well. I'll have Homeland Security alerted. They'll start looking for the other crew on the ground."

"Good luck with that."

"Tiger One, where are you?"

"We are searching. With that boat on top of us, we can't go into the shallows. So far, no tubes, no hatches, *nada*. The water is really deep here, Five. The duck blind is resting on stilts that have to be twenty feet long."

"Keep looking."

What kind of shooting platform teetered on stilts that long? And why build one over deep water?

"Ike, this is Charlie. I have you in sight. You want me in?"

"Keep tacking."

"Five, this is One. We are out of options here. There is nothing in sight. We've searched the bottom from one end of the property shore to the other. We're sorry. There's nothing."

There had to be. There was no other explanation.

"Any radiation?"

"Maybe a little. Some, yes...It's not clear. Something in the area is emitting, but I can't say from where. It's pretty weak. This bottom has been stirred up a lot. It could be background."

"Okay, pull back."

"We thought we'd make a deposit, if you don't mind."

"A deposit?"

"It doesn't make sense to drag these explosive devices all the way back. We thought we might leave them here...under the keel of this yacht."

"I didn't hear that. You can sail in, Charlie, you have some work to do."

Chapter Fifty

Ike slumped back in the thwart and banged his fist on the gunwale. Where had he gone wrong?

"Ike?"

"Yes, Director, I'm here."

"Status?"

"We're in the toilet at this end. If the submarines can take out the four ships we can, at least, minimize this disaster. But five will get you ten this one is aimed right at the Capitol, and I can't find it."

"The Navy is getting some flak from the White House about sinking a neutral merchant ship in international waters."

"You're kidding me."

"I wish I were. Look, the whole operation got off track from the beginning. The CIA had no business messing with a local jurisdiction and—"

"I told you that from the start. Didn't I, Charlie?"

"It didn't start out as anything remotely connected to terrorist attempts at—"

"Doesn't matter, Ike, Charlie, it's where we are now that matters. We have been deemed to be off the reservation."

"Hell, I thought that's why you dragged me in here. To give you deniability—"

"That was the plan, but the President's Chief of Staff, Jack Barksdale, is out of sorts, and he has friends in Homeland Security."

"Good for him. Ask him if he has friends in the undertaking business, because if he screws this up he'll need them."

"Okay, okay. Cool down. We're clear to move but only if we can show something solid and we accept FBI operational control."

"And they will be here when?"

"They are on their way."

"Anything else?"

"He says he needs to be absolutely sure. In the meantime, the FBI and Homeland Security want to start their own investigation."

"Tell them you're sorry, but it's too late."

"It's only too late if we have the wrong date. Even so, they still have two days."

"One day."

"I thought you said Wednesday, Yom Kippur is Wednesday."

"Another slippage in my haphazard reckoning, I'm afraid. Technically, it starts thirty minutes before sundown, or in this case about 6:30 PM, on Tuesday. These lunatics will launch the damned things as soon as they can, and at night. Remember, it will be daylight in Israel and most everywhere else they have eager spectators."

"You mean...Jesus. I'll go see the President."

"Take Charlie with you. He's from Charm City, he can turn on some of that old Baltimore schmooze."

"I heard that."

"Didn't you tell me once you knew the President?"

"I met him back when he was the governor. I knew his sister better."

"There, you see, Director, Charlie's your man."

"Can it, you two. Tell me what has to be done."

"First, show him the map of the ship locations we found. Then, throw the FBI a bone to keep them busy. I can't wait around here to bring them up to speed. Have someone else do it. Get Fugarelli out of bed. We have what's left of today and tomorrow to find and spike the Sunburn, take pictures that we can download to the idiots in the White House, and hope they nod their heads up and down before they get their asses blown to kingdom come."

"Can you do it?"

"No."

"Ike…"

"We can try."

Ike turned to the two SEALs, still in their wetsuits.

"Are you willing to go in again?"

"Hoo, yah."

"Okay, here's what I want you to do…"

◇◇◇

The crew on the yacht waved away the boat with Bunky and his friends. Bunky ignored him and pulled alongside. The altercation had to last at least fifteen minutes, Ike had said. Bunky said he'd stay all day if these were the sons-of-a-buck that burned up the *J. Millard Tawes*. Ike assured him they were. The crew and the watermen had at it for nearly an hour. When it became clear that Bunky and friends were not going to leave them alone, and in the presence of an official Department of Natural Resources boat, they hauled anchor and left.

By that time the SEAL team had returned to the area of the duck blind. Bunky's friends and some more workboats filled the area between it and the shore. Bunky lowered Ike's metal detector over the side and let the craft drift across the property face. The men in the water waited. Each time Bunky got a reading, he dropped a crab pot over and the SEALs swam to it and began to poke through the mud.

On the first pass, they uncovered three tire rims and the radiator from a 1951 Nash Rambler. The rims had been filled with concrete and had once served as mooring anchors. It was unclear how the radiator found its way into the bay.

Bunky moved closer to shore. That drew the guard from the trees. The watermen immediately took up their complaints with him about the ruined crabbing bed. Ike got him in focus and took his picture.

"Tiger Five, sorry, *nada*. We have some suspicious depressions in the area and that low-level radiation, but nothing else."

"Roger that. Bunky, as soon as the SEALs clear out, you do, too."

"Aw, Ike, can't we stay and do something to these dad-burned jerks?"

"Clear out. Now."

◇◇◇

"Any luck, Ike?"

"Director, we're dead in the water. I know the missiles are here somewhere, but for the life of me, I don't know where."

"You said, they. There is more than one?"

"Yes, sir, I think so. If your people were correct in their assessment that six missiles are missing, that would mean two are squirreled away here, and one each on the ships."

"I'm going in to see the President now. What can I tell him?"

"If he wants to keep from having another nine-eleven, he should suck them up and let us do what we have to do; that would include sinking the ships."

"Barksdale thinks we should board and inspect them."

"Then Barksdale is an idiot. These are the same people that gave the world suicide bombers. Does he really think they will even stop, much less meekly turn their ship over for inspection? They will run straight in, open their holds and launch."

"What do you do now? I need to tell the President something."

"You might suggest he remove himself to the Blue Ridge Mountains, or Camp David, or wherever you all stash the President nowadays when the rest of the world is going up in flames. Maybe he can figure out a way to keep those missiles from launching without letting the people whose finger is on the button know what we have. And good luck with that, too."

"I'm only interested in your end. Do you have a plan?"

"Not yet, I'm missing something important. It's right under my nose and I can't see it."

"I need something substantive."

"Do you think we could call in an air strike, maybe put a Predator over that farm?"

"You're crazy. An air strike on the continental United States? No way."

"Then I'll have to think of something else. Have fun with the President."

Chapter Fifty-one

The two SEALs dried off in the motel room while Ike uploaded to Langley the pictures he'd taken of the men on the yacht and on the shore. He turned his attention to the blow-ups of the land. He traced a line from the shed to the area in the water where he'd thought the submerged missiles were.

"Sailor," he said, "What do you make of these pictures? By the way, what are your names?"

"I'm Constantine Papadopoulos—they call me Connie—and this here is Whaite Hungerford."

"I had a deputy once named Whaite. Good man."

"Where's he now, sir?"

"Please don't call me sir. The name's Ike. Whaite died, LOD, last winter. Some moron ran him off the road in a snowstorm. Left a wife and kids." He pointed to the stack of photographs. "Either of you see anything?"

"Jesus, those are satellite pictures of the place we were just at. You guys took all of them?"

"Littoral, that's coastline, Surveillance Scan—photos taken by a satellite in synchronous orbit over this area."

The two SEALs spread the pictures across the two twin beds and studied them. Ike had arranged them in rough chronological order. Charlie knocked and entered.

"Why aren't you on your sailboat?"

"Ike, it's getting cold out there, and besides, there is nothing for me to do. I took the dinghy and rowed ashore. Right now,

I'm beat and plan to take a nap. What are all these pictures doing on the bed?"

"No nap. We are in a mess. Time is ticking away. The movers and shakers in Washington think we're nuts and are about to precipitate an international incident, and I am—"

"Getting grumpy, but that's nothing new. So, what can we do we have not already done?"

"We need to find the Sunburn or Sunburns. Help us out. Study these pictures and tell me what I'm missing. If the launchers are not in the water, where are they?"

The four men sifted through the pictures.

"I have a question, Ike. What is that duck blind doing over deep water? I mean don't they put them in the shallows and shoot over the feeding grounds? This blind ain't worth the money it took to build."

Ike nodded. "I've wondered about that, too. What they have done, I think, is dredge a channel for the *Saifullah*. When they were done with that end of the operation, they stuck that blind in the channel to make us think the water was shallow and cover their tracks."

"Come winter, that thing will wash away."

"The least of their worries. They'll be long gone."

The group turned their attention back to the photographs.

"This place used to be a farm, didn't it? We saw that tractor in the barn."

Charlie nodded. "Yes. I believe it originally included the acreage across the road, but when the place was sold, the house and ten acres were split off. The owners, who held it before our friends bought it, used it for hunting and fishing. Why do you ask?"

Connie waved a photo around, "I was wondering where the silo was at. I always thought farms had, you know, silos."

"Not all. Only the ones that feed cows, dairy farms or farms with a small herd, beef operations, like that. Horse farms, farms that deal strictly in harvested crops might not."

"How come you know all this stuff, Charlie? I never figured you for a country boy. You should move down to the valley with me. On second thought, don't. You cause me enough trouble right where you are."

"Thank you for that vote of confidence. My grandparents had a farm near the Pennsylvania line. When I was small, I would visit them in the summer."

Ike slapped his hand on the table. "Silo," he said. "Silos. That's it. Somewhere out in the wilds of Wyoming or wherever, there are silos. Not the kind filled with molasses covered, chopped alfalfa, but ICBMs. Missile silos."

"Yes, so?"

"They must have built a silo for the Sunburn, don't you see?"

"Ike you all scoured that place. True, it was dark, but you would have found something as big as a missile silo."

"Maybe. Charlie, call your pals back at the store and have them download all the surveillance for the last year again, to our computer."

"You don't have enough memory on this hard drive to do that, Ike."

"Then tell them to make us a new, complete set and fly them here ASAP. In the meantime we'll have to make do with what we have."

◇◇◇

By late afternoon several thousand photographs had been delivered and sat in stacks on the table, the chairs, the beds, and the floor.

"You wanted them, you got them," Charlie said. "Now what."

"We're looking for a pretty big excavation to appear and then disappear. First let's eliminate things we don't want to waste time with, and then concentrate on the possibilities. For example, we assume the *Saifullah* arrived every twenty-eight days, and we can date those arrivals, forward and backward, from the Fourth of July. Since we know the missile was off-loaded on the Fourth of July, whatever accommodation needed to be made for them had to have been completed by then. We should go back from there. I'm guessing they dug a hole somewhere. It would have to be deep and wide so that there could be a system for venting the gasses produced at launch."

Charlie picked up a stack and dropped it into the trashcan. "These are all post-Fourth of July."

"The area is largely wooded except for here," Ike put a finger on the clear area bordering the bay. "I don't think they would have tried to dig in the woods. But if they did, they'd have to cut down trees, and that should be obvious."

They sat in silence and slowly turned over pictures. Connie got up and called for room service to send up a pot of coffee and sandwiches. When it arrived, the aroma of the coffee and the food brightened their spirits somewhat.

"I don't have anything," Charlie announced, and reassembled the stack at his feet.

"They were doing some dredging and built a bulkhead, is that right?" Connie asked.

"Yeah. They had a permit to create a channel for a boat slip. They started to build the dock. You can see it, here next to the bulkhead, but didn't finish it."

"I remember the dock from last night. It's pretty rickety, if you ask me. Big son-of a-bitch, isn't it?"

"Now that you mention it, it is. You'd expect it to be narrow across the face of the bulkhead and then send an arm out into the water."

"I remember walking across it and it, like, wobbled. You'd think they would have secured it to the ground with four by fours set in concrete. That's the way you build a deck. Anyway, the reason I asked about the dredging is because there is something screwy about this bit."

"Where?"

"Well, look. If I didn't know better, I'd swear they were dredging on the wrong side of the bulkhead in this picture and about a dozen after that. See, the hose that's on the removal end of the pump is back behind the stones of the wall."

Ike studied the sequence of shots. "You're right. They are not filling in that area. They are making it deeper."

"There's something else. The next day the hole is gone, filled up or something."

The pictures beyond that showed a smooth surface, as if the ground had been filled and leveled.

"That's got to be it. The wooden platform is not fixed to four by fours because they want it to be moveable. The damned things are underneath it."

Charlie, frowning, waved a picture at Ike. "But this picture shows the ground as filled in."

Ike took the picture and squinted. "Connie, Whaite, you have younger eyes. Is that a line marking the area?"

The two men stared at the photo. "Yep. Looks like a tarp, like maybe they pulled it across and covered the edges with dirt."

The phone rang.

Chapter Fifty-two

"I'm guessing that's the director of the CIA and that he does not have good news for us from his visit to the White House. Either way, I don't think I want to hear it," Ike said. "Connie, you answer and take a message. Charlie and I are not here."

Constantine Papadopoulos picked up. "Hello." Ike could just make out the director's voice but not what was said. "No, sir, they're not here. No, sir, I don't know when they'll be back." Connie winked at Ike. "Yes, sir…yes, sir…I understand, sir. I'll tell him as soon as he returns."

"What's the bad news, Connie?"

"Well, it's pretty much what you'd expected, I guess. He said you, we, were to stand down. You're to wait for some FBI guys to get here, bring them up to speed, and then do whatever they ask you to do. They'll be here tomorrow morning early."

"That's it?"

"No, something else, but it didn't quite fit the rest. He did say you were to use the Paris protocol, whatever that means."

"He said Paris, you're sure of that?"

"Paris. Yes, he said Paris. Does that mean something to you?"

"Oh, yeah. Charlie, it's Paris."

"Lord, love a duck."

"Does anyone know what happened to the ATF's fancy black PBR?"

"It's still in the marina, but I think the crew is gone." Charlie said. "I'm afraid to ask, but why?"

"In a minute. I have to make a call and I need an untraceable phone. Hold the fort and order us up some more food."

Ike left the motel room and searched for a pay phone, a relative rarity in an age of ubiquitous cell phones. But fortunately, motels cling to a service standard that includes the possibility that a guest may not have succumbed to the brave new world of electronic excess.

After he conned the desk clerk out of a dollar's worth of change, he called Bunky, who was less than happy to hear from him again. However, when he heard what Ike had in mind and that he would be thumbing his nose at the government, he jumped at the chance.

"I'll be there, you bet. You want I should bring some of the boys with me?"

"Not this time. See you at nine."

Back at the room, he faced the two hard-eyed SEALs.

"Charlie here says the Paris Protocol refers to a time in the past when, in spite of direct orders, you went ahead and did what you thought was right at the time. It turned out all right and so, after chewing you out pretty good, you got a commendation. Is that it?"

"Pretty much."

"So he's saying you should do what you think needs to be done in this case, but he won't support you if you fail."

"In a nutshell, that's it. Now, I can't do this alone. I need help. I don't draw my paycheck from Uncle, but you three do, so, I can't expect you to risk unemployment and your retirement benefits for a loose cannon like me, but…"

"I don't know about Connie," Whaite said, "but I didn't join the SEALs for their retirement benefits. I'm game. You have a plan, I take it."

"If I understand the threat to the country we're looking at right…well, count me in." Connie added. Charlie sighed and nodded his agreement, too.

"Okay. We need to stay out of sight and out of touch until nine, sorry, twenty-one hundred hours."

At eight-thirty, clouds swept in from the northeast to cover their activities once again. Ike thanked whatever deity might be responsible for darkness. At nine, Bunky met them on the pier. Somewhere he'd conjured up what he supposed must be appropriate covert action attire: black coveralls, watch cap, and burnt cork on his face. To be fair, the two SEALs, Charlie, and Ike looked similar. The only real difference being the professional touches of grease paint and the gadgetry festooned to the belts about their waists.

"Bunky, can you get us out of here?" Ike asked.

"You got the key to this beauty?" Bunky grinned.

Ike turned and looked inquiringly at the others. The all shook their heads. Not a good start.

"No, I guess not."

"No problem. There's a trick to unbuttoning these old boats." He stepped over the side. "Just be a second."

Bunky had his back turned so Ike could not see what he did or how he managed do it, but within minutes, they were aboard, the engine humming, orders barked to the two sailors to cast off, and with Captain Crispins at the helm.

◇◇◇

The prow of the boat bumped gently against the muddy beach. They put ashore downwind from the property, just beyond the stone bulkhead. Night-vision goggles in place, they worked their way carefully along the shoreline, toward the decking that they assumed formed the cover of the silo holding one or more Sunburns. He ordered Bunky offshore, ten yards or so, and told him to hold that position until he saw their signal. Then he was to come in and evacuate them.

If the guard were in position, they would have their work cut out for them. The best they could do, if that were the case, is silence him, spike the missiles, and hope enough time would pass before the rest of the people on shore discovered it for them to call home and have the ships at sea take out the freighters and their deadly cargo.

Like the clouds overhead, the four men drifted along the shoreline. At the bulkhead, they paused and scanned the trees for guards. None in sight. They sidled forward, keeping low and moving with the shadows. At the deck they paused. Ike leaned over and attempted to lift it. It didn't budge. All four of them managed only to move it forward a few inches.

"We've got to get this thing shifted," Ike murmured.

"Not going to happen," Charlie gasped. Ike would have mentioned how too much time at his desk had cost him a step, but that would have to be later.

"Maybe we can lever up an edge," Whaite said, "and then one of us can slip under and take a peek."

Ike couldn't think of a better idea, and he worried that the guard might appear at anytime. "Okay, you three lever it up and I'll slip in."

"Ike, with respect, but either me or Connie should do it. Like, we're sort of used to this stuff and…"

"Whaite, you'd be better, faster, and all that, but I'm expendable, none of the rest of you are. Now find me a lever."

The SEALs hesitated.

"He's right," Charlie said quietly. "Let's get him in and out quick."

It took a moment, but Connie, who'd disappeared into the night, returned with a long four-by-four. Ike paced the deck slowly and then pointed to the westernmost corner.

"Lift here."

The board slipped under the edge, and the deck lifted enough for Ike to roll under. As he expected, there was ample room for him to crawl around after the deck dropped back in place. Somewhere to his left there should be a sharp drop off into the deep excavation holding the silos.

"Ike," Charlie rasped, "We have company."

"Drop out of sight, and wait." He heard the three men scuttle away toward the bay. He felt, more than heard, the booted footsteps as the guard paced across the deck. Ike held his breath and waited. If the guard decided to hold this post for any length of time, Ike would have a serious problem.

Chapter Fifty-three

The footsteps retreated to the other end of the decking. Ike rolled away from the edge. His fingers found the ridge of earth covering the tarp's edge. He paused and listened. Silence. The tarp's edge lifted easily. He slipped under it and rolled forward. Before he could stop himself, he slid down the rough earthen side of the excavation, sending a shower of damp soil and mud before him. He landed awkwardly in the pitch black. He waited, frozen in place, for a reaction, some sign that the guard above him might have heard something.

Ike had slipped the supersensitive dosimeter in the pocket of his jumpsuit. He checked to make sure it hadn't been damaged in the slide. He'd also hung a variety of utilities on a web belt about his waist.

"You look like Batman," Charlie had said. "Does that make me Robin?"

"No, you're the Joker."

He unclipped a penlight and risked a quick scan of the canvas above him. There did not appear to be a gap. The tarpaulin, he knew, was heavy and would not show any light on the other side if it remained in place. He pivoted to inspect the area. He needed to attend to the missiles. He'd worry about the guard overhead later. He swung the light across the interior of the pit they'd seen in the photographs.

The area was a roughly oval hole perhaps fifteen feet deep and thirty feet across. It had not been lined, but some two-by-fours braced against plywood sheets buttressed the wall in a few places. Clods of earth had fallen here and there and built small piles in several locations. A rude, handcrafted ladder leaned against the far wall. In the center were two steel launching ramps, and on them were two Sunburns.

Ike checked the edges of the canvas again. Reassured that no light escaped, he tried the radio.

His voice barely above a whisper, he said, "Charlie, can you hear me?"

The answer seemed staticy but clear. "We have you, Ike."

"You need to tell me where that guard is at all times."

"Roger that. He's still at the far end of the deck. What have you got?"

"I'm in the pit. There are two Sunburns down here on launchers they must have assembled in place." Ike slowly swung the light beam back and forth and searched the floor and the missiles.

"An umbilical runs from each of them and is gathered into a single cable that exits the pit toward the shed. I'm certain it's the same one I tripped over when we inspected the property."

"The guard's coming back. Out."

Ike released the talk key and continued his inspection of the pit and its contents. If he could do it somehow, his job was to disable the hardware in a way as to make it appear as though a failure to fire was accidental.

On the bay side of the pit, the terrorists had dug a two-foot-deep trench and fitted it with a commercial sump pump, complete with a float on a long metal arm that triggered the pump when it rose to a certain level—like a toilet tank only in reverse. Since the pit had been built below the water table, water seeped in from all sides, especially toward the bay, at a slow but regular rate. As he turned back to the pump, it turned on and pumped several gallons up through a white plastic pipe that exited the pit below the topmost edge. It must dump into the bay through the bulkhead.

"He's gone again, Ike. What do you need?"

"In a while I will need a way to get out of here, but for now, have one of the SEALs sidle across the bulkhead to a position somewhere between…" he checked the roof again and made a quick calculation, "…ten to twelve feet from the end of the deck. When he's there let me know."

Ike waited for what seemed an eternity.

"Sorry to hold you up, but our friend came back. Connie had to sink to his eyebrows to stay hidden. Okay, he's there."

"I've found a pump here that keeps this place relatively dry. Tell him to feel for water spurting from the wall somewhere in the area."

"Ike, I can hear you," Connie said softly.

Ike had been holding the float arm down to let water fill the sump. He released it and the pump kicked on.

"Got it."

"Is there a flutter valve on the end, that lets the pumped water out, but keeps the bay water from pouring in?"

"Hang on, I've got to move some stones…Whoa…Wait, got to hide."

Ike swung the light across the floor. As he expected, there were three sensors placed near the Sunburns, also employing a float device, this time on slides. The floats rose and closed a circuit at the top of the shaft to set off an alarm if the water level rose within a foot of the Sunburn's lower fins. If Ike were to only disable the pump and let the area flood, an alarm would send the men in the house there in seconds. First, he would have to cancel the sensors.

"I'm back, Ike. There is a valve. Not a very good one, but I guess it doesn't really matter. If water back flows to the pump, it will hold there until the next pumping cycle."

"Next question. Did you hear the pump when it ran?"

"No, but try it again."

Ike forced the pump.

"No can hear."

"Excellent. Jam that valve open, if you can. Then, while I fiddle around down here, why don't the three of you figure a way to get me out?"

"Roger that."

"I could help," Bunky cut in.

"Stay off the air, Bunky."

Ike pulled a roll of electrician's tape from the assortment of items fastened to his belt and taped the floats on the sensors in place. Then he plastered several layers of tape across the electrical contacts at the top of the slides, to insulate them. That would guarantee that if the floats overcame their restraints, no contact could be made and, at the same time, prevent a short circuit that might also trigger the alarm.

"I have the valve jammed."

"Is that outlet above or below the high water line?"

"Below, I can't be sure but it might be below the low tide line as well."

"Good, get back out of sight. Any idea how to draw off the guard?"

"Working on it."

Ike pulled the commando knife from its sheath on his "Batman belt" and carefully punched holes in the sump pump's float. Then he reversed the blade to its saw-toothed edge, and began to work on the plastic pipe that rose to an elbow and disappeared into the bay. He only wanted to create a leak that would augment the seepage from the ground water into the pit. After a few minutes he managed to produce a steady stream of water from the pipe.

To make sure the pump was completely disabled, he taped the float arm down as well. He made a quick survey of his handiwork, grabbed the ladder, and headed to the spot where he'd entered.

"Any luck up there? I'd rather not be in here when they discover their precious missiles are under fifteen feet of water."

"We have a problem up here, Ike. Sit tight."

Chapter Fifty-four

Ike repositioned the ladder, set the lower end firmly in the mud, and inspected the canvas above him.

"What's happening?" No answer.

He turned and made one last check of the area. The two Sunburns, their noses angled toward the Chesapeake Bay, seemed perversely elegant. They posed a threat to the country that could only be reckoned as incalculable, yet they sat there on their angled launchers, sleek and dangerous, like twin asps, ready to strike. He unclipped the digital camera and fired off a dozen shots of the missiles, the pit, and the pump apparatus. The sump had already overflowed and water had begun to seep across the dirt floor toward the launchers.

"Ike, we've moved off the bulkhead and into the bushes on the adjoining property."

"What happened?" Ike walked back to the Sunburns and busied himself with their aft fins.

"We were about to chance slipping the lever under the deck for you and just then the guard walked right at us. We thought the game was up. Then, there was this noise and he turned away. You know that tractor, the guys spotted in the barn? Well it's on its way down here."

"I'm coming up the ladder and will be at the edge of the deck in twenty seconds."

"Roger. Okay, the guard has left the deck and is walking over to the tractor. They have lights on so, no night vision left for any of them. Ike, hurry, we're putting in the lever now."

Ike scampered up the ladder and rolled out from under the canvas. He felt the edge of the deck, crawled out, and away toward the water.

"What'll I do with this lever?"

"Toss it in the bay. Let the tide take it away."

"Someone signal Bunky."

"Got it."

The bulky shape of the river boat loomed up and beached with a crunch. The four men climbed aboard.

"Let's go, Bunky. Chop, chop."

"You-all gonna have to get back to the stern. We're aground and you sittin' up front just pushes us deeper in the mud."

The men shifted sternward. Their combined weight lifted the bow free and Bunky eased the boat into the bay and turned for home.

The men sat silently, waiting for the adrenaline rush to subside and their breathing to return to normal. Finally Charlie broke the silence.

"What the devil were they doing with that tractor in the middle of the night?"

"I don't know if you noticed or not, but there's an eye bolt on the deck near where we were working. There will be another one at the other end. They are attaching cables to those bolts and the tractor. Tomorrow night or at dawn sometime they will drag the deck away, roll up the canvas, and set up their shoot. They can't do it in the daylight for fear someone will get curious. And they can't do it now, lest some fly-over spot those bad boys sitting in the excavation."

"Please tell me the shoot won't go as planned."

"Charlie, if you are correct about those things needing to dry launch, they won't."

"And if I'm wrong?"

"They will go up, then straight down into the Chesapeake Bay. I bent their guidance fins past repair."

Ike filled them in on the sabotage he'd performed on the pump and sensors. The SEALs gave him a high five. Charlie looked relieved. Bunky started to sing.

<>⟨⟩<>

The director of the CIA had positioned himself, Buddha-like, in a chair facing the door. They burst in, all smiles and roaring the last refrain of "There'll be a Hot Time in the Old Town Tonight." The director's expression brought this hilarity, born of nervous energy and relief, to a screeching halt.

Buddha-like in posture, volcanic in mien, the director pointed a finger at Charlie and, in a voice just short of yelling said, "Where the Hell have you been? I told you to stay put, and you Schwartz, were to stand down and wait for the FBI." He seemed ready to go on, but Ike interrupted him.

"Director, you also said Paris, remember? A few things you need to know before you blow a gasket, or start your ulcer bleeding again. One, Charlie went on this operation because we needed him. Same for Connie and Whaite. We had work to do and your buddies in the White House and the Joint Chiefs weren't bright enough, or gutsy enough, to give a nod in the right direction. If we'd waited for them…"

Ike paused and unfastened his belt. He dropped it on the table and removed the digital camera. He slid it across the table to the red-faced director.

"Two, you wanted absolute proof that what we believed was more than a supposition. There are photographs of the missiles in this. You can upload them to the pussies in the Whitehouse."

Ike worked his way into the bathroom and began removing his greasepaint.

"Three, unless those old Sunburns have been retrofitted to wet launch, they are not going anywhere and the guys doing the launching will assume the failure was accidental. At least they are not likely to stick around to find out otherwise."

He stripped off his wet jumpsuit and donned a pair of olive corduroy slacks, a biscuit-colored turtleneck sweater, and loafers.

"Four, the ball is now in your court. Now, what have *you* done in the last twelve hours to put the toothpaste back in the tube?" He tossed the dosimeter on the table next to the camera.

"I was close enough to the noses of both of those things to expose this. You can check it for radiation. If it's hot, you might want to rethink the idea of an air strike."

The director seemed nonplussed. He recovered. "Just a minute, Ike—"

"No, Mr. Director, no more minutes. We busted our asses for you tonight. We were getting nothing from you—*nada*, zilch. The country was about to go to Hell in a hand basket, and your people wanted to be reassured, for crying out loud. Also, unless you missed it the first three times, I don't work for you anymore and I have no desire to work for you in the future. So, if you have a complaint about my handling of this bit of business you can—"

Charlie stepped between the two men. "We're all a little tired and uptight. Let's back up a little. Director, the missiles here are dead in the water, figuratively and literally. But we do have something for the FBI. Is that right, Ike?"

"They can cordon off that property. The minute they hear that tractor start up, they need to grab every one of the bastards, before they can signal the rest of their friends, and take out the launch panel. If that yacht returns, it's a good bet they're planning to escape in it. Have a Coast Guard cutter standing by to haul them in."

The director swallowed. "You're right. We've all been too close to this and you are right, Washington has a lot to answer for. Okay, I'm sorry Ike. Do you really have the damned things out of commission?"

"As Charlie said, dead in fifteen feet of water."

Ike packed his small duffel and went to retrieve his toiletries from the bathroom.

"Well, on this end," the director said to group, "we have shifted the synchronous orbit of the Littoral Scan a few degrees. We have all four ships in view. At daybreak, we will zoom in. The minute they pop their holds open and we see the Sunburns, the Navy will sink them."

Ike patted his pockets and made a quick survey of the room. "Backup?"

"Ships nearby, radar locked in, antimissile systems up and running. If they happen to get one off, we'll shoot it down within a mile of launch."

Ike headed toward the door.

"Where do you think you're going?"

Ike stepped through the door into the night.

"Me? I'm going home for the holidays."

Chapter Fifty-five

Commander Hank Bellows, captain of the Seawolf class *Connecticut*, studied his target through the periscope. The old freighter looked like something from a time warp. Motionless, on a relatively calm sea, it appeared as innocuous as a cruise liner. A very rusty and seedy one at that. It was hard to believe that the brass from the CIC on down wanted it put on the bottom, no questions asked. Scuttlebutt had it that there were some very bad people on that bucket, and there was a "need to" out on it and three others like it.

He turned to his exec and told him to take a look. The image had to be enhanced in the early predawn. The freighter, at first barely a silhouette, loomed into sharp focus. Its name, in Arabic and English script, could be seen.

"It's the *Saifullah* for sure. You have any idea why we're putting this boat down, Captain?"

"Fleet says it's a target—one of the old Libertys left over from II. It's an exercise."

"I thought all those old hulls were long gone, except the ones in maritime museums."

"That's the story."

"So, tell me again. What the hell is this old piece of iron doing in our sights?"

"All I know for sure is that we are supposed to send a fish into it. Make that four fish. The top wants to be sure."

"When do we do this?"

"We're standing by. I think any time now."

"Crew is on station, and the hardware is loaded and ready. Actually they're pretty pumped."

"Open the doors, Mr. Banning."

"Doors open, aye. It's not every day we get to sink something, even to practice. You did say exercise?"

"That's what I said. You know how command works—need to know and all that."

"Okay, I'll buy exercise as the official story. As the man says, what's the story behind the story?"

"My former roomie at the Academy runs SEAL team four. He tells me that the people on this target were responsible for taking out a guy named Reynolds, a class behind us at the Academy. He served on the *Jimmy Carter* a couple years back. He's one of us."

"No shit, the *Carter*?"

"What he said."

"Anything else?"

"Nothing for sure, but if you listen real hard to the com chatter, you'd swear we are only one of a small fleet of intercepts out to get this ship and, I think, at least three more like it."

"Jesus. Why don't we just surface and blow this one away with an S to S missile?"

"That's the funny part. The orders are to stay out of sight, stay quiet, when told to, shoot and leave the area at flank."

"Follow up run if, God forbid, we miss?"

"With four in the water, that's not likely, but nope, that's covered somewhere else."

"There are more of us out here?"

"Like I said, chatter sounds like ten or more here, surface I think, and maybe three times that number around the continent. It's hard to tell. With all that, you can bet your ass this ain't practice. Give me a range and speed."

◇◇◇

The sun, not yet above the horizon, lighted the shoreline a dim gray-green. Mist, more like low-lying fog, drifted across the cleared area near the bay's edge. The tractor's large diesel coughed to life, sending a puff of carbon black smoke skyward. The driver eased it into gear, and the cables that stretched from it to the decking snapped taut. The man who'd been watching them moved to each eyebolt on the deck and inspected them. Satisfied they would hold, he turned and signaled the tractor's driver, who eased out the clutch. The big tires bit into the sandy soil and the deck began to slide away from the water.

Lights were on in the hut that the briefing had indicated held the missile firing control. FBI Special Agent Karl Hedrick, clad in a black tactical jumpsuit and web belt, and armed with a silenced nine-millimeter pistol, kicked in the door. Before it could recoil from hitting the wall, he stepped in. In the midnight session before they'd loaded up and come to this place, they'd hammered at the seriousness of the operation and the possible consequences of failure. The first of the shed's two startled occupants hesitated and then lunged for a switch on the panel in front of him. Karl shot him between the eyes. The second man, seated beside the first, swung a shotgun upward at Karl.

Karl shot him, too, but his dead hand found the switch and threw it. Karl froze. A second passed, then another. No noise, no flash of light, no roar of rocket engines, only the distant rumble of the tractor's motor. No launch.

Karl's hands began to shake. He wiped his forehead, swallowed back the gorge that rose in his throat, and keyed his microphone. "Hut clear," he rasped, then stepped outside and threw up the two donuts and three cups of black coffee he'd had an hour previously.

With the hut cleared, a dozen men, similarly attired in black and armed with assault rifles, materialized from the shadows and trained their weapons on the men working by the deck, which had by that time been dragged from the bulkhead at the water's edge. Four were attempting to haul away the tarpaulin. The lead agent shouted for them to stand and put their hands in the air. He repeated the order in Arabic.

All of the men looked startled, then dismayed, and finally furious. They made a dash toward the water. There was no other way for them to go. They'd fenced the place to keep intruders out. Now the same fence would keep them in. Staccato gunfire from the road left them the sea as their only option.

The engines on the yacht twenty yards off shore roared to life. Its crew cut the anchor line, and the boat heeled over to speed away. The men on shore shouted and waved at it. It roared full throttle into Eastern Bay. At the same instant, the black ATF boat, now armed with twin fifty-caliber machine guns in its bow, pounded around the point to the west. The yacht's crew foolishly began to fire at it. The machine guns shredded the yacht's hull like tissue paper. It and its crew disappeared into the waves inside a minute. It would come to rest on the bottom not more than ten yards from the remains of Nick Reynold's Cessna.

Some of the men remaining on shore spun and, cursing the FBI, drew their weapons. Only three of them survived the fusillade that followed.

Local residents, awakened by the noise, checked their calendars. Goose season wouldn't open for another few weeks. Damned-fool city people…what did they know about anything?

Bunky Crispins sat up and shouted "hot damn!"

<><><>

The sun cleared the eastern horizon and painted the *Saifullah* a bright red-orange. Men on deck busied themselves with clearing hatches, then jogged aft, and turned to watch.

"It's a go, Captain."

"Very good, XO. Shoot!"

"Shoot, aye. One away…Two away…Three away…Four away.

"Take her to two hundred feet. Right full rudder. Flank speed."

"Right full rudder, aye. Two hundred feet, aye. Flank, aye, Navy takes care of its own, Captain."

"Roger that, Mr. Banning."

Epilogue

Ike had a fire lighted and fresh drinks poured. The smoke from the A-frame's chimney made lazy tendrils across the valley westward toward the Appalachians, which now cradled the setting sun. It hovered, hesitantly, like a ripe tomato threatening to splatter the mountainside. He inhaled the scent of burning pine and oak and smiled. This was the best time of the year in the valley. Days were warm, nights cool and brisk, and the leaves on the hardwoods were changing to gold, red, and yellow. This was the reason he'd built the cabin overlooking the Shenandoah Valley. He stuck out his long legs and exhaled.

"You at peace, Ike?" Ruth sipped her drink.

"Yes. Are you?"

"I'm just happy you're back in *one* piece. You didn't have much of a vacation, did you?"

"It had its moments."

"What happened to the big raid that your Acting pulled off?"

"The parents were upset, he said, but they cooled down. No thank-yous, of course, but no more lawyer threats either. They were more worried about Beyerson and the drugs."

"Beyerson?"

"A teacher at the high school. Turns out he's a registered sex offender in Ohio and was out of bounds here. Didn't bother to register locally."

"How'd he get through the background check at the school?"

"I'm not sure. I guess since he started out as a short-term temp, they weren't too picky. Then, when they kept him on full time, they lost track. The month-old papers from Ohio were found unopened on principal DiComo's desk. The word is he's been reassigned."

"What about the occult? Weren't the kids dabbling in the dark arts?"

"There wasn't much talk about the satanic business. Not the stuff of modern sensibilities, I guess. Blake Fisher was disappointed about that."

"Poor Blake. No respect."

"Well, now he has the makings of a sermon series. Did you know he's getting married on Christmas Eve?"

"No, but then I'm not on the church's 'A' list, either. Any other local good news?"

"Esther Peeper's cat came home, looking a little worse for wear, after a prolonged tomcat absence."

"I'm not quite sure that qualifies for the AP wire." Ruth swirled her drink around in her glass. "So you managed to stop the baddies from destroying civilization as we know it?"

"Charlie says the whole business was shut down, so, yes."

"What were you doing up there, anyway?"

"You don't want to know."

"You already told me the rough outlines Saturday. I want to know how you managed to fix it."

"You know me—skillful application of cunning and duplicity. How else?"

"Will you stop jerking me around and answer my question? You're not on their payroll. You don't owe them anything, Ike."

"You're right. I don't but…"

"But what?"

"It never ends, Ruth. All we did was stop one complex, and moderately sophisticated plot. They learned from it and will not make the same mistakes the next time. On the other hand, I'm not convinced we learned anything."

"The next time? What do you mean the next time?"

"Those people are fanatics. They may represent only a tiny fraction of the population at large, but they hate us enough for a multitude. They will not be satisfied until they have destroyed this country, one way or the other. They will try again."

"But now we know what the possibilities are and can prepare for them."

"This plan was nothing like September 11. The next will be different, and the next, and the one after that."

"Different? How?"

"Who knows? We have locked down our airports but there are still thousands of miles of unpatrolled borders, unsecured drinking water reservoirs, and seaports…then there are bridges, railroads. Imagine what they could do by pushing an abandoned railroad car over the border. God knows, the list is endless."

"You are scaring me, Ike. When will it end?"

"When they win, or we wake up to the fact that we cannot forever be apologizing to our friends for wanting to secure our borders and destroy our enemies."

"Surely they will change over time. This is the twenty-first century."

"These folks do not live in the twenty-first century, or any recent one for that matter. I hate to disillusion you, but this has been going on for a thousand years. There is no end."

"Ike, diplomacy is the way to end it."

"For most folks, it would be. But when you deal with fanatics, it's an entirely different game."

"If we put their leadership away, then the rest will—"

"Years ago, when oystermen discovered that starfish were the chief predator of shell fish, they would chop them up into tiny pieces in an attempt to kill every one they found. Later, they discovered that all the separate little pieces they'd thrown overboard grew into whole starfishes. Instead of reducing the population, they unwittingly increased it by the thousands. These people are like starfish."

"You sound particularly pessimistic tonight, my friend."

"I've had a discouraging run-in with the powers that shape the democracy. I don't see an end to this lunacy."

"Well, you can chalk up one for your old pals in the CIA, anyway."

"Actually, they didn't score. The agency has a mandate to stay out of domestic operations. The government wishes to continue that illusion, and since the director is already under all kinds of heat from oversight committees for one thing or another, they handed the credit off. The president's chief of staff nominated Homeland Security to receive the plaudits for foiling the attempt. Their people all got commendations and a lot of press for their successful action against terrorists."

"I would have thought the FBI would be the nominee."

"They get the credit for rounding up the men in Talbot County, Maryland—which in fact they did. No complaint there. The CIA received *bupkis.*"

"There has to be a way out of this craziness."

"In my humble opinion—"

"Since when has anyone accused you of humility?"

"I said humble, not…whatever. It is my opinion that the wonks inside the Washington beltway are, as a class, clueless about what's going on outside it, particularly in the 'flyover states.' Something happens to them when they take up residence in the vortex of power. I want to believe they're better at grasping international things, but…"

"But what?"

Ike shook his head. "We live in hope."

The two sat in silence for a while. Ike fixed them each a fresh drink.

"Well, at least you're back safe and sound, and just as irritating as always, and with no obvious permanent damage done. I can be thankful for that. Are you going back to the beach now? You have week of vacation left."

"No, I came back for Yom Kippur with Pop. I think I'll stick around."

"What did you do with your cute little airplane?"

"Charlie had someone fly it back to Georgetown and square the accounts. Why don't you stay here for the rest of the week?"

"I can't. I have all kinds of—"

"Work to do? Don't you have a second-in-command, someone who watches the store when you're out of town or sick?"

"There's no one. I mean there are the deans, of course, and Agnes."

"So, who runs the place when you're away?"

"The dean of faculty."

"Is he any good?"

"He's a she, of course she's good. I don't appoint slackers."

"How do you know?"

"She…I just know."

"Call in sick. Get Agnes on the phone and tell her you have a bad case of the screaming mulligrubs brought on by an overdose of her amazing asparagus roll-ups, and crash here for a few days."

"I can't. Who'd…oh, I see what you're up to. You're not as shrewd as you think, bubba. You are trying to make me admit I can't delegate. Well you are wrong."

"So, you are going to call in, or not?"

"Just watch me, smarty, and wipe that grin off your face."

Ruth disappeared into the relative gloom of the cabin. He heard her make the call, give Ike's phone number to Agnes, and hang up.

"There, that's that. This will make up for the weekend we lost to international terrorism or whatever it was." Her expression softened. "I was worried about you, Ike."

"To tell the truth, I was worried about me, too."

Her face brightened. "Okay, I've done one for you. What are you going to do for me?"

"Anything you ask."

"You said you were going to buy me a present down at the beach. Did you?"

"Yes."

"Is it a blender?"

Ike withdrew the box containing the canary-colored diamond ring, flipped open the lid, and laid it in her lap.

"You could say so."

Agnes' Asparagus Roll-ups

Ingredients:

Loaf of white bread (Wonder is best)
Canned asparagus
Mayonnaise
Salt and pepper

Directions:

Carefully remove the crusts from the bread slices. Slather on mayonnaise liberally. It will help keep the asparagus spears in place. Drain the canned asparagus and pat dry on a paper towel. Lay one large or two small spears on the bread slices and roll the edges together. Season to taste. Cut into two or three bite-sized pieces. Fasten each with gay party toothpick, especially if the bread won't stay in a tidy roll.

Serves ten.

To receive a free catalog of Poisoned Pen Press titles, please contact us in one of the following ways:

Phone: 1-800-421-3976
Facsimile: 1-480-949-1707
Email: info@poisonedpenpress.com
Website: www.poisonedpenpress.com

Poisoned Pen Press
6962 E. First Ave. Ste. 103
Scottsdale, AZ 85251

LaVergne, TN USA
01 April 2011
222482LV00004B/2/P